CRITICS RAVE FOR DIA HUNTER, *ROMANTIC TIMES* REVIEWERS' CHOICE AWARD NOMINEE!

THE GENTLE SEASON

"This love story is wonderfully reminiscent of 'Annie Get Your Gun' but also an original. . . . An all-around good read."
—*Romantic Times*

THE BEHOLDING

"Fast paced and full of adventure, *The Beholding* rightly weaves these threads together with a steaming sexual tension to create a powerhouse of a story."
—*Rendezvous*

"*The Beholding* lifts your heart and steals your soul."
—*Romantic Times*

"Travel across the West of the 1800s with Dia Hunter in search of truth and love. A heartwarming read."
—Jodi Thomas, national bestselling author and two-time RITA winner

LOST

He was so close, she could feel his breath brush the top of her nose. He smelled of soap and potions and man.

"Shaw," she whispered and saw the question in his green eyes. "You said you were attracted to Naomi *and* Prima. Whichever one of us you didn't kiss before, needs to be kissed now so the two of us have both said our proper thank-yous." Drowning in sensations as potent as hundred-year-old whiskey, she went gladly into his arms. She had dreamed of his kiss, longed for it every moment since experiencing the first one yesterday.

The soft perfection of his lips blazed a welcome path at her temple, against her cheek, the bridge of her nose, driving reason from her whirling thoughts. He paused, only an inch from her lips, and she knew if she allowed the kiss to continue, her heart would never be her own again.

VAM

MOONBOW IN THE *Mist*

DIA HUNTER

LEISURE BOOKS   NEW YORK CITY

A LEISURE BOOK®

July 2001

Published by

Dorchester Publishing Co., Inc.
276 Fifth Avenue
New York, NY 10001

ISBN 0-8439-4891-4

The name "Leisure Books" and the stylized "L" with design are trademarks of Dorchester Publishing Co., Inc.

Printed in the United States of America.

*This book is dedicated to those of us who remember
what counts most in life . . . love.*

*And to Chris Keeslar, editor extraordinaire,
a man of infinite patience and wisdom.*

ACKNOWLEDGMENTS

I gratefully acknowledge Kentucky's McCreary County Public Library District; Kay Morrow, District Librarian; and Wilma Waters, Processing Clerk, for their help with the research on moonbows.

MOONBOW IN THE
Mist

Chapter One

June 1859
Blueberry Bluff, Tennessee

Some things a woman never forgets. Her favorite dress. Her first kiss. The man who steals her heart.

The man flatboating down current through the gossamer mist that blanketed the Cumberland River was a stranger. Just as the man predicted to steal Naomi Romans's heart would be. But did this one have the eyes of a wolf, as Annie had also foretold? Naomi couldn't tell from this distance.

She tried to shake the image from her mind, but it would not leave. Annie's description of those eyes had branded itself into Naomi's thoughts. Yellow-green. Eyes that would look into her soul and reveal its hidden truths. Eyes that didn't belong to Cooper Kingsley.

From her position on the sheer bluff that rose above the river's west bank, Naomi could see little more than hair the color of sunset on a pumpkin patch and a powerful-looking stretch of buckskin-clad legs. Muscular shoulders dug the single oar deep into the Cumberland, then rotated it backward with an ease that spoke of many days spent honing the skill.

Curiosity filled her. She needed a closer look to determine whether he was as tall as he seemed, to discover the color of his eyes . . . to find out what it was about him that made her stomach feel as if it were full of flitting hummingbird wings.

"I'm just hungry," she announced, realizing how long she'd been gone. Annie would fret if she didn't return soon with the blueberries. The sound of her voice made Naomi aware of how quiet the forest had become. Too quiet. Skillet and Jug were up to something.

She swung around to check on them. "Just look at you!" she admonished, picking up the now-empty basket that had been brimming with ripened blueberries—berries she'd picked since sunup. Gone, every last one of them. Eaten! "You know Annie likes morning berries better than evening ones. Now she'll have to wait till tomorrow to cook the pies." Naomi frowned at the pair.

"She's gonna skin you two furless. What do you have to say for yourselves?"

Always the first to repent, Jug remorsefully covered his masked face with his paws. Blueberry juice dribbled down the raccoon's fur. His tongue darted out to lick away the evidence; then, as if the animal realized he'd just sealed his guilt, his mouth snapped shut. Naomi laughed, too charmed to stay angry with him.

Mischief gleamed in his partner's dark eyes as the smaller of the two raccoons brushed the five black rings around her fluffy tail, making a point of showing that not a drop of berry juice stained her fur. With a detached air, Skillet rested on her haunches and glanced away as if totally innocent of any wrongdoing.

"You little bandit. Think I don't know you put him up to this?" Naomi reached out to tickle Skillet's soft gray belly. A few dozen blueberries had rounded it considerably. The female raccoon chirred softly.

Jug's pointed nose sniffed the air, and he trilled tiny sounds at his cohort. Skillet's ears stood erect, her eyes alert. She chattered something back. Both raccoons darted past Naomi.

She immediately turned, remembering the stranger. "Finally smelled him, didn't you?" She'd quit being amazed at the pair's perceptiveness a few weeks after she found them. While kits, they'd been balls of boundless curiosity.

Now that they were nearly two-year-old coons, few creatures were as cunning or courageous.

Already the mist began to vanish, the sun heating the Tennessee hills with the first blush of summer. The boat floated close enough now that she could see the loaded-down cargo of oddities riding low in the water. Straps looked like rawhide spider legs, securing crates and a large trunk to the raftlike conveyance. A tent had been erected at one end, probably for sleeping quarters or protection from the afternoon sun. A coffeepot hung on a tripod of iron that stood over a bed of rocks and sand in front of the tent, obviously the remnants of the man's morning cookfire.

A river peddler, more than likely. She'd seen them on several occasions: men hawking their wares, living on the river, finding the Cumberland and the settlements along its watercourse a profitable market for goods brought down from St. Louis.

Sunlight shone on one of the crates and reflected off something shiny inside. With a palm, Naomi shielded her eyes from the glare.

Skillet squealed, trilled low in her throat, then lit off down the mountain at a rapid clip.

"Oh, no, you don't. Leave the poor man alone." Recognizing Skillet's command for the other coon to follow, Naomi grabbed the empty basket and immediately gave chase. She knew exactly what the greedy little thieves planned to do. They would wait till the stranger pulled ashore, then catch him off guard and raid his wares.

The image of the first time they'd searched through Annie's shelves of remedies came to mind. The search had been thorough, her organized concoctions so mixed up that Annie had ranted for days.

Naomi ran along the bluff, working her way down to the bank. Pebbles scattered beneath her bare feet, making her skid slightly. The path to the prized blueberry patch was steep and slippery when she was walking, much less when trying to run.

"Hold up, Jug!" she yelled, watching as the male raccoon raced ahead of his partner. "You'd better not steal him blind!"

A shout from the river distracted her.

The man had locked his single oar into place and now shaded his eyes. Slowly his hand lifted into the air and waved.

He'd obviously spotted her and said something. She wasn't certain whether to stop and answer him or keep running after the coons. If she didn't follow Skillet and Jug, she'd never catch them in time. *At least wave back,* she finally decided. *So he'll know you saw him.*

She waved, noticing immediately that her hand . . . no, both hands . . . were stained with blueberry juice. Naomi instantly shoved them

17

behind her. If he was the man of her dreams, she sure hoped he wasn't expecting to marry a paragon. Blueberry stains were nothing compared to some of the other misadventures that seemed part of her daily routine.

In her exuberance to hide the berry stains, she stumbled. Her body fell forward. The basket went flying. Her feet began to skid. The edge of the bluff seemed inches away. Naomi's toes deadlocked against the earth. Her heels rose inches off the ground, and her body teetered forward. Desperately she backpedaled her hands and rocked on the balls of her feet, trying to regain her balance. Naomi spun right, praying for earth or something solid to break her fall.

The massive branch of a hickory tree loomed in front of her.

Pain splintered across Naomi's right temple as her head hit bark. A scream—her own—echoed through the blackness that engulfed her.

Chapter Two

A high-pitched scream pierced the air. *Damn, a woman?* Shaw Lawson's eyes focused on the sheer cliff rising above him where he'd seen the stranger dressed in men's clothing disappear from sight. He shouldn't have distracted her, but he'd learned pulling ashore and introducing himself to one of the people living on the fringe of a settlement always made for easier connections to others in town later on. Since his first foray into the Appalachians, he'd discovered the mountainfolk were friendly but wary of strangers . . . especially those with Eastern accents. He seemed less "strange" if somebody had already made friends with him. "Lady, are you all right?"

His shout echoed off the rocky outcroppings bordering the river. No answer.

"Lady, are you hurt?" he hollered louder.

Still no answer.

Shaw grabbed the oar and pulled backward with all his might. The paddle lifted high above the surface. Water streamed down to dampen his leather gloves. Quickly he dug deep into the Cumberland, shifting directions and propelling the flatboat to the west bank. "Hold on!"

That was all he needed—to cause injury to one of the locals. His heart sped up as if it were racing on white water . . . or worse. *That's the way to win their trust, Lawson!* "I'm coming!"

Minutes seemed like hours as he fought the current and finally pulled ashore. Shaw studied the distance between the boat and the bank, then pushed aside his wariness of having to get wet. The woman's life could be at stake. Hell, his entire future was.

Grabbing one end of the hitch rope, he leaped into the river. Shaw jerked as the current wrapped icy fingers around his thighs and filled his boots to the brim. The riverbed seemed to clamp down on his ankles, making it difficult to lift each leg as he trudged toward shore. He gritted his teeth, cursing at the vivid imagination that made him feel as if he were being pulled backward, down to a watery grave. *You're not thirteen anymore, so just get on with it.*

An eternity of a minute later, he finally reached the bank and secured the rope to a nearby tree. Exhaling the tension that flooded him, he began the climb that led up the bluff. His boots sloshed and squished with each step, the wet soles sliding along the rocky path. "Hold on!"

Two balls of fur ran toward him. *Raccoons!* Hell-bent to run him down, from the looks of them. He didn't know much about coons, but he'd been told they were the worst for passing hydrophobia—a disease too vile for man or beast. The largest had a blue tinge to its fur.

Shaw jumped and grabbed an overhead branch, testing its sturdiness. It held.

Not that hanging like moss or forcing himself to remain quiet would keep him out of harm's way. Coons were climbers. He knew that much about them. Maybe they weren't jumpers, though.

When they ran past him, Shaw breathed a sigh of relief. His attention focused on the path that lay ahead, and he realized how dangerously close it ran parallel to the cliff. Minutes might count for the woman. Hanging here until the coons got farther out of range was no option. Shaw let go and hoped that something else had distracted them and would take them along their merry way.

A few yards farther, he saw that his haste had proved wise. He found the woman sprawled backward beneath a hickory tree. Her eyes were shut, her feet and knees dangling dangerously over the bluff. If she were simply unconscious

21

and she stirred, she might slide off the edge. But if she was worse off . . . Dread and the need to see if she still breathed hurried his steps.

The lady moaned, touching her temple with one hand.

"Don't move, miss." Shaw knelt down behind her, reached out to touch her . . . then paused. Moving the woman might cause greater injury.

A closer look revealed no cuts or blood other than on the side of her head. None of her limbs seemed positioned at an awkward angle, but there was no true way of knowing until he checked further. He took off a glove and felt her neck for a pulse, but his own was pounding so hard he wasn't sure if he could distinguish the two.

Her cheeks were pale, a clear difference from the sun-bronzed skin at the opened collar of her blouse, but she was warm. Had her fingers moved?

He glanced at her hand. Although the back of it looked discolored, it didn't seem to be scraped or bleeding, as he'd first thought. Some sort of stain, it seemed. The other hand looked the same.

"I've got to . . ." She tried to raise her head and neck. "Ooh, it hurts."

"Lie still," Shaw warned. Assured that her back couldn't be seriously hurt if she could move her fingers and neck, he shoved his forearms beneath her shoulders to link their arms and pull her backward into his lap. He shouldn't have shouted and startled her. But being the self-serving bastard that he was, he'd thought he'd save time by hailing the stranger from the boat instead of waiting until he pulled ashore. Save time, make money.

When her calves scraped against the rocky outcropping, he was glad she wore trousers instead of a dress. At least they offered some form of protection. But a glance at her forehead reminded him that she wasn't completely out of danger.

A knot the size of a chestnut was forming just above her right temple, already turning a nasty reddish blue. Wisps of hair that had pulled away from her raven-colored braid served only to show the ashen color of her face.

Shaw estimated her weight and size and wondered why such a slip of a woman was out here by herself. He gathered her up in his arms and decided that a cool splash of water might speed her recovery.

The return pathway proved even more slippery.

He searched the woman's face for a moment, thinking she looked vaguely familiar. But that was impossible. He knew no one along the Cumberland.

Dark lashes. High cheekbones. Freckles across the bridge of her nose. The woman would launch no ships with her beauty, yet she wasn't unpleasant to look at. But she might become so if she woke and found him staring at her like a store-keep gauging the quality of his inventory.

Shaw's attention returned to the dangerous path. A moment before he reached the shore, he discovered he'd wished himself into more problems. Something else had definitely distracted the raccoons. His supplies! "Get out of there," he demanded in a deep growl.

The beasts ignored him, and the woman didn't awaken despite how loudly he'd voiced the command. Shaw gave in to traces of panic. She should be opening her eyes again, saying something.

His flatboat bobbed as the river's surface rippled, warning him that boarding the craft would require a balancing act. Fortunately the woman could barely boast a stretch of the galluses over her calico blouse. Her modest weight would make the balancing act a lot easier to accomplish.

For a split second, Shaw battled with indecision. If he left her on the bank, he couldn't protect her from the coons after he chased them aground.

The sound of breaking glass echoed over the countryside. His jars!

Shaw ignored the sound of the river lapping at the shore. He didn't have time to replace those jars, and he'd be damned before he'd let two ring-tailed raccoons beat him out of the best chance he'd had in years to prove he wasn't the rogue everyone thought him to be. He had to protect those jars at all costs.

Gritting his teeth, he waded into the water. The flatboat bobbed and swayed, sending a rush of cold against his ankles, another against his knees. Though she was light, the added weight of the woman made him feel off balance, his steps less sure. One boot slipped. Another.

His knees slammed against the soft riverbed. The current rushed up to soak the woman to her shoulders and splash against Shaw's neck, making him sputter a curse as it sprayed against his face. His knees slid a few inches before he could regain a shaky footing. He stood there a moment, trembling, cursing the current, vexed by his luck. Now she was not only unconscious but wet. He was not exactly what he'd call being helpful.

He lifted his burden closer, shifting her weight to get a firmer hold. Her cheek nestled against the curve of his neck. The warmth of her gentle breath and the touch of her soft, wet skin seared through him, making him instantly aware of how the calico clung to her tiny waist . . . of how each bead of water glided along her skin as if it were made of pure silk.

For God's sake, man. She's far from choice. He liked his women more full-bodied. More than a handful. Shaw stared at the galluses rising and falling with each of those gentle breaths that tickled his neck. It would serve him right if the waif revived and slapped him into a new respect for little women.

He shifted his gaze back to the task at hand. Managing the remainder of the distance without further mishap, Shaw finally reached the boat and deposited the woman safely aboard.

Suddenly a crate toppled. Jars clanked together, then fell. One rolled across the planked flooring. A high-pitched squeal warned that the raccoons had escalated their search.

"Get out of there!" he commanded, looking around for something to use as protection for the woman while he chased the coons away. His personal trunk—light enough to move, but large enough to form a blockade. He grabbed the ornately carved trunk and shoved it closer to her. The boat rocked at the shift in weight. Shaw's heels dug into the boat bed, his feet bracing to ride the current. If those animals dumped the woman in the brink or made him lose any of his cargo, he'd have two coonskin caps by nightfall.

The raccoons raced forward. He instantly reacted, diving to the boat bed to grab them. The large one darted one way, the smaller another. His arms flailed and missed.

"Wake up, lady!" Shaw grappled to regain his footing, swinging around, only to stare in utter amazement.

One of the beasts rested against the woman's hip while her hand reached out and stroked its head. Tittering something low, the other raccoon pressed its paws against the lady's forehead and cheeks, as if feeling for a fever.

"I'm all right, Skillet." As the coon's paw pressed against her lips, the woman kissed it and sighed. "I just hit my head, girl. I'll be fine."

The raccoon near her hip pushed its head further into her palm, demanding another stroke. She granted its wish, only to frown. "There's no need to cry, Jug. I'm really quite myself now. Or . . . at least I will be. I just need to lie here a moment more. I feel dizzy."

To Shaw's surprise, the raccoon's black eyes shimmered as if truly filling with tears.

When he bent to help the woman stand, the smaller of the coons, the one called Skillet, bared its teeth. Shaw stood still, leaving his hand linked to the stranger's. He might get bitten, but he couldn't let the woman go until he was sure she could stand on her own. "I'm not going to hurt her. I just want to help."

Eyes the color of the blue mist that often crowned the Great Smoky Mountains opened and stared at him. Remarkable eyes that far made up for any ordinary aspect of the woman's other features. Definitely eyes worth waiting to see, he decided.

Her forehead creased. Dark lashes blinked several times; then she squinted. "Do I know you?"

The other raccoon grumbled, the eyes in his mask narrowing into slits.

"I'm a man about to be bitten by two raccoons if you don't call them off."

"Raccoons?" She bolted upright, her hand instantly jerking away from the coon she'd been petting. She squealed and crossed her arms, pressing them protectively against her. "Oooohhh! Get them away from me!"

The one named Jug bumped its head against the lady's elbow, as if asking for more affection.

Possibilities fired rapidly through Shaw's mind. She had hit her head. She knew the raccoons, then didn't. She'd said she felt dizzy. Did she have her true wits about her?

"Don't worry; I'll distract them," he reassured her, deciding she must still be confused. Searching for something to draw the animals' attention away, he reluctantly retrieved the object of their earlier interest. One less jar to prove its worth. One less to make his fortune. But apparently it was the thing the animals found most appealing. This new resolve to be a better man was costing him in more ways than he'd expected.

Jug took interest and chased after the jar. Skillet wasn't so easily fooled.

"Will it bite?" the woman asked.

"I don't think so. At least not *you*, anyway. You called them both by name." He repeated what she'd said. "They even tried to defend you when I approached, as if they thought I meant to harm you. Sorry I startled you. I meant only to introduce myself and maybe share a cup of coffee. I wanted to find out how much farther to the nearest settlement. I heard you scream, then didn't see you anymore."

She looked puzzled.

Once again Shaw felt frustration at how long it had taken to reach her. "I pulled ashore as quickly as the current allowed. Found you with that nasty bruise." He touched his temple to indicate the bruise on hers.

Her hand reached up to feel the injury, then came away with blood on the fingertips. She examined her hands, puzzlement deepening the furrows in her brow. "It *looks* bad, but nothing feels bruised or broken."

"I'll get you a cloth. Hold on a minute." Shaw quickly searched through the valise that held his belongings. His hand instantly locked on something that might appeal to the female raccoon—his shaving mirror.

Grabbing a washcloth from the bag, he dipped it in the water and wrung it out quickly. He placed the mirror a few yards away from the smaller raccoon. "Here, Skillet. Take a look at your pretty self. That's right. You're a fetching little furball, aren't you?"

Instead, Jug took notice of the mirror and investigated. Skillet voiced her objection and grabbed the mirror. A tug-of-war began in earnest.

Shaw didn't waste any time. He helped his patient stand. When her legs wobbled slightly, he wrapped a protective arm around her shoulders. "Any pain?"

She started to shake her head, then seemed to think better of it. "No . . . yes . . . I'm not sure. Kind of dull." Her blue eyes searched his. "Why am I wet?" Her gaze swept over him. "Why are *you*?"

"Let's move over here, out of their way. You can sit on this trunk until you get your bearings." He offered her the cloth, then an explanation about how he'd slipped getting her to the boat.

She accepted the cloth. "Thank you, Mr. . . . ?" She looked startled. "I'm afraid I don't quite remember your name."

"There's no reason you should. We've never met." Yet Shaw couldn't shake a feeling that he had seen her before. He simply didn't remember where at the moment. "I'm not from around these parts. Name's Shaw Lawson." He motioned to his inventory. "I'm peddling goods downriver. I waved to you from the river." Seeing her confusion, he explained his reason for waving once again.

"That accent. Philadelphia?"

Shaw stared harder at the woman. Her speech

wasn't flavored with the same backwoods twang as that of other people he'd met along the Cumberland. "Yes, it is. You've got an ear for language."

"After Dialect Interpretation at Miss Parmelady's Finishing School, I'd certainly better have. My father . . ." She seemed to grow increasingly uncomfortable, shifting on the trunk. "He would demand his money's worth of—" She glanced at Shaw's labeled inventory and frowned. "Goods, you say? Rainbow seeds and wind flakes? Glass jars? Who would buy such folly?"

Although he suspected her swift change of subject was a product of whatever unhappy thought she'd suffered regarding her choice of schooling, the woman's criticism of his choice of profession annoyed Shaw. He'd had his fill of high-toned disbelievers lately. The rainbow seeds, wind flakes, and happy ash required someone with a good imagination, a sense of humor, and a bent for adventure. But the Mason jars served a very real purpose. A purpose that would change the lives of the people along this waterway, if they'd just listen to him. A purpose that would help him reclaim his soul.

Not wanting to waste the possibility of a sale, he added a bit of challenge to his voice. "Such merchandise is bought by someone just like you. Someone willing to take a risk."

31

"You don't know a thing about me." Her chin tilted slightly.

Little as the woman was, she still had a big look of stubbornness about her—a willful risk taker. It was a dangerous trait in anyone, Shaw knew from past experience, but in a woman it could be an even more dangerous—or advantageous—prospect.

"Not true," he continued, taking a risk of his own in contradicting her. She could be someone important in the territory. Someone who might persuade others not to order. Someone who could destroy the timetable the financiers had set for him to prove himself. "I know your hands are stained with ink or some kind of berry juice, from the looks of them."

She blushed.

"And you're daring"—he pointed to the place where he'd found her—"because you weren't afraid to climb up that bluff all by yourself."

He liked the way her eyes sparked with appreciation for his compliment. Willful, a risk taker, and competitive. "And I suspect you aren't afraid of stirring up gossip, if you have to."

The spark blazed to blue fire. "And just how did you arrive at that conclusion?"

He pointed to her legs and grinned. "You're wearing trousers."

She glanced down, then back up again, the blue fire slowly kindling to a glow. She finally rewarded him with a smile. "I am, aren't I?" Suddenly her smile disappeared. She stared at him and whispered, "You have the strangest eyes. Yellow-green."

"Wolf eyes," Shaw admitted. She was not the first to express surprise at the odd bits of yellow that flecked his green eyes, but her voice held something more akin to amazement. "At least, that's what my sisters call them."

"Just as Annie predicted."

"Who's Annie?"

The woman appeared suddenly perplexed. "I have no idea."

The blow to her head had obviously produced a sense of confusion within her. Shaw studied his patient closely. He'd heard of such a malady. A severe head wound or a terrible fright could cause someone to lose her memory. The loss might last for months, even years; other times, only days. Either way, he had no idea how to remedy it.

Duty called to him as it had many times long ago. He had vowed to ignore its summons ever again. For years he had, putting his own needs first, serving only himself. But now . . .

He'd known the minute he saw her disappear from sight that his life had just taken an unalterable course. The minute he'd found her lying unconscious—the minute his mind told him he could not turn his back on yet another innocent person he had harmed because of his own selfish needs.

Redemption for Shaw Lawson, rogue, lay in helping this woman.

To determine her alertness, he met her gaze squarely. "Do you know where you live?"

"Of course." Indignation replaced bewilderment. "In New York City. Across from the new park." She glanced around at the countryside and seemed startled by what she saw. "But . . . this isn't New York."

Something was very, very wrong. "What's your name, miss?"

"Prima." Her shoulders squared, her spine straightening as if she were being corrected by the teacher at the finishing school she'd mentioned earlier. "Prima Powell, of the Manhattan Powells."

Shaw stared at her hard and breathed out a long, low whistle. Had he heard her correctly? Prima Powell?

If what the woman said was true, he'd just solved a two-year-old mystery.

Chapter Three

The scent of something clean, woodsy, and indefinably male emanated from the broad span of buckskin-clad shoulders that blocked sight of anything beyond them. Prima struggled to make sense of her surroundings and the presence of the stranger standing in front of her. Her head hurt tremendously, and she hardly would have been able to keep her eyes open if it weren't for the fear that she had no idea where she was or how she'd gotten there. The fact that her safety at the moment counted on the good graces of a total stranger served only to increase that fear.

She watched a bead of perspiration trickle down the man's neck, moistening his sun-bronzed skin until it shone. Her gaze traced the admirable slope from shoulder to narrow waist, the swell of his muscular thighs, the brace of his steady feet.

At any other time in her life, he would have been a vision of temptation, someone she would have enjoyed meeting. Today she needed to proceed even more cautiously than usual with strangers. Not trusting any of her senses at the moment, Prima glanced at the sun and its position in the sky. Midmorning. The fact that she had to reassure herself about the time of day concerned her. How long had she been in this condition? This unfamiliar place? With him?

Her cheek suddenly quivered. Prima reached up to smooth away the frustrating sign of nervousness, only to discover that a wisp of her hair was doing its best to take root in the corner of her mouth. Vapors! She must look a mess.

He could be a madman, and all she worried about was how she looked. Still, she was woman enough to like what she saw in the man if he was genuinely what he professed—someone who had tried to rescue her from a fall.

Quickly anchoring the wisp of hair behind her ear, she was surprised to find the rest pulled back into a single braid. A long one at that. She grabbed the braid and examined its length closely. "I think I'm . . ."

She willed herself silent, finishing the statement in her head: . . . *missing something here*. The last time she'd looked, she had short hair.

She'd cut it to her shoulders, a deliberate defiance of her father's wishes because he had refused to let her join the transcontinental railroad crew as a photographer—employment usually reserved for men. Now her hair was almost waist-length!

Prima took stock of the other oddities in her appearance—trousers and galluses, and she was as barefoot as a newborn baby. Though she prided herself on her unconventionality, this was even beyond the boundaries she normally tested. She'd been here—wherever that was—for a lot longer than just this morning. The length of her hair was proof enough of that reality.

"You think you're what?" her rescuer asked. Curiosity deepened the green of the man's eyes, making the yellow streaks dim in comparison. Sheltered in lashes the color of pine roots, his eyes seemed hypnotic, mesmerizing.

Wolf eyes, he'd said. Eyes that captivated, lured. The instincts she'd relied on for most of her adult life warned her to proceed cautiously with how much she revealed to this man until she had more presence of mind about her current situation and his intentions. She'd learned early on that being born the daughter of a wealthy man had its advantages and disadvantages . . . and always a price. She didn't know anything about him, and so she had no way of knowing how much he knew about her. "I think

I'm capable of taking care of myself now. I've troubled you enough."

"Then you need no further help?"

He sounded relieved. Too relieved. Despite her discomfort at being in the company of a stranger, she couldn't help feeling a bit incensed that he would so readily leave her to her own defenses. "I wouldn't dream of detaining you any longer."

He glanced at his wares and frowned at the two beasts who played tug of war with one of the jars. "Time is money, as they say."

She would be neither a burden nor an obligation to any man. Prima rose from the trunk, her spine stiffening as if someone had poked her with the barrel of a gun.

When he faced her again, apology instantly softened his expression. "I meant no offense, Miss . . . Powell. I'm sure being the daughter of your father makes you more than aware of how losing time can affect a man's success."

So he knew of her family's fortune. How fortunate for him that he'd come along just at the right time to rescue her from mishap. Distrust hardened her tone despite the continued dizziness she fought. "Yes, I'm well aware of the many incentives that drive an enterprising businessman such as my father. Making use of time is just one of them. I would be glad to pay you for your troubles."

The apology fled from his features even as he

slipped an arm behind her to steady her. "I'll take no pay for helping to right a wrong I caused in the first place. You wouldn't have fallen had I not distracted you. And . . . now you can hardly stand."

"I'm perfectly—" Her protest died as she stood without moving for a moment, trying to separate the need to be indignant from the dizziness that spread in waves from her temple.

"I'm sure you're quite capable, miss." His arm tightened behind her, creating a buttress of iron that protected her from falling backward. "But sometimes it's wiser to rely on others."

Something in his tone pierced the misty fog that threatened to overtake her. Strange, but he sounded as if he *needed* her to accept his help. Her body demanded what logic and reason scorned. She felt less wobbly with the support of his arm.

But it was a long minute of unsteady breaths before she could rid herself of the acute awareness of his uncommon height, tapering body, and sun-bronzed skin. "You're right," she finally admitted, taking a step away to test whether he would challenge her freedom. To her relief, his arm returned to his side, allowing her to move any way she wished. She sank to the top of the trunk, grabbing its edge to steady herself. "It would be best if I had someone accompany me to the doctor. But I can't, in good conscience, take any more of your time. I understand your not wanting to accept any money, Mr. . . . ?" Her cheeks reddened in embarrassment. Perhaps there was, indeed, reason for more concern. She was not usually this dull-witted and was having an unusually hard time concentrating. "I'm afraid I've forgotten your name again."

"Lawson. Shaw Lawson." He eyed her carefully.

"I'm feeling better by the moment, Mr. Lawson," she reassured him. "If I sit here a few more minutes, I'll be fine." She averted her gaze to the single oar used to steer his craft. "About our discussion regarding payment . . . I would very much like to hire you to take me to the nearest doctor. That would be additional time away from your pursuits, and I can't, in good conscience, ask for further help without paying you for the kindness."

"Perhaps I should take you home first. Let your parents know what happened and let them send for a doctor." Lawson plunged into the water, wading to the tree on shore that moored the boat, and unknotted the rope.

On his return, he looked disgruntled. The way he brushed the water from his pants leg after he boarded made her wonder if he wished he could wipe away the obvious responsibility he must feel toward seeing her safely home.

Home? Wherever she was, she had a feeling

New York was far, far away from this place. She didn't want him to know just how frightened she was at the moment at knowing that her parents weren't within close proximity. A twist of irony was that she'd spent most of her twenty years trying to keep them at a distance. "The doctor first. Otherwise Morgan will ask me why I didn't take care of necessities first."

"Morgan, is it?" Lawson secured the hitch rope and unlocked the oar, jabbing its end against the bank and shoving off. "You call your father by his first name?"

The flatboat shimmied, its front end shifting to the left to glide into the current. Prima's hands gripped the trunk harder with each powerful plunge of the oar into the river. The tug-of-war between the raccoons stopped, both animals sitting on their haunches like frozen statues.

Prima pretended her interest was riveted on the raccoons, not wanting to answer the man's question about her relationship with Morgan. Not wanting to scream that Morgan refused to let any of his children close enough to warrant such an affectionate endearment as *Father*. *Change the subject. Your head's already hurting enough.* "Why didn't you chase the raccoons off before we left?"

"As I said earlier, you knew their names. I assumed they were your pets."

Pets? Raccoon hair on one of Morgan's Aubus-

son rugs? Perish the thought! "I've never even owned a dog. What would I do with raccoons?"

As if they sensed they were being discussed, both scurried over and took a seat beside her.

"Oh!" She had to pry her fingers loose from the trunk to throw her hands up in front of her face.

The larger of the two creatures looked up at her, its dark eyes rounded. Puzzled? No, something else. Was it possible the beast was frightened?

The strong sense of daring that had caused many an argument with her parents and afforded her an equally long list of adventures to boast about to her friends in Quest spurred Prima to reach out and tentatively touch the animal. If her friends in the thrill-seeking club could see her now! They'd surely lift a toast in her honor.

The raccoon bumped its head against her palm, then settled against her side. "You're scared, aren't you, little one?" she cooed compassionately. "See there. We can be friends."

The other raccoon began to make a soft sound, almost as if it approved of Prima's compassion for its cohort.

Lawson turned around. "You called that one a him and said his name was Jug. The one that's chirring is a girl—Skillet, if I remember right. If they were going to bite you, they already would have. They seem to like you well enough. Looks like you don't have anything to fear from them. If you're all right with them, I really need to watch what I'm doing here until we're farther out. Lots of things could snag us." When she nodded, he turned his attention back to the current.

She allowed Jug to lean against her, stroking his soft fur until he began to make the same sound as the female. "Skillet and Jug, huh?" Prima let go of her grip on the trunk and stroked Skillet's belly. The chirring grew louder. "Like that, do you?" she whispered. "That's quite a name you've got for yourself. Both of you."

It amazed her that the animals did, indeed, seem to know her well and allowed her to touch them. Such trust would have taken time to achieve. Time that seemed lost to her now. Time that eluded her even as she tried to recall it.

The effort of gaining the middle of the river, and the craft's speed, caused Lawson's shoulders and arms to flex, rippling powerful muscles that had obviously been honed from great experience with the task. Prima tried not to stare at his backside, but he had an astounding physique for a man of his profession. She'd always thought of peddlers of potions as thinkers, men who spent their time reviewing costs and inventory, dreaming of ways to make quick money or swindling people. She'd never pictured them as outdoorsy men honed into muscle and sinew. The fact that he was incredibly strong-looking didn't diminish her concern with how easily he might subdue her if he were a man with ulterior motives.

She might be small, but he wouldn't find her a willing captive.

The need to know more about him made her bold. "You said you're a peddler. Why here?" Perhaps by finding out why he'd chosen this place she could discover exactly where *here* was.

"I have a month to peddle those jars," he informed her over his shoulder. "My partner and I heard there was a bumper crop of goods along the Cumberland this summer. A man goes where there's more use for his products."

The Cumberland? She was somewhere in Kentucky or Tennessee! Panic engulfed Prima. Her mind strained to recall the hours previous to awakening in this stranger's presence, even the day before. "Are you s-sure?"

His laughter drifted back to her. "Yes. Otherwise how would he expect to be a success at what he does?"

Realizing that he was not privy to her thoughts and assumed they were talking about his work, she pretended to mean something else as well. "No, I meant the bumper crops. Are you certain they were along the Cumberland?"

"Very sure. I've been traveling it for a couple of days and the crops were good in Kentucky, but people upstream have said they're even better ahead. Supposed to be a place called Moonbow.

44

But the map I have of Tennessee is an old one from Boone's time. Moonbow must be a bit farther around the bend than mine shows."

Tennessee. She was in Tennessee, riding the Cumberland River on a flatboat with a stranger. How in Lewis and Clark's names did she get here? Fear coursed like a frosty current through her bloodstream. She trembled. The raccoons huddled closer.

"You said you've only got a month to sell your jars." How could she ask what she needed to know without letting him learn more than she wanted him to? "Why the time limit? Is something going to happen by a certain time if you don't?"

"Our backers will pull their finances by August first if we don't prove the usefulness of our invention."

August first. That meant it was the end of June or the first of July. Hadn't yesterday been March? Just how much time had gone by? Was it the same year, for heaven's sake? How could she get that question by him without sounding totally addlepated?

"An invention, you say? The jars?" They looked like glass jars to her. "Is there something different about them?"

He turned halfway around and pointed at the container the coons had left lying against one of the crates. "The zinc caps can be used repeatedly,

45

and the threads that end below the top line of the jar and before the shoulder help to increase the vacuum." Pride filled his tone. "The seal is tighter that way and keeps the food good for years."

"For *years?*" she asked incredulously. If what he said was true, the man and his partner would make millions. But the worthiness of his invention wasn't the issue here. It's patent date was. "Have you had it patented? You know it's wise to keep close watch on the date so the patent doesn't run out."

"You sound like Morgan Powell's daughter now. Yes, Miss Powell, Mr. Mason patented his jars. Last November, in fact. It's good for several years. Take a look at the jar the coons were playing with. You'll find the date stamped on the bottom. These are some of the first." His attention returned to steering the boat.

She shifted on the trunk to see where the jar had rolled. It was not so far that she couldn't make it, but far enough to make her need to grab on to something for balance. Finding out the date seemed worth risking another bout of profound dizziness. She stood and was pleased that the coons didn't make a fuss.

A glance down at the trunk where she'd been sitting made her promise herself to ask him about it later. Right now she had to make it the distance from trunk to jar. Prima took a tentative step, testing the firmness of the boat bed. Lawson was an accomplished oarsman. She could barely feel the current beneath them. If she hadn't already been dizzy, she might not feel it at all.

A few faltered steps later, she bent and retrieved the jar. She immediately turned it over and read the words imprinted on the bottom: *Mason, Nov. 30, 1858.*

The jar slipped from her fingers, shattering into a handful of pieces against the boat bed.

A cry escaped Prima as reality spun a dark web around her. The world careened, and she grabbed hold of the crate nearest her, finding the shrouding darkness that threatened to overtake her.

Last November, in fact. Lawson's words echoed in her head? November 1858? That meant this was June or July of 1859. She was no longer twenty years old, as she'd been before the fall. She was twenty-*two!*

She'd lost more than two years of her life.

Chapter Four

The sound of shattering glass spun Shaw around. He watched the woman grab hold of the crates as if she were going to faint. "Hold on!"

He lifted the oar and let its handle slide down to his foot, leaving the broad end in the air and the flatboat adrift in the current. All he could do was pray the craft remained midstream while he looked after her. He couldn't do both.

"You shouldn't have gotten up," he admonished, grabbing her by the waist and threading his arm beneath hers. Gently he pulled her closer, angry at himself when she trembled and laid her head against his shoulder for support. She could barely stand. "I shouldn't have made you look at the jar."

He'd let his pride show about the Mason project and forgotten her unsteadiness. A fine way to make amends—causing her to hurt herself even worse.

"It's not your fault," she whispered against his chest. "I wanted to look."

She was such a tiny thing. Fragile. His inconsiderate nature these past few years felt more prevalent than ever. "I should have been watching you more closely."

Whether or not she paid him, he'd see her not only to a doctor but home where she belonged. Even if her claim to be the kidnapped heiress who had been missing for two years was simply a product of her bruised mind. He'd take her as far as she needed to go to recover. That was the least he owed her. The least he owed for everyone he'd mistreated—to take the responsibility of his actions once more. "Here, let's seat you somewhere you'll feel comfortable. Or . . . I have a bedroll in the tent if you think lying down will help any."

She tried to shake her head, but immediately stopped. "I don't want to lie down right now."

"Good. I think it's best to keep you awake until a doctor sees you and says you're okay. Want to sit on the trunk again?"

The flatboat shifted abruptly, the current taking on a choppy pace. An extra step kept them balanced. "I'm gonna have to grab the oar again. Feels like we're heading into some rough water."

"Here's fine." She slid from his arms, sinking

onto the boat bed next to the trunk. "I wanted to look this over anyway." She ran her fingers across the carvings on the trunk. "I can't do that if I'm sitting on it."

"You'll find a blanket inside if you need it. Just undo the latch."

"I'm not cold. Go ahead. I'll be fine," she assured him.

The boat was definitely gliding faster. He couldn't dally any longer. Shaw took his station at the oar, reluctantly leaving her to her own defenses.

"This carving is extraordinary."

His mind filled with the varied images that graced his trunk. Dragons and wizards. Lightning bolts and rainbows. Whimsical fancies graced every side. A roll of thunder sounded as if from the distance. They would soon be approaching either a stretch of rapids or a waterfall. His mind tried to recall the map he'd looked at only minutes before spotting the woman on the cliff. *Waterfall.*

Though not as dangerous as rapids, a small waterfall could be just as devastating to a boat . . . depending on its force. He needed to keep her distracted so she wouldn't become frightened as well as being injured. "Any particular carving?" he asked.

"As a matter of fact, yes. The rainbow that arches over the latch." Her voice echoed with appreciation. "Just now when we passed beneath those overhanging cliffs and it shaded us from the sun, the rainbow looked white, almost opalescent. But now in the sunlight, it has several colors. It's beautiful."

"It's called a moonbow."

"I've heard of that before . . . but I'm not certain from where."

She didn't sound sure of anything. Hitting her head must have really scared her more than she was letting on. Not that he blamed her. She'd awakened to a stranger she didn't know from Adam. "When I found out about the moonbow, I was just as fascinated as you are."

Shaw remembered listening to the old Scotsman who'd told him and a saloonful of others about the legend of the moonbow. Most had teased the Scot, saying he'd been sharing a bottle too often with the leprechauns, but the man had sounded convincing enough to Shaw. Shaw had gone to the smithy the very next day and had a moonbow carved into his travel trunk. He needed good luck just as much as the next fellow. God knew being a workhorse hadn't been enough. Everything he did met with a measure of success, but never quite enough to make him *feel* successful.

"Moonbows supposedly occur in only two places in the world." He repeated what he'd been told. "One of them, and the town named after it, is not far from here, according to those who know about such things. I've never actually seen a moonbow yet, but I plan to."

"At Cumberland Falls. Just over the Kentucky line. And in Africa. There's a large waterfall there, too. Those are the places to look." She sounded as though she were repeating text from a schoolbook. "It takes a large waterfall to provide the right conditions for a moonbow."

"You know a lot about them." Learned from an exclusive school or a saloon? She didn't seem the kind of woman who frequented saloons. Then again, surely anyone who lived in these parts would know of such a unique local phenomenon. The likelihood that she was Prima Powell, socialite and heiress to an immense fortune, seemed more and more unlikely.

"They happen when a full moon sits at a certain angle on a clear night filled with stars," she continued. "The moon shines on the mist of the waterfall at the base and arches either downstream or toward shore. Night rainbows, they call them." The tone of her next statement was questioning. "They must hold some significance for you, since you had one carved on your trunk."

Shaw laughed bitterly. Others had laughed at his dreams of becoming his own man, making his own successes. They'd thought his hopes as fanciful as the carvings on his trunks. The bitterness had not taken hold until he'd never quite achieved what he'd sought. It wasn't that he was tired of chasing the dream. He just wondered if he had taken the right steps or detoured somewhere he shouldn't have. He needed new direction.

His oar took on a broader sweep. His shoulders strained more with each rise and fall of the paddle. "I'd like to think the legend about them is true," he told her.

"That's a part I'm not familiar with."

"The light of its bow is supposed to be able to lead you out of the darkness and toward your life's true path." He wished there were a measure of truth about that part, but he'd been chasing one pot of gold or another since he'd set out to make his own way in the world. The only path he'd found so far was one that had deeper pits to cross than mountains to climb. "Can you think of a better symbol to guide a peddler's travels? What are we but wanderers, steered by the whim of others' needs and cravings?"

God, he sounded bitter. Even to himself. What would she think of him? What did he care? She was a stranger. He hadn't hurt her yet. He had to see her home before he did.

"I don't mean to be rude, but I've got to pay attention to what's ahead. Sounds like we're approaching a waterfall. That probably won't be a problem, but we had best not take any chances. Why don't you grab that blanket I told you about and hold it over you in case there's a lot of spray?"

"No need. I'm already wet."

He'd forgotten. He started to apologize, then decided against it. He didn't want to talk with her any more, didn't want to know more about her than he must. Forget that she might be someone to help introduce him to locals and make a quicker sale. Hell, she didn't even know who she was. If she introduced him to anybody, he wouldn't know whether to trust the information she gave him. So what if he could use the money she'd offered to see her to a doctor? He wouldn't take it.

Now that was something different: turning down easy money. Shaw felt the seed of redemption planting itself in his will. He was plowing new ground here. A month ago he would have charged her three times whatever she'd offered.

For a few minutes more, the river wended its way through the forest of hardwood, hugging a granite slope as old as the world on either side. Finally it rounded a bend and opened to an inlet of emerald waters cutting deeply into the gorge. To the right of the boat, a waterfall cascaded down a ninety-foot bluff, billowing peacock-colored prisms of mist into the river. Everywhere he looked, the countryside was thick with scarlet rhododendron, mountain laurel, and vegetation.

Chestnut boughs laden with nuts awaited the

picker's basket. Persimmon and hickory trees were ripe for the plucking as well. He shaded his eyes against the flare of the afternoon sun and gazed at the peaceful township nestled close to the riverbank. Dotted with cabins, barns, and split-rail fences, it looked like a dozen others he'd seen back on the balds and in the hollows of the Appalachians. Green pastures along the flatter ground provided cropping grass for stock. Along the gently rising foothills, brown furrowed fields caught enough sunlight to warm the newly planted seeds. A clear spring that sparkled like a satin ribbon wound behind each homestead, offering life-giving sustenance to man and crop alike, then found its way to the Cumberland. Peach orchards looked like patchwork squares, lending a fruity fragrance to the headier scent of rhododendron.

The road to the township was clear-cut and dry—an easy transference of his goods from boat to rented cart. The foliage along the way was lush and green with mountain vitality. Blackberries and pearl onions grew wild and plump. Shaw's mind spun with all the possibilities abounding here. If ever there was the place to test the jars, this seemed to offer an abundance of opportunity.

This promised to be the kind of sweet afternoon Shaw had dreamed of ever since he left Philadelphia, the kind of day when he might stroll up to a homeowner and convince the man how fate had stepped in by sending him to show how not to waste a single edible leaf. And once he'd convinced the man that the jars were the next best thing to salvation, he'd simply stroll down the path to the river, sit on the flatboat, and reconnect with his soul the way he needed to do. Someplace like this he just might be able to hear his innermost thoughts and find something still good about himself. Something not to be ashamed of.

"Moonbow," he announced, pointing to the settlement. "The town, not the legend. Bet we'll find a doctor there. Or someone who knows where we can locate one if there isn't one available." He steered the boat away from the spraying mist and toward the opposite bank. "Does any of it look familiar to you?"

"Why should it? I'm not from here."

She sounded convinced. Still, he wasn't quite ready to believe she was the missing heiress who might be worth a fortune to the man returning her to her father. That incident about calling him Morgan and living across from the new park . . . all of that could have been part of the articles written about her in the papers back east. Every newspaper of any standard had told the story of the abduction and ransom demanded for Prima Powell's life. He'd read them himself, but with no more interest than wondering what he might do with the kind of reward Morgan Powell had offered for her safe return.

Thinking along those lines would only get him into trouble. The old Shaw Lawson would be intrigued by what he could get out of escorting her home. The new Shaw said to listen to his gut instinct, get her some help, and be about his own business. From the looks of the crops, there was plenty here to prove the jars' worth and to ensure his fortune. He didn't need the trouble of dealing with a man who might make a wrong assumption about his connection to Prima's abduction.

"I'll pull ashore and tie off the boat. Can't leave it unattended too long. You never know when someone might come along and think it's been abandoned and claim it for their own. I've got a lot invested."

"I won't keep you any longer than is necessary, Mr. Lawson. As I said before, I intend to pay you for every moment of your time."

"That's not what I meant."

"Then what did you mean?"

"That I hope you *do* recognize someone here or they, you. It would make things a lot easier."

"You mean *faster*—so you can go about your business." She looked irritated.

She certainly had the famed Powell temper. "What's tied your bonnet string too tight?"

"Nothing you'd understand."

"Try me."

"No."

"Why not?"

"Ever heard of being careful what you tell strangers?"

"Who better to discuss your problems with than someone with no biases toward you? Someone you don't have anything invested in?"

She frowned at him. "You either have a mighty high opinion of yourself or you don't get along with your relatives."

Her sharp-tongued comment had a lick of truth to it. A Powell trait, as well? "I just don't have as low opinion of myself as you apparently do at the moment. I can understand as well as the next man, and I haven't done anything to you, lady, but save you from keeling over in a faint and hitting your head again."

"Mr. Lawson—"

"Shaw."

"*Mr.* Lawson, I appreciate that you've been kind in your treatment of me so far, but I think it best that we each go our separate ways. I've found that the less you know about a person, the easier parting with them becomes. Don't you agree?"

He liked the way her eyes frosted like sapphires glazed with ice when she became irritated. He wondered what they'd look like pleased . . . really pleased.

His attraction to the woman surprised him.

She was prettier upon closer inspection. Smaller than he liked women he courted, but still pretty in her own way. Maybe it was her temper, the challenge in her voice. God knew he loved a challenge. "I used to agree with that; then I discovered that it made a man a lot lonelier than he was meant to be. The thing you think I don't understand, by the way, is that you dislike business interfering with whatever your current needs or wants may be."

"What makes you say that?"

The frost in her eyes hardened, chilling him even from this distance. "If you're who you say you are, it makes sense. Being the daughter of a business magnate like Morgan Powell would prove daunting when you want Papa's attention, and business comes first."

She stood, her spine as rigid as the tilt of her chin. "You understand nothing about me or Morgan. And it's none of your business."

She was more than convincing. More than ever since he'd met her, Shaw wondered if the woman actually might be who she claimed. Was it possible Prima Powell had been wandering the Tennessee backwoods, unaware of all that had transpired to her?

No . . . it seemed easier to assume she was exactly what he thought of her—a woman who'd unfortunately hit her head and, for whatever reason, now believed herself to be a missing heiress.

The only sure way to discover the truth was to find someone nearby who recognized her. Moonbow was, after all, the closest settlement. She and the coons couldn't have strayed too far this morning. He'd seen no horse or watercraft to have carried her far from home.

But she was right. He had concerned himself too much with her welfare. "This *isn't* any of my business, but I intend to complete what you asked me to do. I'll find a doctor." He pulled ashore, waded out, and tied off the boat. When he returned, he offered her a hand.

To his surprise she accepted his help. He lifted her off the boat, cradling her in his arms like a newborn. This time he was aware of everything about her. How light she was in weight. How her breasts rose and fell gently against his chest. The scent of her hair. He managed to get her to the bank without dropping her or slipping, but when he started to release her, she pressed a hand gently upon his chest to stop him.

"As much as I would like to walk on my own, I'm still feeling pretty dizzy. If I'm not too heavy, would you mind carrying me? Maybe before we get there, my head will have stopped spinning and I'll be clear-minded enough to go the rest of the way by myself."

When he hesitated, she added, "I'll be glad to pay you for the additional service."

He started walking toward the town at a brisk

pace. The coons ran alongside. "I don't need any money, madame. My help doesn't come at a price. What kind of man do you take me for?"

"A surprising one," she said softly. "I didn't mean to insult you."

At least she had the good graces to know when she should back off. "Apology accepted."

A silent truce ensued, making the walk to town quiet but pleasant. Soon they approached the outskirts. Two gangly boys spotted them, waved, then ran up and fell into step alongside the coons.

"Hiya, Skillet. Jug." The smaller boy tried to pet the larger coon, but Jug ran around Shaw's leg, almost making him trip.

Seeing that the coons weren't going to tolerate any petting, the child introduced himself to Shaw. "I'm Willy Boy, and I'm six." He pointed to the taller lad, who tried to match each of Shaw's strides. "That there's my brother, Cob."

"Pleased to meet you boys. Name's Lawson. Shaw Lawson."

Willy Boy took three steps for every one of Shaw's, so Shaw slowed down a bit. The child managed to corral his curiosity for about two seconds longer than Shaw expected.

"What'cha doing carrying Naomi like that, Mr. Lawson?"

"Yeah. How come she ain't walking on her own?" Cob chimed in. "Her legs quit working or something? My cousin, Tuber, his legs quit working that day he jumped off the—"

"You know this woman?" Shaw knew better than to let one of the locals, particularly one just learning to spin a good yarn, get started. One good tale demanded another until everyone within earshot felt compelled to join in. He didn't have the time to be polite at the moment, and Shaw was pleased that he'd been right about his patient's identity.

"Tell him, Naomi," Cob frowned. "Tell him I know you pretty good."

"My name is not Naomi." Every muscle in the woman's body seemed to grow rigid with indignation.

Willy Boy chimed in. "Why, sure it is, Naomi. Just ask Hazel Annie. That's what she calls you allah time."

Hazel Annie. Annie. Naomi—or whatever this woman's name was—had mentioned an Annie earlier. Shaw grabbed at the one straw that might explain her confusion. His gaze locked with the smaller boy's. "Can you show me where this Hazel Annie lives?"

"Uh-huh. For a penny."

Enterprising little devil. "Deal. But you'll have to wait until I can reach into my pocket and get it. I've got my hands full at the moment and—"

"I'll get it for you. See?"

Willy Boy jammed his hand into the pocket of

Shaw's trousers before Shaw had time to finish his sentence. "Now wait a minute!"

"A whole twenty-dollar gold piece!" Willy Boy held up the prize he'd claimed. He looked at Shaw with new curiosity. "Are you a rich man, Mr. Lawson?"

Before Shaw could answer, Cob ran ahead and told others about the rich man who approached, and who he carried. The next thing Shaw knew, Willy Boy squealed. Skillet had snatched the gold piece out of the boy's hand, and now Jug and Willy Boy were weaving in and out of the growing entourage, chasing the animal to try to claim the prize for themselves.

Shaw had no idea where he was headed, but everyone else seemed to be following him.

That's just about the way it always goes, he grumbled inwardly. Forget the fact that he had no clue to his destination ... he was still expected to lead. A fact that had been his call to duty all his life. "I'll get the coin from the coon, Willy. If you'll earn it and show me where I can find this Hazel Annie person."

"Oops. I forgot, mister."

"There seems to be a lot of that going around today."

"Put me down."

Naomi tried to break free from his hold, but this time he refused to let go. She was in clear sight of several people and had nothing to fear

63

from him. She might think he was criticizing her lack of memory, but he wasn't, and he wasn't sure she should be standing, much less walking on her own. "Not till you're safe with this Annie person."

"I won't be left with anyone other than the doctor. I've had quite enough of strangers today, thank you."

"Miz Annie's the best healer this side of the Smokies," Willy Boy informed Shaw. "Ain't nobody better at fixing folks than Annie."

By the time Shaw reached the general store, several people had joined the entourage, all curious about what had transpired.

"There she is!" Willy Boy waved at the aging woman sitting in the ladder-back chair in front of a rickety-looking cabin. A thick braid dangled past one shoulder, a startling contrast to the suntanned hue of her wrinkled skin. She seemed to be sleeping, but Shaw noticed smoke drifting from the corncob pipe nestled in one side of her mouth. One eye opened slightly, squinting against the afternoon glare.

The two coons ran up to the chair and played chase around the old woman's skirt hem. She reached a hand down as they made a pass in front of her and magically came up with something shiny in her fingers. The gold piece. The coons instantly stopped, lay at her feet, and hid their faces.

"That's mine, Hazel Annie!" Willy Boy shouted, then seemed to remember his obligation. "Something's done gone wrong with Naomi."

Long strides ate up the distance that separated Shaw from the healer. "Are you Hazel Annie?"

"That I be." The eye remained open, a hazel orb appraising Shaw from toe to eyes. "I've been expecting ye."

Willie Boy accepted the coin the old woman handed him and whispered in awe, "She kin tell what's gonna happen 'fore anybody knows it."

"Be mindful of that, boy, and don't be buying too much of that sassafras."

"How'd you know I's gonna . . ." Reverence filled Willy Boy's expression. "Yes, Miz Annie. I'll just git me a lick or two."

Shaw respected the mountainfolk's ways enough not to mock the woman's proposed talent. He had his own beliefs—that telling the future wasn't something he believed many people were good at. And the one thing he needed to know at the moment didn't need a fortune-teller. "Is this woman's name Naomi?"

"Naomi Romans, 'tis a fact." The hazel eye did a swift inventory of Naomi's condition. "I reckon we be obliged to ye now for seeing her safe."

Naomi started to protest, but Shaw hushed her. "If you'll point me the right direction, I'd be happy to take her home."

The woman stood and blew out a ring of smoke. Though she couldn't have been any taller than four-foot-eight, she had the bearing of someone twice her height. "She lives here, and I be her grandmother, Annie Romans. Hazel Annie to most around here. Her only relative."

Naomi—Prima, whoever she was—gripped Shaw as if he were a lifeline about to shred into pieces.

She clutched him in desperation and insisted, "I've never seen this woman before in my life."

Chapter Five

Though the Tennessee sun was warm, Prima felt a chill in her bones. She didn't know the woman claiming her as relative any more than she recognized this small hamlet of hill people. "Put me down!" she demanded, struggling to break free from Lawson's cradling arms.

"You'll fall."

"I insist you put me down . . . now!"

"Ye ain't yourself, are ye, gal?" The one-eyed woman's forehead wrinkled with concern. She grabbed the cane propped against the wall next to the chair she'd been sitting in and hobbled inside the cabin's open door. "Bring her and let her lay down a spell."

"I don't want to go in there. I don't know that woman!"

"Now quit struggling, Miss Romans." Lawson's

grip remained tight around her. "I'll let go soon enough once you can lie down instead of fall down."

She continued to struggle, straining one way and another in an effort to make it so difficult for him to hold her that he'd have to let go. But the man had the arms of an oak, and the effort served only to make her head feel even dizzier. She ceased her battling for the moment, closing her eyes to let the world quit spinning.

"You'll have to let me down sometime," she thought she shouted, but the words came out only as a faltering whimper.

"Only too glad to, miss, once there's somewhere to let you rest."

Murmurs echoed from behind them, drawing her attention away from her anger at the man. It seemed her predicament had drawn the attention of most of the inhabitants of the little mountain hamlet. She felt like the latest medicine show rolling into town. An ironic image, she admitted, since her so-called rescuer was a peddler of such potions. "You'd think they had nothing better to do than watch a woman being kidnapped against her will."

"Versus kidnapped willingly?"

The chuckle that rumbled deep from his chest forced her eyes open. Despite her fury about the abduction, she found herself pleased by how the lines around his eyes crinkled with humor. She felt a traitor to herself. "You know very well what I mean," she said as she fought off the attraction. "You'd think you were a mother goose leading her goslings."

"No, I don't know what you mean. And I'm not even sure *you* know at the moment." His gaze locked with hers. "But I did think the same thing a few minutes ago. It's kind of hard for people to expect you to lead when you have no idea where you're going. Sometimes a man would just like to be a goose and let someone else point the direction. It'd be nice to coast a little. Know what I mean?"

What had happened in this man's life to compel him to make such an observation? Her curiosity about Shaw Lawson was sparked. Perhaps she needed to make a point of finding out a little about the peddler. Morgan could easily set his hounds to investigating the matter. She would definitely send a message to her father as soon as she had regained her freedom and this exasperating brain ache subsided.

She was, after all, her father's daughter, capable of her own measures, despite what Morgan thought. "I wonder, when you're paid for your troubles, will my father find you more a sinner than a saint?"

"I've had my stint at both. But right now I'm trying my hand at a little redemption. You see, lately I've been too much of a sinner."

"Such animosity. And here you are expecting me to trust my well-being to such a person? I think you should put me down before you have more to repent for."

"My full name's already engraved in brimstone. One more sin or less won't erase a letter of it."

Her nostrils flared, his animosity toward himself almost palpable. It was then that she noticed the scent of drying herbs hanging heavy in the air. It wasn't altogether unpleasant, but uncomfortably familiar in some way. Unnerving.

She studied the shelves upon shelves of pottery, jugs, and baskets that lined the old woman's cabin. Pots bubbled on the cast-iron stove in one corner of the large room. A large curtain made of scrap material cordoned off a section of the house that must go deeper into the hillside that formed the cabin's back wall. The two raccoons scampered off in that direction, disappearing beneath the curtain's hem.

"Ready for a nap, they be," the old woman announced. "Ye kept them out a lot longer than usual this morning. Ain't natural, them coons wandering the woods come daylight. Ye're going against their nature, ye are."

Two years' worth of this morning, Prima thought sarcastically, then tried to imagine herself as this Naomi person who had raccoons for pets. Trying to conjure such an image only made

70

her head hurt worse. She was finding it hard to concentrate, feeling the edge of sleep creeping in to overtake her.

Take note, her mind warned. *Know where you are.* She had to learn more details about this place where she was being taken, so she could escape it more easily.

A hickory surface bereft of any cloth to adorn its top stood in the middle of the room with quilts spread over two work chairs sitting opposite each side. Prima knew suddenly that it was not a table, but an old sea trunk that had been brought over by one of the original settlers of the thirteen colonies, and it provided a setting for a prized crystal tea set. It was a fact she couldn't possibly know, yet sensed was true somehow. "It c-can't be," she whispered.

"You remember something, don't you?"

Though she wanted to deny it, Lawson's tone sounded pleased and she saw relief in his eyes. "Of course not," she lied softly, unwilling to admit her continued confusion.

"Back here." The old woman pulled aside the curtain under which the coons had disappeared. A tunnel journeyed deep into the mountain, lit by candles glowing overhead in lanterns. Two curtains on either side of the earthen hallway sectioned off four rooms from visitors. A large wooden door with an iron rod stretched and bolted across its center ended whatever access there was to deeper inside the mountain.

"Her room be the first on the right."

Feeling herself sinking more into despair with each step farther into Annie Romans's house, Prima wondered if she had lost her mind and she had awakened into some kind of remembered hell. Just as the woman pushed aside the curtain to her supposed bedroom, Prima gasped at the exquisite beauty before her.

The fragrance of rhododendron filled her senses. The crimson flowers, interwoven with garlands of ivy, encircled the ceiling, then cascaded in four compass points to the floor. A dark quarried stone of some kind unfamiliar to her formed an incredibly shiny flooring beneath their feet, while a cream-colored comforter on the massive chestnut bed that took up much of the room offered a welcoming ordinariness. Skillet and Jug lay on handwoven rugs of a color matching the bedcoverings, napping just as the old woman had predicted.

Above them, opening onto the hillside itself, were windows shaped like full moons that bathed the room in beams of light—moons made of the same crystal seen in the main room. It was as if a sunlit garden had been carved out of the hill.

Clean, fresh, rich fragrances of polished chestnut and flowers revealed that Annie Romans might look like destitute mountainfolk, but the

woman had the refinement of someone more re-
gal.

"It's quite lovely," she admitted as Annie
turned back the bedcovers. This room would do
quite nicely as an interim place to plot her escape. Quite nicely, indeed.

" 'Tis." Annie motioned Lawson over to place
Prima on the bed. "Took ye nigh on six full
moons to see it finished."

"*I* did this?" Even as her senses reeled with the
quality of the room now at her disposal and the
tenderness of the man's touch as he propped her
gently against the pillows, a strangeness enveloped Prima. This place felt right. It felt as though
it were hers. It looked like something she might
design. She felt some sort of sense of accomplishment in the effort. But it couldn't be. She couldn't
have.

Morgan had never allowed her to lift more
than an embroidery needle. And that only to add
monograms into the lace kerchiefs sewn for her.
She was a Powell. Waited on by servants. A deb-
utante of New York society. Groomed to become
a doting wife to the lucky man Morgan chose to
increase the Powell coffers. She was no stone
lifter or flower arranger.

The need to cry engulfed Prima. She almost
gave in to the overwhelming impulse, though not
for the fact that she was totally confused about
what had happened to her and that she now lay

in an alien bed in the presence of strangers bent upon "helping" her. She almost relented out of a deep sadness that came from knowing she had truly lost her senses and somehow become this Naomi person everyone claimed her to be, that it had taken a stranger to give her what her own father would not—the freedom to discover what she could do on her own. Despite her effort to fight them, tears brimmed in Prima's lashes.

"Ye're just tired, child. Close yer eyes and rest. Yer deliverer here kin tell me what ails ye."

A caring touch pressed against Prima's forehead. The woman's aged hand smoothed back the wisps of hair from Prima's brow. "That looks like a nasty lick ye took, sprite. Grandmother will have it seen to afore you can say 'two bald brothers bandied a beer barrel.' "

"I'm not who you think I am." Prima blinked back the shades of gray creeping into her vision. She mustn't go to sleep. She mustn't. She searched the old woman's discerning hazel eye. "I'm really not."

The old woman patted Prima's shoulder. "Ye're exactly who I know ye to be, child. Now let the angels kiss yer dreams, lass, and we'll take up the talk upon yer waking."

"I'll let your grandmother know how I found you, then check in on you later." Lawson turned to leave.

Prima's hand shot out to Lawson. "Please don't

go. Don't leave me here, Mr. Lawson. Shaw." She tried not to sound frightened, but she was. More frightened than she'd ever been in her life. "I-I don't belong here. I'm not who she says I am. I don't know why she's saying it. Maybe she thinks she can get something out of it." She couldn't meet the woman's gaze any longer, unable to ignore the look of hurt she saw dart across the hazel eye.

"Contact my father," Prima insisted, trying to sit up but finding her head becoming dizzier with each effort. "Tell him to send someone who knows me. They'll verify my identity."

"Now what kind of da would not come see his wee one's true self?" Annie frowned, sharing a glance with Lawson that said she thought the hit on the head had truly scattered her granddaughter's wits.

"One who's so busy with business that he hires others to tend to . . ." The blackness clouding Prima's mind deepened in hue. She was tired. So very tired. ". . . lesser matters." She willed her eyes open one last time. "You can't leave me, Shaw. You promised to see me home safely. I'm not safe."

Chapter Six

"I'll stay. For a little while." Shaw watched relief ease the furrows in his patient's brow. He couldn't leave her. As much as he wanted to—and needed to be about his own business—he hadn't fulfilled his own promise to himself about her. She'd required only that he take her to a doctor. In these tiny hill-country settlements, a local healer was considered the next best thing to a real doctor. But he'd promised to see "Prima" safely home. The fact that she didn't yet *feel* safe demanded that he remain.

Shaw ran a hand through his hair and exhaled a long breath. But before he could ask the old woman if he could impose for a few hours, she disappeared past the curtain and returned with one of the two chairs he'd spotted in the main room.

"Sit a spell beside her. She won't go to sleep unless ye do. She can be all-fired stubborn if she puts her mind to it. And from the looks of her, she needs to rest her mind." Annie handed him the chair. "I'll make some ginger tea. It'll ease that head bruise of hers when she wakes up, and help ye make a clear decision."

Annie retreated from the room, leaving Shaw alone with Naomi. Was it possible the healer could hear his thoughts? More likely her years allowed the old woman to be a discerning judge of character. Either way, she was right. He needed to decide how far he was going to carry the obligation he felt toward Naomi.

He placed the chair beside the bed and took a seat. Naomi's eyes stared at him, making him shift in the chair. A couple of times her lashes drifted closed, then immediately flashed open as if she'd been startled. He realized she was fighting sleep, afraid he wouldn't keep his word and stay. "Go to sleep, Naomi. I'll be here when you wake up. I promise."

"My name's not Naomi. It's Prima. Prima Pow—"

Her eyes and lips closed in midargument. Giving in to sleep eased her features, making her skin look even paler against the darkening hue of her bruised forehead.

"That was quite a hit you took." Shaw reached over and pulled the comforter up, tucking it around her shoulders. Her head turned toward him, the bruise and one cheek nuzzling against the pillow as she settled in. The scattering of freckles across the bridge of her nose seemed more noticeable now, and he thought they made her look younger in sleep. Young and prettier than he had first imagined.

Just your imagination. It's that big-brother protector thing you have within you, Shaw reminded himself. *You're feeling guilty about causing her harm on top of feeling ashamed that you haven't seen Hannah and the others since . . . well, in too damn long.*

He wondered what his sisters would say if he suddenly showed up after five years. Would they welcome him or tell him to get out of their lives, as he had done to them on that horrible day?

Maybe that was what this was. Maybe he thought by seeing Naomi safe, he could somehow make up for hurting Hannah. His hands slapped down on his knees with such force he was sure it could have awakened the dead. He stood, muttering a silent oath to be less stupid. But he'd been stupid on too many occasions. What was one more?

The rattle of teacups warned of Annie's return. Shaw watched the curtain move back as she entered with the crystal tea service clasped in both hands. He moved to take it from her. "Here, let me help."

"Thank ye kindly. I'll go fetch the other chair."

"I would've done that if I'd known—"

Before he could finish his statement, she had left. He didn't see anywhere he could place the tea set, so he simply held it and awaited his hostess's return. It didn't take her long.

Annie brought in the chair and moved it close to his. Then she bent beneath the bed and pulled out a trunk. "Ye can set the tray on that. Don't rightly have much room in these tommyholes. My JickJack ran outta spunk digging as many rooms as he did. Couldn't convince him all we needed was a couple of big 'uns. But you know a Scotsman. He wanted a brood of lads and lassies." As she straightened her bearing, she groaned. "These old bones are a misery," she complained. "Good thing I got me a fine crop of corn to heal what ails 'em."

She pulled out a flask from her skirt pocket and took a sip. "Course, me and the Lord ain't presently in agreement on whether or not whiskey is the best remedy for the ailment, but I got every confidence when the time comes for Him and me to settle up old matters, He'll be fair and fiddling." She took another sip, then cocked an eyebrow at Shaw. "Care fer a swig?"

Shaw shook his head. He'd shared a jug of corn whiskey with one of the traders he'd met in Kentucky, trying to make quick friends and quicker money. He'd suffered a sour belly and couldn't remember where he'd tied off his flatboat for a day and a half. "Tea sounds good right now."

He placed the tea set on the trunk and waited for Annie to take a seat. She stood there looking at him. He continued to stand. He was, after all, his mother's son. Ladies, whether born or city bred, were seated first.

"Well, outlander, take a seat. It ain't polite for mountainfolk not to let you settle in before we gawk at ye."

Despite her frankness, Shaw liked the woman immediately. He laughed and did as he was told. "I take that to mean you're going to interrogate me about why I'm with your granddaughter."

She returned the flask to her pocket and sat, reaching down to pour from the teapot.

"Let me." Shaw poured the tea into the cups, surprised that it didn't shatter the delicate crystal. He handed Annie a cup and took one for himself. "I was expecting something hot."

"Cold as a duck's butt on the Cumberland come January. Ginger, when its wild and cold, heals different than when it's dried and boiled hot." Annie took a sip. "Cold clears the senses."

"And counterbalances those clouded by warm whiskey?"

The hazel eye winked at Shaw and he laughed. He was beginning to like Annie Romans a lot. He hoped when Naomi woke and spent some time in the woman's company she'd feel the same. But liking someone and trusting them were two altogether different matters.

"Ye got questions, son. About me and my Naomi. Go ahead and ask."

Shaw took a sip of tea as he thought not about what to ask, but how to do so without offending the old woman. "Say, this is actually cold. How did you get it that way?"

Hazel nodded to the back wall. "Got me a artesian spring that runs underneath part of the back room. I store milk and perishables there. Don't even have to boil snow in the dead of winter. Temperature doesn't change much in the tunnel, come summer or winter. Don't worry 'bout the spring freezing up."

"And the room across the hall? Is that your bedroom?" Shaw wondered why there were so many rooms in the tunnel. She'd said she was Naomi's only relative. That meant those rooms had other uses than children's bedchambers.

"That one's for patients who have to stay a spell. Mine's the one just past it. It's warm, and drier than the others. I 'spect there's a vein of ore over its roof that ain't in the others. JickJack couldn't dig no sky views in it, bless his departed soul, so I made it my dry house."

"JickJack?"

"My husband. Dead twenty-one years past." The one eye closed as grief aged the woman's face further.

Shaw pretended to sip his tea, letting her gain control of whatever depth of emotion she was feeling.

In a solid voice, she continued. "Jick said if we wasn't gonna have no more babies, then by gumption I should have me a place where I could baby my herbs. The ones that sun and dewdrops make poorly. Jick knew how to please me fine. I love that old room. Now me and my herbs sleep there, warm and snug as water ouzels what crawled up on a rock to dry in the sun."

She loved the room, but it was clear she loved the man even more. Four rooms, each one offering a glimpse at Shaw's hostess's personality. One, an imaginative way to keep perishables, which said she was practical and competent. Two, a room to house patients, which proved she was compassionate and respected in the community. Three, a room that housed her obvious life's passions. And four, a room she allowed a beloved granddaughter to decorate the way she'd wanted. They were the signs of someone who knew how to let a person grow and develop into herself. All these aspects made Shaw even more certain Annie Romans was someone Naomi should trust.

"Tell me what happened."

Annie's directness surprised him. There was no judgment in her tone. Why that should have surprised him bothered Shaw. Was he so ready to judge himself lately that he expected everyone else to do so, too?

Shaw watched Annie, wondering if she could read his thoughts, and what she would think of him. "I waved to her. Apparently distracted, she fell. Must have hit her head on the way down."

"Must've hit a hickory tree. There's a few slivers under the skin. I'll take them out once she's rested a mite. 'Twould be best to wait till she has a bit more sense about her afore I numb her."

Shaw studied Naomi. "Has anything like this ever happened to her before?"

Annie glanced toward the raccoons. "Can't say for certain that it has."

For the first time since he'd met her, he wondered if the healer was being evasive.

"Them coons any part of the trouble?"

She hadn't turned away to mislead him. She'd simply wanted to gauge the animals' role in the fall.

"I can't say as they were, although they ran toward me from the same direction I found her."

"I told that child the pair of them would be the death of her if she didn't start treating them like coons instead of chillun. Coons are night creatures by nature. She's got them running the woods with her at all hours. It ain't right to make a body do what others do, just 'cause they be kin. The child is stubborn as a mule with no git in his gait."

"Has she been that way all her life?" All of this was fine and good to find out about Naomi, but he needed to start asking the pertinent questions—the ones that would let him feel comfortable leaving her with Annie. How long had she lived with her grandmother?

"She's been more set in her ways the past couple of years."

"That why she hasn't married?" If Annie was her only relative, Naomi wasn't wed. She looked young, but she had to be long past marrying age . . . especially here in the hills, where some folks paired up at age thirteen.

"She has a beau rightly enough. He'll be a wad of worry when he hears about this."

A beau. Naomi was being courted by someone. It shouldn't have mattered one bit to Shaw, but he found himself wondering what kind of man attracted her. What he looked like. How much she really liked him. He hadn't pictured her with anyone.

It's no concern of yours, he reminded himself. "Then he'll be back soon? She'll remember more once she sees him, I'll bet."

"Ye can stay in the room across the way. I've got a bed made up for patients. That way, if she wakes, ye'll be close and hear her."

"I can't stay, ma'am. I have a flatboat full of goods I can't just leave on the open river. Somebody'll claim it as their own and—"

"It be safe enough. I'll tell folks ye're staying with me till the sprite's better."

"Why would you do that?" Shaw knew the power of such hill women. The Appalachians were settled by Scotch-Irish folk who'd traveled from the old country to find new homes here in America. They were a clannish lot, superstitious about and unrelentingly faithful to their women healers. Such a woman ruled not only the place where she lived, but several hills and hollers of people in every direction. If she wielded such power, he and his belongings would be guaranteed safekeeping while under her hospitality. And she would not be someone he wanted to annoy. . . .

"Ye need to stay as much as she wants ye to."

Shaw slid the healer a long look. "Trying to tell my future, are you?"

"Ye aren't here just to peddle goods, lad, or ye'd have pitched yer banner afore ye stepped two feet in town. Ye need something else from Moonbow. From Naomi. Maybe a little rescuing yerself?"

Maybe there was something to this talent she had. "Why do *you* think I'm here?"

Annie sipped her tea, then replied quietly, "You need somewhere where people accept you for what you are now."

Very close. Too damned close. "Why's that?"

"Seems to me that you want to atone for something, perhaps because ye didn't rescue someone ye thought ye should have."

Enough was enough. "If that's so, then I've done my part. I rescued your granddaughter. That should make my conscience clear of whatever you think I didn't do . . . right? I should be free to go."

"Unless"—Annie reached out and patted Naomi's hand—"it's yer calling to help her accept who she is now."

Chapter Seven

Prima awoke unconvinced that she hadn't experienced a long, disastrous nightmare. She reached up to test it in the one sure way to discover if it were all true or just an overactive imagination. Her hand expected to touch flesh, but instead felt cloth. Her fingers traced the material, discovering that it encircled her head. A bandage.

Slight pressure at her right temple revealed that the wound was still tender to the touch.

Shaken, she forced her eyes open. A dim glow illuminated the room, giving it a soft, reassuring atmosphere. Light shone from overhead crystal orbs built into an earthen ceiling that rose over a room she'd prayed she wouldn't wake up in.

Prima lay without moving for a moment, trying to separate dream from reality. But necessity demanded that she attempt to sit up. She needed a glass of water . . . anything to take away this terrible sense of being stranded alone somewhere without hope of anyone believing her, without reason for being there, without a life to call her own.

She had barely slipped her legs from the covers when one of the shadows shifted and came alive. Someone stood from the chair next to the bed. Her eyes pressed closed, willing the man's image back into the remnants of her dream, but his tawny hair, broad shoulders, and wilderness-hardened physique made mistaking him impossible.

Shaw Lawson and his rescue of her was no dream. That meant everyone thought she was Naomi Romans. She had not dreamed the nightmare, but awakened to it.

He poured amber liquid into the cup that sat alongside a teapot on a trunk she hadn't noticed before. One of his knuckles gently curved beneath her chin, urging it upward so he could hold the cup to her lips.

"Sip this."

Her hands reached up to hold the cup herself, but he didn't let go. "It's the least I can do for you."

She took a sip, staring at him over the brim, surprised that he was still there. If her memory of what had transpired had been true, she'd expected him to hit the trail the moment she'd given in to sleep. The liquid was unexpectedly cold. It had a bitter taste, but was not so disagreeable she couldn't endure it. "What is it?"

"One of Annie's remedies. Wild ginger, I think. Supposed to make your head quit throbbing." His knuckle uncurled and he let go of her chin long enough to push away a strand of hair that had fallen over the bandage. "Does it still hurt much?"

"A little. Not like before." *Not like in yesterday's dream*, she wanted to say. But it hadn't been a dream. She handed him back the cup and stood, trying to get her bearings and see how much she remembered of this so-called reality. "How long have I been sleeping?"

"Three days."

"*Three?*" She gasped, noticing the shadow of whiskers that darkened his jaw. Had he sat there watching her all that time? Suddenly it dawned on her that she wore a nightgown. The braid she'd been so surprised at wearing now hung down her left shoulder instead of in back. Her hands were no longer colored with whatever had stained them. She crossed them in front of her breasts as if he were seeing her naked. She was not prudish. After all, there had been times her Quest team had stripped down to their long johns or chemise and pantaloons to swim, but the choice to be unclothed in front of someone had always been her own. "I hope Annie was the one kind enough to do the changing for me."

"She was."

Prima grabbed the coverlet and wrapped it around herself. With what little light there was in the room at the moment, he couldn't have seen through the linen gown, but she felt naked to his view all the same. No matter that Morgan thought his own daughter was quite a hotspur; she didn't invite men into her boudoir.

All this movement was making something critically necessary. Something unladylike to discuss in polite society.

"Feel up to walking or would you prefer I carry you?" Lawson took a few steps toward the door.

"Where are we going?" Wherever it was would have to be her second destination.

He grinned. "I think we both know where."

Her cheeks blazed with embarrassment. He knew. "*We* aren't going anywhere!"

"I just want to make sure you're steady on your feet." His gaze studied her from bare toes to bandage. "You look like you could still use some help."

Holding the mass of covers that protected her from any more intimate examination, she took a tentative step, testing her weight. She took another one, then another. Her body was stiff from lying in bed for days, but not so weak that she couldn't do at least this one thing on her own. By the time she reached him at the door, she met his gaze squarely. "If you'd be so kind as to show me the way, that'll be sufficient. I assume since you've been here, you've found the . . . where Mrs. Romans . . . you know where I mean!" she finished in exasperation.

Shaw chuckled.

"Your humor eludes me, Mr. Lawson." She moved past him in a huff, pushed aside the curtain that formed the doorway to her bedchamber, and headed into the main room.

"Wrong way."

She spun around to face him and wished immediately that she hadn't. The world careened. Her hand shot out to anchor itself against the wall.

He wrapped an arm around her waist to offer support. "No need to waste that feistiness on me, Naomi. I'll be long gone from here as soon as you're better."

She allowed him to help her, her feet shuffling forward where he led. "I'm sure it would be wasted on Naomi as well, whoever she is. Now, if you'll cool that egotistical fire you've built for yourself, you could be finished with me a lot sooner by showing me where to go. Or better yet, fetch Mrs. Romans. Perhaps I could pay her to help me find the place."

"Stand here." His tone was brief, angry. "I'll unbolt the damn thing for you." The strides carrying him down the tunnel were long and powerful. "Don't worry. No charge."

He slammed back the iron rod and swung open the door to the end of the tunnel, revealing another curtained-off room several yards deep into the hillside, but well lit all the same.

"The necessary." Lawson motioned toward the room.

"*That's* her outhouse?"

"A single-seater. The cabin is self-contained even in winter. Probably too uncouth for the likes of you, Miss *Powell*." The air vibrated with his mockery of her proposed identity.

"I've made you angry."

"Brilliant deduction. Your head must be feeling better."

"Were you *fond* of this Romans woman?"

"You didn't see her taking care of you while you were sick. That woman loves you with everything she is. Where the hell do you think she is right now?"

Prima had wondered why the woman had left two strangers alone in her house. She was apparently a trusting soul. "I have no idea."

"Up in one of the meadows at church with the circuit preacher." Lawson's gaze had turned the color of the evergreens at twilight, almost black, it was so piercing. "She's got everyone from here to Nashville praying for your recovery. I won't have you insult her, either. If you so much as

92

offer her a single penny for helping you, I swear I'll pull you across my lap and spank that spoiled backside of yours with my own hand."

"You wouldn't dare!"

"Try me, lady. You don't hurt the people who love you. That's a price too high for anyone to pay. Now, be done with what you must so I can see you back to bed. Maybe a little more rest will clear your senses better, or at least give Annie some time to rest herself. If everyone hadn't said no, I could believe you were the spoiled child of a rich man."

She felt she'd been slapped. "I may be Morgan Powell's daughter, but I'm spoiled only because he insisted upon it. God knows I've tried to be something more than just a pretty arm piece for his proposed heir to the empire. The man unfortunately was blessed with daughters instead of sons. I will not stand here and be blamed for repercussions of my personality that have been forced upon me, sir!"

Though shocked by her own vehemence, Prima felt somehow cleansed by her reproach of the man's judgment. How long had those words been embedded in her soul, waiting for the opportunity to scream them to the heavens? She'd wanted to be different from her sisters, who thrived on their father's expectations. She had ached to find out how "ordinary" people lived, how they learned to cope with how life challenged them. The biggest challenge as a Powell, more often than not, was to choose a flavored pastry for breakfast.

"Then I suggest you make good use of the time you're with this healer. She could teach you a few things that would serve you well . . . if you return to your so-called father's home."

Annie Romans had made quite the impression on Lawson—or, from what he'd said about not hurting people you love, someone had disappointed him badly. Prima couldn't resist satisfying her curiosity. "You must have been hurt yourself by someone close to you. Mind if I ask who?"

Shaw's jaw stiffened, looking more chiseled from rock than the tunnel that surrounded them. His eyes refused to meet hers, his voice echoing with a distance that nothing could cross. "Someone as full of it as yourself, Miss Romans."

The people of Moonbow were guarded against Shaw's questions about Naomi. When he discussed his jars and what they could do to preserve foodstuffs, he made a point of learning anything he could about the woman. If a comment was made about her and the coons, he asked how long she'd owned them. When he inquired about Naomi's unique accent, someone said she'd visited from back east and decided to stay. That led to his investigating exactly when she'd first paid the visit. A few agreed that it had been at least two years ago. But word must have gotten around that he was asking too many questions. He might be under Annie's hospitality and had the privilege of community that allotted him, but Naomi was one of their own. A protective unity of silence had ensued, and Shaw knew he would glean no more information from the hill people.

None of what he'd gathered had been enough to prove she was Prima, yet there was enough evidence to make it possible that this was the last place the missing heiress had spent her time these past two years . . . but why? Everyone thought Prima Powell was dead, killed by whoever had sent the ransom note to her father. If she was alive, what was she doing here . . . and why did everyone think she was Naomi Romans? This was too much of a puzzle, if true. It was too unbelievable to think Annie Romans might be part of such a conspiracy.

Though he'd stayed in the Romans cabin at Annie's insistence and out of a sense of obligation to Naomi, Shaw was ready to put an end to the matter. He'd watched Annie for days. Naomi was safe in her hands. He needed to be about his business. Not that he needed to go farther downstream. There was plenty of food to put up for the coming winter, and his jars were badly needed here. Just yesterday he'd watched a woman throw out a crock of pickled beets after only a month of storage. If he made a success of the jars here, news would reach Nashville before he could. Customers would wait at the riverbank to meet his flatboat instead of his having to peddle them in town. Not having to transport them from boat to rented cart would save lots of time—and money.

The Pumpkin Patch, the name given to the local general store, was doing a brisk business when Shaw wiped his boots across the doorstep and entered. Willy Boy and Cob were arguing over who would be the first to make enough money to buy the new whittling knife the storekeep had laid on the counter in front of them. Two ladies stopped their examination of a bolt of cloth to turn and look at Shaw. The buzz of conversation dimmed when the four men sitting in the chairs near the potbellied stove in the corner took notice of his presence. He'd discovered the first day that the circle of chairs offered a great place to visit with friends or share a bit of news. He'd found a different audience to hawk his wares every day since. Today was no exception.

"Evening." He remembered his manners and took off his slouch hat, nodding in acknowledgment to the ladies. Both offered a smile, then turned their attention back to the cloth.

"Outlander." The burliest of the four hill men

returned Shaw's greeting and nodded toward a chair hanging on the wall. It was a silent invitation to join the circle.

Willy Boy spotted Shaw and quit arguing with his friend. "Hey, Mr. Lawson. How's Miz Naomi? She better?"

He could almost feel everyone's ears perking up to learn of Naomi's condition, though no one looked at him directly but the two boys. "She's up and around this morning. Looking much better. Mrs. Romans has done a fine job of caring for her."

"No one better." Respect radiated from the burly man's tone, warming the chill of silence.

"Hazel Annie can cure any misery," piped in another man. "A body should be proud to call Annie grandmother."

"Ain't everybody Annie holds such fondness for," replied yet another. All four men nodded in agreement to the last statement.

"Why, I remember when old man Whip was spilling mortal gorm that time and she—"

"Buford . . ." With a single mention of the burly man's name, one of the women had the code of silence set into place again. Everyone in the store seemed to share a glance, then went back to what they were doing before Shaw had entered.

There was something that wasn't being said here. Or worse, something that *was*. Shaw had the feeling that these people were trying to convince him of how lucky Naomi should be to have Annie for a relative. Maybe trying too hard.

A tug on Shaw's pants reminded him Willy Boy had initiated the question about Naomi. He'd been so busy listening to the others he'd forgotten the child. "Mr. Lawson, you got another gold piece?"

Shaw chuckled and tousled the boy's sandy hair. "No. But I might have a penny or two."

"That won't buy me a knife." The sigh that exited the boy's mouth deflated his gangly frame.

Shaw glanced at the blade the two boys had been arguing over and realized that Willy must have set his heart on owning it. "What happened to the first eagle I gave you? That was enough to buy you and your friend a knife and then some."

Willy Boy shrugged and held up a few pennies. "I gave all but this much to my papa so he could give it to Miz Annie."

Puzzled, Shaw knelt and looked the boy squarely in the eyes. "Why did he give the rest to Miz Annie?"

Tears welled up instantly in Willy Boy's eyes, and he couldn't speak. He just shook his head.

" 'Cause he owed it to her, mister." Cob ran interference for his friend. "Ain't been able to pay her for nigh on three years now. He owed her lots more, what with Willy's ma being sick ever since

Willy was borned. Now me and Willy don't gots enough to pay for the knife."

"I t-thought maybe if Pa gived her the money, she'd be able to buy some more of them hard-to-get rem'dies for Mama." The tears deepened the color of his eyes to chocolate. "Annie says it takes more than mountain seed to cure what ails my mama. Said it's something she's got to get from back east."

The boy's sacrifice heightened Shaw's own sense of painful dishonor at having neglected his responsibility to Hannah. Never before had he felt such shame for his past behavior as he did then, standing there in front of a boy no more than three feet tall.

He had to do something for Willy Boy and his family. Something that would make a difference. Not to make himself feel better, but because it was the right thing to do when something was within his power. Shaw vowed to talk to Annie about the matter when he checked on Naomi later this afternoon.

Right now there was something else he could do to make things right. "Mister?" He motioned to the storekeep and his counter. "You got two of those knives?"

"I have."

"Give one to each boy. I'll pay whatever they don't have."

Willy's eyes instantly brightened, and he ran a

sleeve across the tears that had dripped to his nose. "Golly, Mr. Lawson! Thank ya kindly."

"No, Willy." Shaw swallowed back the lump of emotion knotting his throat. "Thank *you*. Your mother should be proud of her son."

Shaw paid the storekeep, then walked out. Forget hawking any wares or finding out anything more about Naomi and her relationship with Annie Romans. Right now what he needed to do most was something his own mother would be proud of.

Something he hadn't done in a very long time.

Chapter Eight

Prima sat in the chair outside Annie's cabin and watched the last of her morning visitors head down the hill toward their homes.

"Good folk, those McGregors," Hazel Annie complimented, removing the cob pipe from her mouth to blow out a ring of smoke. "Malovera be with child again, ye know."

"That's news to me." Prima caught the sarcasm in her own tone and flashed the healer an apologetic smile. Annie had been kind to her since her arrival. No matter that there was some reason to suspect her hostess of duplicity, Annie had acted nothing but the caring grandmother. If what Prima suspected was true, a suspicion that grew with every visit she'd received from a townsperson this morning, then she owned Annie Romans a wealth of gratitude.

Watching the expectant mother waddle down-hill, her brood of children in step behind her, Prima wondered how well she was supposed to have known the McGregor woman and her children. Six of all sizes and ages, the oldest no more than eight years old, if she were guessing, had paid call. Each child, one at a time, had wanted to kiss Prima's cheek.

All around them the people of Moonbow went about their afternoon chores. Prima had thought she would feel nothing but resentment toward these folks who had misidentified her, but she found herself, instead, speculating on how well she got along with each and how they had played a role in *Naomi*'s life.

The noise of the smithy's maul hammering against iron, the sound of children laughing as they played, the sight of a woman hanging newly laundered clothes to dry all lent an atmosphere of peacefulness to the afternoon and the decision she'd made upon recovering her full senses.

How she had longed to experience such an atmosphere of ordinariness.

Prima's fingers rubbed the soft chambray blouse she wore, admiring its softness against her skin. The nankeen trousers, though a brownish color she didn't prefer, were surprisingly supple. Annie had said she washed them in chamomile and bitterroot, knowing Naomi would want to wear her most comfortable clothes the first day she felt like being up and about.

"Would ye like more tea, sprite?" Annie held the teapot, ready to pour more.

"No, thank you. I've had enough." If she was going to set her plan into motion, then she needed to be sure that her strength was her own and not assisted by an herbal concoction.

"Then ye're feeling yerself enough?"

Prima met the old woman's gaze, wondering if she'd heard an edge of caution in the question. "I'm feeling totally myself, thank you."

"Good." Annie studied her closely, her eye blinking once. "Then 'tis resuming yer chores we'll do tomorrow. I kin use the help with the remedies. I'm a bit lacking in bitterroot and some others. Them coons of yourn been running wild while ye's abed. No time to coddle 'em and even less to keep 'em out of me crocks."

She'd not thought about how she would manage the raccoons. During the night while she'd slept, they'd been absent from her room. During the day they'd lain curled up on their rugs by her bed. It might be interesting to see how well she got along with a pet, since they obviously already liked her. "I'll see what I can do with them," Prima promised.

"Ye've always been an enterprising child." Annie reached out and patted Prima's hand. "I'm sure whatever ye take on, ye'll do with sure hands and a willing heart. God-given talents ye have, girl. A pride to all of us who want to see ye well."

Prima stirred uncomfortably beneath the woman's palm, pretending to stand simply to stretch her legs. But it was as if Annie Romans had looked down into her soul and read the secret wish she'd carried inside for so long; a wish to learn and to do and to test herself. And here she was, being offered a chance to do just that. "I'm going to walk down to the river and see if I can spot Mr. Lawson. I've never really thanked him for rescuing me."

"I willna tell ye not to go, but watch yerself around that man. He is a charmer, working on yer wants and convincing ye of needs that may not be so. But more important to watch than his ambition, ye must be careful of something else, sprite. A man who doesn't know his own heart be in a far worse condition than one not knowing his own mind."

"I'll watch myself around him," Prima assured her. *Around everyone*. Annie's warning lingered in Prima's mind as she waved good-bye to the old woman and headed down the path that led toward town and the river beyond.

She didn't have to be warned about men like Shaw Lawson. She'd met men like him all over the East. Men who wanted to become her friend for only one reason—to win her affections and access to her inheritance.

104

She thought she might even have recognized Shaw's name in regard to some nefarious dealings he'd once made. It seemed her father had once mentioned reading about someone named Lawson, and now that she had a clear enough head to think past the most recent days, she recalled a newspaper account that had not been very flattering, and was quite critical of the man's actions.

In fact, Lawson reportedly had lost his inheritance because of whatever he'd done. Morgan followed only the pursuits of enterprising young businessmen who might one day become advantageous employees of Powell Shipping. For Shaw to be mentioned by name, the peddler must have been on the list for an important position in the ranks of Morgan's employees.

Odd, but the Shaw Lawson she'd known these past few days seemed a perfect gentleman.

Watching the pathway carefully, she tried to recall more of what her father had said about Shaw. The man was reputed to be both arrogant and a lady charmer. Morgan had laughed and said both traits were good for business.

"Hey, Naomi. Good to see you up and around," hollered a man who was loading bags onto his wagon in front of the general store. "Tell Hazel Annie my missus is feeling much better. Gonna fix up a mess of greens and bring 'em by later."

"I'll tell her."

Several other people waved, so she waved back. Naomi seemed well liked in the town—a fact that pleased Prima. Not that she wasn't liked in New York. Many people she knew liked her well enough for the good time she could show them or from fear of reprisals from Morgan. But Annie and Naomi didn't seem to own more than the cabin and the few belongings housed therein. People apparently liked the two women for themselves, a possibility that would make her plan for the next month very interesting.

Excitement hummed in Prima's veins. She could feel the current of curiosity coursing there. She loved an adventure. Thrived on it. But now she was looking forward to the ultimate quest: an adventure into the mundane. She was about to learn how ordinary people lived.

Anticipation put a liveliness into her step. Hurrying toward the flatboat, she couldn't wait to find the peddler and tell him what she had planned. Surely he would take her up on the offer.

She found him at the riverbank, adding more supplies to a wagon.

At her approach, he set down the crate he'd been handling and dusted off his hands. Though the sun shone behind him, casting his eyes in shadow, she could feel the welcome in the relaxed stance he took and the thumbing up of his slouch hat.

"You're looking stronger," he complimented. "Glad to see you on your feet."

"Thanks to you." She thought him more handsome than her recollections. Seen through a blinding headache and lapses of consciousness those past few days had made him seem more phantom than real man.

Sweat streamed down his shirt, plastering it against his skin, revealing rippling muscles beneath the cloth. Visions of him taking off the shirt to relieve himself of the heat made her lips go dry, her throat feel suddenly parched. She swallowed hard, willing the images away and reprimanding herself harshly for pondering such folly. The attempt to clear her mind and find out what was real had her imagination working overtime. She needed to give it a rest.

He took off his hat, wiped a sleeve across his brow, and glanced at the sun. "About time for me to take a break. Want some water? I don't have anything else to offer at the moment."

"Nothing for me, thank you." Prima pressed a hand against her tummy. "Mrs. Romans is a generous hostess."

"Still Mrs. Romans, is it?" He motioned to the flatboat and his tent. "Care to sit a minute? I've got a canteen of water cooling in the tent so it'll be out of the hot sun."

"Lead on." Prima followed him and discovered that he'd pulled the boat close enough to shore that no water had to be forded in order to board.

Once on the craft, she studied the flatboat with new interest. Though most of the supplies had been moved into town somewhere, the boat still looked river-ready. As if he could leave at a moment's notice. But she supposed that was an event most peddlers faced—being run out of town. The tent didn't look much bigger than enough to lay out a bedroll and store a trunk or two. "You *live* here most of the time?"

"When I'm working a river. I don't need much. A place out of the sun. A sky to think."

Shaw bent and disappeared inside the tent, bringing out the canteen. "Violà! Still cool, thanks to Annie. She kept it in that room used as a springhouse and told me to keep it in the shade most of the day. Said it would still be cold this afternoon. She was right. Your grandmother's quite an amazing woman."

"She's not my grandmother. That's what I've come to talk to you about, Shaw."

Shaw glanced at the wagon and then back at Prima. "I promised to meet Mr. McGregor in about an hour. Thought I'd run down and get this last load so I'd have it off the river before I do. But I can stay awhile before I have to meet him." He motioned to the boat bed and the wagon. "Any particular place look good to sit?"

"Are there snakes near the bank?"

His laughter echoed over the countryside.

"You're afraid of snakes but not snake peddlers? That's what I'm called, you know."

Prima smiled. "Should I be?"

"Once," he admitted solemnly. "But you've had a stroke of good fortune, miss. I've turned off my charm for a while. You're safe enough at the moment."

She waved to the boat. "Then by all means, let's sit on the edge of the boat. I want to roll up these trousers and dangle my legs over the side. It's really hot, you know."

"You really want to do that?" He didn't look at all pleased.

"Unless there are real snakes about."

He seemed to be mulling over his answer.

"I can tell if you're lying, you know."

"Have some of Annie's talents, do you?"

"Will you please quit trying to convince yourself that I belong here? I acquit you from any guilt. In fact, once I tell you what I've come to say, you're going to realize you had no part in any of this."

He watched as she chose a place to sit and started rolling up her trouser legs. She felt his gaze upon her and looked up. "What? You've never seen a woman's ankles before?"

"I've seen my share."

She would just bet he had. A man his age and with his rugged handsomeness would have had his share of women. "Then you don't object to my lack of propriety?"

"If you're comfortable with showing your legs to a stranger, far be it from me to disapprove of such a lovely spectacle."

She quickly dipped her legs into the river, enjoying the refreshing coolness that took away the heat of his words and the afternoon sun. Her legs were two of her best assets. Her legs and her derriere. She thought of all three features as a sort of repayment for the lack of cleavage she'd inherited from her mother. It pleased her that he thought they were lovely.

When she noticed him still standing there, she asked, "Aren't you going to roll up yours? It's really quite refreshing." The image of him stripping off his shirt and rolling up his leggings was all too appealing a prospect. She turned her attention to the water, not wanting him to see the flush of heat the image had aroused in her cheeks.

"I prefer to stay dry." He sat beside her, turning his back to the water and stretching his legs out across the flatboat. He took a sip from the canteen. "Sure you don't want some?"

She watched him lick the moisture from his lips. All of a sudden she felt terribly parched . . . as if she hadn't had a drink of anything in years. "Yes, thank you. I believe I do."

Lifting the canteen to her lips, she pressed her mouth against the rim and drank. The taste of him, warm and slightly tangy, still lingered there. A twinkle of yellow-green eyes challenged her, exposing his awareness of the intimacy she felt in the sharing. Prima started to return the canteen, to ignore his dare, but she couldn't. She'd never let anyone but her father get the better of her. She wasn't about to now.

Prima drank again, this time long and deep. "Nothing gets better than this, does it?"

"I can think of a thing or two that might best it," he teased in return.

This time she took a drink to keep him from seeing her blush.

He threw back his head and laughed. "You've got a lot of spit in you, whoever you are."

"You had better hope not," she said, handing him back the canteen.

He glanced at the water container, then back at her. "You wouldn't dare."

"Do you know me so well that you could make such a statement?"

He took the canteen and closed it. "Point taken."

"What?" She feigned a hurt expression. "You're not thirsty anymore?"

"I believe I'll wait until another time."

"A wise man you are, Mr. Lawson."

"Because I won't drink after you?"

Her smile disappeared. "No, because you're smart enough to admit that you're not convinced

111

you know me. That you don't know me well enough even to say whether I'm Naomi Romans."

He placed the canteen on the boat and gave it a push toward the tent. It slid under the shaded tarpaulin like a polished stone gliding across a frozen pond. Shaw stood and excused himself. "Sit there a minute; I'll be right back. I want to show you something."

He went to the wagon, dug inside one of the trunks, and lifted out something that looked like writing parchment. When he returned, he handed the pieces of paper to Prima, then lowered himself beside her. "I like to think I'm a smarter man than most. I want you to read these."

Names lined the paper with notes about how they related to Naomi. Some just had a single word or a title beside them: *Parson. Friend.* Some had statements the person had apparently made. Under Annie's name, a long list of notes had been taken. But each note was something said by someone else, not what Annie had said herself. "What does this all mean?" she asked, handing him back the curious collection.

"They've all got to do with Naomi Romans and how long you've—she's—been in Moonbow. Near as I can tell, Naomi paid Annie a visit about two years ago. Came from somewhere back east."

Prima's heart beat faster. She watched him scan the notes again. He suspected there was something amiss about her identity or he wouldn't have taken the time to go to so much trouble to talk to everyone and write down what he heard. If she'd had any reluctance to share her proposed plan with him before, now all objections were gone.

Still, she needed to proceed with caution. If he were a fortune hunter, like most of his breed, he could use the information she was about to share with him to make himself a very wealthy man.

Cautiously she asked, "What do you make of all this?"

"That either you are exactly what they say you are—a granddaughter who came to visit and stayed," he answered gently, "or you're who you say you are, and there's some sort of explanation why everyone is determined to convince me you're Naomi Romans."

Delighted, Prima breathed a sigh of relief. She hadn't realized how alone she had felt in proving her theory right until she suddenly felt less so. "What made you consider the second possibility?"

"Because everyone seems too ready to prove that Annie is the best thing that could possibly happen to you."

"Exactly." She kicked her feet back and forth in the water, finding it difficult to contain her excitement. Water splashed on Shaw and he grumbled.

"What's the matter? You don't like to get wet?" She laughed.

"Not particularly."

Puzzled, she looked at him. "You make your living on the river. Why would a man choose such a profession if he dislikes water so much?"

"It's called meeting a challenge. Facing one's fears."

"You're a strange man, Mr. Lawson."

His eyes met hers. "And you, miss, need to tell me exactly what you remember so I can determine how strange I think you are."

They shared a laugh before her smile faded and she sobered. "Please keep in mind that I've questioned myself a hundred times since you rescued me. Every doubt that enters your head has already entered mine."

"Go on."

"I guess what I need to know first is what you know about amnesia. Are you familiar with the word?"

He nodded. "I thought that might be what happened to you. A hard hit on the head. Memory loss."

"Good, then keep that in mind while I tell you what I think happened to me. Of course, I can't be certain. But I now know most of what occurred—up to a point—and feel fairly certain about the rest."

How could she begin to explain what had driven her away from her father's home two years ago? She couldn't possibly explain the years of estrangement between her and Morgan. But it was not her duty, at the moment, to persuade Shaw of the right or wrong of it—only that it had happened.

She sighed deeply. "I left my father's home in New York because of an argument we had. As was common practice when we couldn't tolerate the sight of each other for a while, he banished me to our summer home in Nashville. Oh, don't look so sorry for me." She waved away his sympathetic expression. "I could be quite the disagreeable tart when I didn't get my way. And that's what had happened. I hadn't gotten my way in a matter. All we Powells have a ferocious temper."

"So I take it you *are* certain you're Prima Powell, the shipping heiress?"

Did he have to say it that way? Was that all she was ever to be known as in this world—daughter of shipping magnate Morgan Powell? "Yes, I *am* she."

She swung her legs back and forth, making ripples upon the water's surface. "Anyway, I was unwilling to follow his orders yet again without comment. He wanted me to follow in my older sisters' footsteps by becoming society matrons par excellence." Frustration filled her tone as she tried to convince Shaw the way she'd never been able to convince her father. "He didn't understand my need for independence, my desire to be different from the rest. When he refused to let me become a photographer for the railroad, I gladly packed for Nashville. But then I heard of the excursion a few of my friends from Quest were making to the Cumberland."

"Quest?"

A longing to see her old friends pierced Prima to the quick. "A society of thrill seekers I belonged to. We all had parents who indulged our diverse whims, and we often traveled together as a group. We went places that excited us. Found new adventures. In March of that year, we received news that the Cumberland would thaw early, and that if we wanted to see something extraordinary that occurred in only a few places in this world, we would need to make a quick go of it. That extraordinary something was the moonbow you discussed earlier. Ironic, don't you think, since I've ended up here in, of all places, Moonbow, Tennessee."

"That still doesn't explain why everyone thinks you're Naomi Romans."

She nodded. "I'm getting to that, but first things first. The timing couldn't have been better. I decided to punish my father by not telling him about my detour with Quest down the two hundred miles of river. After all, he needn't know. I was headed where he'd told me to go. I'd just get there a little later and not in the manner he expected."

"Why did your friends leave you here?"

"That's something I don't know yet. What I remember is . . ." The images of that last day together with her friends were still a bit fuzzy. Two years had elapsed. Two years of not remembering anything else as Prima Powell.

"The last thing I remember is that we were all in canoes on the Cumberland. The guide we'd hired to head our expedition had not yet returned from his foray downstream to see if there was a better place to camp for the night. A storm had come up suddenly that afternoon and made everything incredibly muddy where we'd originally planned to rest for the night."

His mouth crooked at one corner.

"Oh, now, don't laugh," she argued in her own defense. "We were tired and wet and quite cranky at the time."

"Roughing it, were you?"

"By our standards, yes, very much so." She wanted to wipe the smirk from his lips. "Anyway . . . someone dared me to stand up in the canoe without turning it over."

"And you had to do it."

"We were always taking such challenges. It's

why we called ourselves Quest. To seek out new experiences."

"Sounds precious." His eyes were lit with amusement.

"You can laugh if you want. But we had more fun than you can imagine. There, with each other, no one told us what we could and could not do." Satisfaction filled her momentarily at recalling the success of accomplishing various tasks. But she was not here to fight with Shaw. She was here to gain his support.

"My triumph was short-lived," she admitted. "Someone tilted the canoe on purpose. I didn't hear the shout of warning until it was too late. The next thing I knew, my feet were tumbling over my head. Something hard struck my head, and the current rushed me away. All I remember is fighting the water around me and the blackness that threatened to overtake me. Until I woke up and saw you after you said I fell, I don't remember a thing in between those two moments. Try as I have to understand and recall anything else, there seems only one explanation that makes any sense."

She lifted her legs from the water and stood, needing her feet planted firmly on something solid so she felt solid in her reasoning.

He stood beside her. "And what is that?"

"I must have suffered amnesia," she announced, looking up into his eyes to gauge his reaction. "Not after the fall on that bluff where you found me, but after the hit I took when I fell from the canoe. I've apparently awakened to reality after a memory loss of two years! That would explain why everyone here believes I'm Naomi Romans. I've been her for two years and didn't know it."

Chapter Nine

The more her words sank in, the more they made sense. The girl believed she had awakened from a bout of amnesia and lived the last two years as Naomi. "There's only one thing that still puzzles me," Shaw announced as he searched Prima's face for any sign of indecision. She seemed sincerely convinced of her conclusions.

"Why Annie claims to be my grandmother?" Prima shrugged. "I know. I've asked myself the same question. She's the only one who would know for certain that I wasn't Naomi." She bent to roll down a pant leg.

Shaw tried not to watch, but her long, slim legs sparked a growing awareness of her femininity. He'd observed her sleeping, counted every freckle, knew that her forefinger had a habit of pointing whenever her brow furrowed during a troubled dream—as if she were reprimanding someone. He could guess accurately how many seconds it took for her to stir from sleep to the actual opening of her eyes. The past few days had given him time to study every nuance of her delicate features, and he found himself attracted to her despite his previous predilection for more amply endowed women.

When she caught him staring now, he attempted to play down his interest. "You didn't wear any shoes again, I see."

"It's apparently a habit of Naomi's." She lifted one sole and frowned disgustedly at the callused heel. "My mother would have to use smelling salts if she saw these feet. When I think of all the money she's spent on perfumed liniment and fine stockings to make sure we don't have workwomen's feet . . ."

When she saw Shaw's sneer, she scolded him. "I know. I know. I've had a hard life. Poor little rich girl." She unrolled her other pant leg. "It's just difficult to believe some of the differences I've noticed in what people say about Naomi versus my real personality. How could I have been so different? You wouldn't have caught me dead barefoot!"

Shaw thought her statement was more true than she realized. "It seems that's what everyone back in New York thinks of you. They believe you must be dead." He told her about how her father had received a ransom note from someone who'd said they had abducted her. "When he left the money at the place where it was supposed to be dropped off, no one ever showed up to claim it. Your father waited for a couple of weeks longer, thinking something had caused the kidnapper a delay. Maybe his horse threw a shoe or a wagon wheel broke on the way there. No one showed. Still hasn't. He even left a stone marker at the place—somewhere in Kentucky, I believe. It says that if a note is sent stating that you will be left safely outside the front door of the sheriff's office at a given time, the ransom will be waiting at an arranged place at the exact same time. No one would be there to try to cause the kidnapper any trouble. There'd be no questions asked."

Shaw watched her face for a reaction to the lengths her father had gone to, but found it surprisingly unaffected. "According to *Harper's*, it seems your father has allowed the ransom to remain in that local bank ever since. No one's ever taken him up on the offer. *Harper's* has done an update four times, that I can recall. Your father was quoted saying that by his keeping it in public memory, the abductor might change his mind about returning you, if you indeed still are alive."

Tears moistened her eyes, turning them a twilight blue. "Poor Morgan," she whispered. "He must be so angry."

Though glad that there was some indication of

feeling for her father, Shaw had still expected her to say *sad* or *grief-stricken*. A word of compassion. "*Angry?*"

She nodded. "Yes, angry. Angry at something so out of his control."

"I think you misjudge your father, Miss Powell." Shaw remembered too well his own parents' fear when they'd heard about what had happened to Hannah. They'd waited for hours while the surgeon tried to repair her broken little body, had poured their hearts out in grief when they received the news that, though alive, Hannah would never walk again.

Yes, there had been plenty of anger later—anger at *him*. But not while Hannah's well-being was in question. He'd known better than to take the other boys' challenge to go over the falls in a barrel. He should never have been at the falls in the first place. He was supposed to have been doing his chores. But he was tired of being called Do-Right Lawson, Sure-as-Shooting Shaw, Mama's good little son. All he'd wanted to do was prove he wasn't afraid to try something daring. All Hannah had wanted to do was prove she was able to do anything her brother could.

He'd been thirteen and ignorant. And because of it, now his sister was crippled for life. "If he's angry at anyone," Shaw announced, "it would be whoever kidnapped you . . . and perhaps your friends at Quest for not letting him know what happened. Whoever kidnapped you must have found you when you washed ashore. I don't know when Mrs. Romans came into play in this story, but I don't envy what charges she'll face once you tell your father where you are. I sure hope she came into your life sometime after the kidnapping."

"You like her, don't you?"

Shaw nodded. "If she's innocent, I wouldn't want to see her hurt."

"Don't worry. I'm not going to tell anyone anything . . . yet. I'll give her plenty of time to prove her innocence. I'm going to stay around here for a while."

Shaw grabbed Prima's arm, then realized how tightly he gripped it and instantly loosened his grasp. "You can't. You've got to go home. He thinks you're dead."

"I'll tell him." She pulled her arm away, frowning. "But I can't go yet. I can't even let him know I'm alive. I want to be sure of more of the facts first. You don't know him the way I do. He'll want answers. Answers I don't have. He'll come down here and start running people's lives. I need to find out more about Annie. About why she wants me to be Naomi and, if necessary, what part she might have played in a kidnapping. The only way I can do that is to find out who I was as Naomi and how I fit into the scheme of things around here. You know these mountainfolk. Also, if my father sends a team of investigators down here asking questions, no one will tell them anything. Then we'd never discover the real reason all this happened."

It didn't sit right with Shaw, letting her father suffer needlessly, but he did see some sense in her argument. "I've run into that wall of silence, myself. They won't talk easily to outsiders, if at all."

"Then you know I'm right about staying, about how I should proceed. I need to resume my role as Naomi and pretend nothing's happened but a bruised head. You'll be selling goods here for a month. That ought to be plenty of time for me to find out what I need to. Then I can just travel back to wherever you're going and send a message to Morgan from there." She shaded her eyes with one hand and looked at the wagon. "Looks like there's still room for me. Care if I hitch a ride into town? I don't look forward to mud on my feet. They're still wet."

He did need to be about his business, but not before he made one thing clear. "This sounds like you've thought it all out, Miss Powell. But you've forgotten one thing."

"What's that?" Her blue eyes met his gaze and held it.

"Annie Romans knows you don't believe you're really Naomi. She's going to wonder what you're up to if you suddenly accept the role of her granddaughter. As much as I like it, I can't wholly

125

discount her as the conspirator—or one of them. From what I've seen and heard, she holds a lot of power in the community. I think it's best we contact your father right now, today. As soon as you're ready to travel."

"What about your jars? You'll lose business."

He'd thought of that. "Yes, if I don't sell these, I'll lose what backing I've been promised."

"I couldn't let you do that. If I decide to leave before your month is up, then I'll see that Morgan reimburses you for whatever money you're out."

"He won't be sorry, if that should be the case."

"I don't think you need worry, though. I believe a month is enough time to find out what I must."

From all she'd told him about her relationship with her father, he doubted anything could dissuade her from arming herself with every fact she could before she approached Morgan Powell. "We've got to be careful how we proceed."

"We?" Prima's face lit with appreciation, her breath taking on the quick rise and fall of excitement. Relief in her voice mixed with a look of gratitude. "Then you agree to help me?"

Though the swell of her bosom had to go a long way to measure up to others he'd admired in the past, her enthusiasm helped define the enticing view. Temptation shattered Shaw's resistance as if it were a stone thrown against glass. He might have been a cad, might truly want to redeem himself on many accounts. But he was a man, after all. "Unfortunately, you leave me no choice, Miss Powell. I'm against this delay. Against it with every ounce of logic I can muster. Yes, I'll help you, if that's what it takes to let me see you safely home, but . . ." He watched the smile of gratitude broaden, revealing a full bottom lip still glistening from the water she had drunk from the canteen. "I insist on one condition."

"Name it."

"This," he said, gathering her into his arms and branding her with a searing kiss.

Something indefinable changed between them as Shaw kissed her. With her insides trembling, Prima unwound her arms from about his neck, unaware of how they'd gotten there. Her fingers ached for one last touch of the silken hair that framed his handsome face. Yellow-green eyes, which moments ago had been filled with demand, now stared at her with a searing intensity. She felt the heat of their desire melting away any sense of propriety that might have told her it had been wrong to allow the kiss.

She squeezed her eyes shut, hoping against hope itself to silence the sensations that coursed through her bloodstream. But every nerve ending pulsed with the erratic beat of her heart. Her every breath mingled with his. Every fiber of her being cried out to move closer and be cocooned in his warmth.

Never before had she believed any man could make her lose all sense of herself, all sense of where she was, but here she stood in the middle of Tennessee, kissing him as though she had nothing better to do, nor belonged anywhere else but in his arms.

"No slap?" he murmured, one hand pressed against the middle of her back, the other threaded through hair.

She shook her head and moved away, instantly missing the warmth of his fingertips. Glad that he offered no resistance to her escape, she asked breathlessly, "Why did you do that?"

His gaze seemed to bury itself deep within her. He reached out and toyed with the ebony braid dangling over her shoulder. "The truth?"

"Always."

"Because I wanted to see if your lips tasted as sweet as they looked."

Prima prayed for a gust of wind to fan her cheeks and cool the rush of longing that flooded her skin. The man was indeed a man of persuasive words. Words and actions that seduced and lured an all-too-willing victim. She could almost believe him capable of conjuring rainbow flakes.

No matter the confusion of her mind lately, her body knew exactly what it needed. It wanted him to hold her and kiss her senseless again. All because his eyes tempted her with adventure hidden in their depths, and his lips dared her to discover even more about herself.

But she had one troubling thought of her own: not Shaw's concern about how much to trust Annie, but how much to trust what he'd just done. Who had he kissed—Prima or Naomi? He knew neither woman well. For some reason it was important that she knew which of her identities intrigued him more. "Do you often go around kissing anybody who catches your fancy?"

He smiled and swooped her up into his arms, cradling her as he had when he carried her into town. "Can't stand it, can you?"

"Can't stand what?" she demanded, wondering if he intended to kiss her yet again. "What are you doing?"

"Exactly what you asked. You said you didn't want to get your feet muddy. I'm carrying you to the wagon." He chuckled. "And what you can't stand, Miss Curious, is not knowing whether I'm attracted to you as Prima or as Naomi."

"You certainly have a high opinion of yourself, Mr. Lawson."

"Not really. I've just been around you long enough now to know that you like to be the center of attention. Ironic little twist of fate, don't you think, that the woman you're competing against is yourself?"

He lifted her onto the driver's seat, then

climbed aboard. Gathering the reins, he slid back the break and commanded the team into action. "The fact is . . . right now I'm undecided. I like you both pretty much the same."

Chapter Ten

It's the quickest way, Prima told herself while standing in front of the Pumpkin Patch. Voices discussing Shaw Lawson jarred her senses, causing her pulse to race faster. She didn't want anyone to see her standing out here eavesdropping.

She swallowed the nervousness that threatened to tighten her throat and tested every button that fastened her blouse. Prima took a deep breath, then pushed open the door. For the first time in her life, she stepped inside a store simply to associate with others . . . not to purchase anything.

The scent of spices and tobacco smoke assailed her, layering the air with hazy images and a combination of odors she wouldn't soon forget. The shelves were brimming with neatly arranged goods.

Several pairs of eyes focused on her at once, their intense regard heating her skin in a blush that surely matched the color of the hair on the head of the little boy who stood at attention while his mother measured a length of fabric against his leg. His eyes rolled upward as if he were praying for the roof to cave in and free him from his parent's assessment. Prima knew exactly how he felt at the moment.

"How do, Naomi?" the blond woman said as she glanced up from the fabric to see who had entered. "Annie says you're feeling a mite better today. We're all mighty pleased to hear it."

"Thank you." Prima didn't quite know what to say without drawing more attention to herself. She couldn't remember the woman's name but was certain she must have been one of the group of ladies who had paid a call that first day. She recognized the bonnet the woman wore, its color the bright blue of the sky. The boy's name sounded something like his hair color, if she remembered correctly. *Ruby. Rudy.* "Planning to sew Rudy some new pants?"

"Wore his britches to the seam. Patched his Sunday-go-to-meetings one time too many. He done wore 'em plump through the pew. Growing so fast, I can't keep up with 'im."

A circle of men in the corner laughed. Prima noticed that two of them held knives and were carving designs in pieces of bark. Shavings were piled in tiny mounds beneath each man's fast-moving fingers. Their cohorts cheered and challenged each other with bets.

"Don't pay them no mind, Naomi." Rudy's mother frowned. "They's betting who can whittle a squirrel the fastest. I say they's wasting good wood. Ought to be carving a good sturdy pipe or ladle. Something useful."

"Ahh, Dawnabelle, squirrels got their uses, too." The tallest of the men winked.

Dawnabelle wagged a finger at him, but gave a conspiratorial wink at Prima. "They sure do, Jubal. They show a gal how to spot a group of nuts."

The men took the chuckling good-naturedly. Prima smiled back at Dawnabelle, setting her name in her memory.

"Annie out of something?" asked the storekeep as he stepped from around the counter and brought a basket to Prima.

She waved away his offering. "No, thank you. I mean . . . I ain't here to shop." She'd have to get used to this hill talk and try not to sound so proper all the time. Still, Shaw had said he could tell she didn't sound like a local because of the difference in her speech pattern.

Wouldn't Miss Parmelady's corset stiffen if she could hear her now? "I was wondering where I might find my grandmother," Prima continued. "She wasn't home and I haven't seen her most of the morning."

"She's out at Cooper's place . . . like she is every Monday," Hank announced.

"That's right." Prima acted as if it had been only a slip of the memory. She must make it a point to find out exactly who Cooper was. Pressing her fingers to the bandage, she deliberately sought everyone's sympathy. "I guess things are still a bit jumbled up here."

"I remember the time I took a lick on my haid," the tallest man interrupted again, beginning a long-winded tale of woe.

After a few lengthy minutes, Dawnabelle complained loudly. "Now, Jubal, you ain't gonna start that stone arolling again? It gets bigger with every telling. If you'd had that kind of festering, you wouldn't have the sense to remember so much of it."

Hank stopped whittling. "Now, Dawn, sugar honey, you know yarn takes on a better weave if you throw a broader warp ever' time you spin it."

Everyone laughed at Jubal's defense, Dawnabelle the loudest. An affectionate glance shared between the two made Prima wonder if they were husband and wife.

"Could I talk to you a minute, Dawnabelle? Outside?" Prima motioned at the smoke that layered the room, pretending that she needed the air. "I'm afraid I'm still a bit queasy."

The men seemed all ears now.

A glance at the room made Prima realize the

men had every intention of eavesdropping on her conversation unless she could find a way to embarrass them out of doing so. "Women things, you know."

One man cleared his throat. Another began to discuss something manly like swinging a broadax. Prima smiled, knowing that she'd guessed right. Men everywhere were the same: give them one inkling that the discussion might be on the functions or workings of a woman's body and any red-blooded male would instantly go deaf.

"Rudy, sit with your pa a spell. Me and Miz Naomi will be right outside if you need us." Dawnabelle bent down and wagged a finger at her son. "And mind you, no lick-candy. It'll ruin your supper."

"Yes'm." The boy looked so relieved to be freed that he didn't care what he had to agree to in order to be done with the measurements. He hurriedly took a seat next to Jubal.

Dawnabelle followed Prima outside. "Women things, you say?" She eyed Prima from blouse to pant hem. "You ain't missed your monthly, have you? That Mr. Lawson fella's a right strapping hunk of man."

The woman's insinuation brought heat to Prima's cheeks. She hadn't expected these people to be capable of such lenient thinking. "Of course not! I haven't known him but for a few days."

Then she wondered how well Dawnabelle knew Naomi. Well enough to suggest Naomi might be easily swayed by such a man? Had she become a jezebel?

Prima's pulse beat noticeably stronger in her throat, and she attempted to swallow her nervousness. She ran through her plan mentally, making certain it was well thought out. Carelessness would arouse everyone's curiosity, much less that of someone like Dawnabelle, who seemed to be one of Naomi's closer friends. And Annie. Annie would immediately know if anything was amiss. The woman was reportedly a reader of the future. Not that Prima believed in such things, but it still was better to be even more cautious around Annie.

"The woman thing I didn't want to talk about in front of the men is a gathering. That hit on the head I took made me remember that I hadn't shown my friends how much I appreciate them lately. I'd like to invite everybody—well, the women, at least—to tea. Thought maybe you'd help me spread the word." She played for sympathy by touching her temple. "I don't really feel up to much walking or traveling. Of course, I'll have to get Annie's permission, but tomorrow or the next day would be a fine time to have it."

The sooner she started getting to know everyone, the more quickly she could determine what exactly was happening here in Moonbow—and how exactly she had acted as Naomi. "You know how we all get so busy. I just don't want too much time to go by and us not get together." She laid it on thick now. "It's weighing heavy on my heart, and I just won't have peace of mind until I've shown you all what you mean to me. I nearly forgot you for a few days. That was a mighty scary thought. Now, I just want to make sure I do remember everyone like I should and kind of have a reminiscence of old times. Do you think you could possibly let all the women know about the party?"

Dawnabelle nodded. "I'll get Rudy to tell all his friends, and they'll tell their mothers. If you wait till Sunday, you could tell 'em all yourself after church."

Prima shook her head. She wanted to be further along with her fact-finding by that time. Part of Shaw's month had already gone by while she'd been recovering. Time was too precious to waste any more of it. Besides, if she waited until Sunday, she would have to greet each person by name—names she didn't yet know. A party before that time would let her know how well she knew each, or at least give her a minimal knowledge of them all and how they related to Naomi.

"I really want to do this sooner than that," Prima stressed. "Sunday's a time for family gatherings, and I hate to take everyone away from their families on that day. I think an afternoon tea will be just the thing. Tell them to bring their children. We can put them down for naps while we all talk."

Dawnabelle held a hand over Prima's bandage. "You shore you should be up and about? I think you've still got a touch of the hickory fever."

"What makes you say that?" Alerted that she might have said something to make the woman suspect there were ulterior motives behind this tea party, Prima silently reviewed the conversation. Nothing she could recall should have been misconstrued as odd.

"If you think for one minute that you're going to get all our young'uns to bed down for a nap when you're gonna bake your prizewinning cookies"—Dawnabelle wagged a warning finger at Prima—"then a few of your wits ain't mixed right. You best ask Annie to give you a bigger slug of medicine."

"Children and my cookies. Not something to forget, huh?" Prima pretended to laugh, realizing with a sinking feeling what she'd just committed herself to. Naomi obviously knew how to cook.

She—Prima Powell—did not.

Chapter Eleven

Waking before dawn and actually getting up that early had been one of the hardest things Prima had ever done, but she needed to see how Annie heated up the stove. She'd watched her father's servants do so on occasion but had never paid close enough attention to feel comfortable doing it on her on. This morning she studied every detail.

"Planning to cook, are ye?" Annie asked, loading up the valise that traveled with her and her mule wherever the day's doctoring took them.

Prima yawned, confessing to the planned tea party. "Since I almost forgot who I was, I thought it might be nice to share an afternoon with my friends again."

Annie nodded approval. " 'Tis a good thing to show others how much ye like 'em."

Prima waved the old woman off to work, glad that the healer's business took her away from the cabin most of the time. That would give Prima time to make mistakes and not appear totally inept.

How easy it was to fit into Annie's world. The healer made no demands of Prima but those she made of herself. She hadn't asked Prima to do anything, but then she didn't do anything for her, expecting Prima to automatically fend for herself. Prima had gotten up and made up her own bed. Well, *Naomi's* bed. After all, she was a guest in the woman's home.

Last night she'd helped Annie peel potatoes for their evening meal and washed dishes side by side with her. She had been thankful when Annie had let her scrub, and Annie dried. She had no clue where everything went yet.

Later she'd helped Annie sort through the drying herbs and boil some of them for future salves. They'd worked long past twilight and probably would have continued on if she hadn't caught Annie snoring. She helped the old woman to bed and tucked her in, finding the task little effort and somewhat heartwarming. She'd gladly fallen into Naomi's bed then, after taking a bath in that delightful underground spring. It had been almost too cold, but the water and the work had invigorated her, making Prima feel better than she had in years. The sense of accomplishment the evening had given her far outweighed the exhaustion she'd felt just before slipping off to sleep.

She very much looked forward to trying her hand at cooking this morning. But by the time she'd learned where everything was stored and got accustomed to Annie's cookstove, she was completely frustrated. She had burned several batches of cookies. The latest batch weren't inedible, but they surely were nothing to brag about.

Uncertain how successful Dawnabelle had been in spreading the news, she had no idea how many visitors to expect. But how many wasn't what worried her. How *good* everything turned out was. If she fell short in quality, and she obviously would, was it too impossible to hope that those who knew Naomi would think her deterioration in cooking ability was simply due to a mind not yet able to think as effectively as it would once she recovered?

Despite the awkwardness of being in an unfamiliar kitchen and having to cook for an uncertain number of people, it still felt good to have labored so hard when the work was for someone else instead of herself. That sense of accomplishment could not be taken from her.

A glance at the assortment of cookies gracing the platter on the worktable urged her to untie the apron from around her waist. She deposited it on one of the wall pegs that hung next to the stove.

"What time is it?" she muttered, wishing Annie owned a clock, but the woman didn't. Annie awoke, arrived, left, and went to bed by the position of the sun or moon in the sky—or her own internal rhythms.

Taking a peep outside, Prima thought it might be close to noon. The sun burned brightly overhead. Hopefully there was just enough time to pay a last-minute visit to the Pumpkin Patch. If she hurried, she'd still have time to get another bag of flour and prepare an even better batch of cookies.

Checking her clothes for signs of flour, she found none and decided she still looked presentable enough not to have to change before she went out. She headed for the store.

The high wind felt good on her skin, cooling off the long morning of baking she'd endured. Above the canopy of shade provided by the trees everything looked shrouded in a blue-gray mist. Clouds climbed high into the sky, like gigantic curling waves of wind. Though full of the scent of pine and cookfires, the air felt somehow heavier, making it more cumbersome for her to move.

You're just tired, she told herself. Once she finished her cooking and took a bath she'd feel better. Purposefully enlivening her steps, she headed the same direction she'd taken yesterday.

As Prima turned the corner onto Main Street, she noticed a lone man standing in the shade near the church, watching her. For a moment a sense of alarm washed the exhaustion from Prima. He seemed to be watching her intently.

Unwilling to be ruled by fear, she took her courage in hand and waved, making sure whoever he was knew with all certainty that she had seen him. "Hello, there. Good to see you!"

He waved back, but didn't say anything. Instantly he moved from where he leaned against the church and hurried inside. The only thing noticeable about him from this distance was dark, shoulder-length hair.

"Probably just curious," she decided aloud, needing to hear the sound of her own voice to calm the rapid rhythm her pulse had taken up. "Can't blame him. *I'd* like to know a whole lot more about Naomi myself." Prima took a deep breath and hurried about her business. Perhaps some of her curiosity would be satisfied this afternoon at the tea, and she would learn some of Naomi's past from people who knew her.

"Forget something?" a voice asked as the fierce wind drove her inside the general store. "Annie told me you were cooking this morning. Not to disturb you."

Pushing the hair out of her eyes, she turned and saw Shaw, with Willy Boy tagging along beside him. "Yes," she admitted. "But I've burned

143

more than I've left edible. Need some flour, maybe some cinnamon. I'm not sure I made enough." She turned to the child. "I bet you can point me in the direction of the cinnamon, Willy."

"Yes'm."

"I appreciate it." Prima anchored a lock of hair behind her ear, realizing she must look disastrous. She hadn't seen Shaw since their shared kiss, and she certainly didn't look kissable at the moment. She needed to occupy her thoughts otherwise. She flashed Shaw an apologetic smile. "I'm sorry I don't have more time to visit. Best hurry before my guests arrive."

"I was wondering if I could walk you home, discuss something with you along the way."

What could she say but yes? He'd agreed to help her. Maybe he'd discovered some important information. Her heart certainly didn't want her to deny him, for it pounded a steady answer— *Let him, let him, let him.*

Prima accepted his invitation, unwilling to throw away a chance to enjoy the man's company alone. "It's noon. I haven't much time before guests start arriving. But you can walk with me, if you like."

When Shaw grabbed a basket from the counter to hold her purchases, his fingers lightly touched hers. Heat skimmed the surface of her hands as his hot skin brushed against hers.

Startled by the sensation his touch aroused within her, Prima discovered that her body refused to obey her mind. Her mind warned her to move far away from the next possible touch and get busy filling the basket with needed items. Her body stayed rooted to the spot, and her eyes stared into the yellow-green eyes that would forever alter the way she described her now-favorite color.

"Want anything in particular?" He stood only inches away from her.

You, she answered silently but attempted to blink herself into full concentration. Why did his eyes start blinking, too? "Two ounces of cinnamon and a pound of flour."

"Anything sweet?"

She sighed. *You,* she wanted to say again, but resisted the impulse. "Any molasses? I like the taste of it in cookies."

Prima watched him gather the requested goods, admiring the way his fluid movements showed he was a man of fine form.

"How much do I owe?" She dug into the pocket of her trousers, then realized with great distress that this was not New York, where she could put everything on her father's accounts. Here she had no money to call her own.

Seeing her distress, Shaw spoke up. "I'll settle up for you." He took the basket and waited as the clerk added the sum of the purchases. He quickly

145

paid for the goods and told the man to add a stick of candy for Willy Boy. When he finished, he offered Prima his arm to escort her out of the store.

Several of the men holding court near the visiting circle scowled at Prima. She'd overstepped some boundary by accepting the outlander's arm. "What do we do?" she whispered low, hoping no one but Shaw heard.

"Just keep walking. They know I rescued you. Whatever you've done, you can simply say you were repaying a kindness."

"Good afternoon, Willy Boy." She noticed the boy wasn't going to follow them out. Perhaps she could appease him at least, and maybe he'd sway his parents. "Come by later and I'll have some cookies for you."

"I might," Willy stated noncommittal.

"You seen Cooper today?" one of the scowling men stepped forward and asked. "Is Annie with him?"

Prima realized he was asking *her* and saying something more than what his words implied. "Can't say as I have. But if I do, I'll let him know you asked."

"Good. I'd like to talk to him about a thing or two."

She left the store in silence. The midday sky had taken on an unhealthy amber glow. Tiny splatters of rain warned that the swollen clouds intended to release their burden. Lightning ripped the skyline horizontally and vertically. Wind-driven sand stung her face and hands.

"Looks like we're in for a storm," Shaw warned. "You might want to call off the tea. If it's bad out, the women won't chance it. Especially if that lightning storm gets any worse."

So intent was she on protecting her eyes from the stinging sand, Prima missed a step coming off the sidewalk. As she stumbled, Shaw's fingers tightened over her hand, protecting her from injury and guiding her back to safety at his side.

They managed to make it as far as the end of Main before rain began to pelt them. Lightning flashed, and thunder splintered the heavens with a mighty roar.

"Gotta get to shelter!" Shaw shouted through the deluge. "Head for the church!"

He handed her the basket and pulled her closer to him to protect her from the rain's icy sting. Prima held on tightly, too busy running and trying not to slip to think about the sensations raging through her from his nearness.

"We made it!"

The declaration rumbled against her cheek, and she found it pleasant to feel the vibration of his words as he spoke.

"Good thing they keep the door unlocked."

Shaw's warm breath rushing over her head as she passed him sent a chill down her spine that had nothing to do with the cold rain. She shivered.

"Cold?" He started to pull off his shirt, then chuckled. "I'd offer you my shirt, but I believe it wouldn't be any drier than what you're already wearing."

"That's all right. I'll just sit here in one of the pews and rub my arms. That'll stir up some heat."

For the first time since entering the sanctuary, she wondered if the man she'd seen earlier was still inside. A glance at the rows of pews and the altar assured her they were alone. Shaw moved to a nearby closet and disappeared, only to come out again shaking his head.

"No luck. Thought there might be a robe hanging in there, but there isn't. Guess we'll just have to dry the best we can. Hope that rain lets up soon, so you don't catch a cold from the dampness."

"And so I can be home when guests arrive," she reminded him, taking a seat in the last pew.

"How's everything at the cabin? Everything going well with Annie?" He took a seat beside her and placed a hand over hers. "Anything I can do for you?"

She allowed it to remain. He was the one person whom she could trust, and she was glad of it at the moment. "You've been too kind already, Shaw."

"I'd like to be kinder."

An awkward moment ensued. She didn't dare speak first. Her heart was creating a list of questions that had nothing to do with those that might be shared while waiting out a storm. Her pulse beat rapidly beneath the palm that enveloped her hand.

"Why did you—" They spoke in unison, then chuckled with embarrassment.

"You first," Prima insisted.

"It's your turn. I've already asked several questions."

"Well, I was wondering why you are so ready to help me, when from what I've heard about you, you're the kind of man who's usually only self-serving."

"What have you heard about me?"

She related the articles she thought she remembered her father had read concerning Shaw Lawson—if it was the same man.

Shaw let go of her hand and leaned forward, resting his elbows on the next pew. She followed his gaze and wondered if he was staring at the large crucifix that graced the back wall at its center.

"I hurt someone once because I was self-serving. I can't help her anymore, so I thought maybe I could redeem myself a little by helping you."

His answer was so casual Rachel didn't react

149

at once. He hadn't said, *Because it's the Christian thing to do.* He'd stated a reason that explained some of the offhand things he'd said that hadn't made any sense before now.

Suddenly admiration rose from the deepest part of her. To help a total stranger because he'd wronged someone else showed a man who was basically good at heart. The wall of indifference she'd built around her heart since watching her father take whatever means necessary to see to his success, and his success alone, cracked open and made Prima wonder if maybe there wasn't at least some hope left for this world.

The admiration she felt for Shaw warmed to something more adventurous. She leaned forward and placed her elbows on the next pew, just as he had. "I think I forgot to pay you something," she whispered.

"For the goods?" He waved away her concern. "Pay me back later."

He was so close she could feel his breath brush the top of her nose. He smelled of soap and potions and man.

"Shaw," she whispered, and saw the question in his yellow-green eyes. "You said you were attracted to Naomi *and* Prima. Whichever one of us you didn't kiss before, needs to be kissed now so the two of us have both said our proper thank-yous." Drowning in sensations as potent as hundred-year-old whiskey, she went gladly into his arms. She had dreamed of his kiss, longed for it every moment since experiencing the first one yesterday.

The soft perfection of his lips blazed a welcome path at her temple, against her cheek, the bridge of her nose, driving reason from her whirling thoughts. He paused only an inch from her lips, and she knew if she allowed the kiss to continue, her heart would never be her own again.

Bands of iron encircled her slender waist as he stood, pulling her up and closer so their bodies would meld together. He felt so good against her, thigh to thigh, breast to chest. Prima fought the urge to tear open the buttons of his shirt and follow the impulse to press her lips against the heat radiating from beneath his clothing. Instead she took a step backward.

"Is something wrong?" he whispered, tracing the outline of her bottom lip with his finger.

"Please stop."

Shaw let go, staring down at her. Annoyance and disappointment battled for a moment before leaving him with a wounded expression. "Hell, Prima, you *asked* to be kissed. Now you look at me as if I was taking unwanted liberties."

She couldn't explain what she felt. She wanted him to kiss her senseless. To press his mouth—hard and demanding—against her own until he stole her very breath. But she had to end this now. End it before it started. Before she knew for sure if it was the real her he wanted to kiss. She'd had her share of false beaux. She wanted a man to care for her as Prima, ordinary Prima. Not as what he thought she was.

Prima grabbed the basket and moved around him into the aisle. "The rain's stopped. The parson might walk in—or that other man. We wouldn't want them to find us kissing in church. I-I don't know what I was thinking when I asked you. Besides, I'll never get the cookies done in time now."

"What other man are you talking about?"

"The one who was watching me earlier. I waved at him, because I assumed he knows me." She explained what had happened earlier, but left out the circumstances about the note.

"And you say you couldn't tell much more about him than the color of his hair?"

She nodded, grateful that this new subject was giving her time to regain her composure.

"Just be careful, Prima. Moonbow seems like a safe place for most, but someone has a reason to keep you here. I'll find out who that is."

He offered his arm and she accepted it awkwardly. The walk home was fraught with the uncomfortable silence that had risen between them.

Shaw bade her good afternoon, planting a kiss on her forehead before she could object. "That's for letting me walk you home. You go on in. I'll take a look around and see if I can spot that suspicious-looking character. Just remember, Prima: trust no one but me." He gently cupped her chin with his hand. "You're starting to mean something to me."

Chapter Twelve

Prima's mouth ached from forcing a smile, and her hand hurt from trying to swat away Skillet's and Jug's thieving paws. The two little bandits had pilfered more cookies than she had decent ones to serve. She doubted that as Naomi she'd had much more control over them than she did now, either. They did anything they wanted.

Her visitors had laughed at the coons' mischievous antics to a point, but now the cookie platter was nearly empty. The party would have to end soon or she'd be forced to see if Annie had anything else to serve her company. She'd rather not go through Annie's stored goods without asking, and the woman had not yet returned.

Concern filled Prima. The old healer worked far too hard, and if she was on her way back, she might catch her death in the downpour outside.

She wished the rain would stop for many reasons, and not the least of them was to assure Annie's safe return.

Her neck hurt from nodding too often to pretend she was actually listening to the unimportant small talk being shared by several of the women. If the men of Moonbow truly did everything of which their wives accused them, they'd have been bachelors before the sun set. Prima offered the remaining refreshments to everyone. "More cookies? Tea?"

"Had my fill," one woman said.

Another waved away the platter. "Won't eat supper, if I eat more."

"I got to be getting," announced Dawnabelle. "Guess I'm gonna slide on back to the house. Don't look like it's gonna let up any."

That initiated a lively discussion regarding how many floods each woman had survived in her lifetime.

Prima was glad for the others' distraction while she thanked Dawnabelle for her help in arranging the party.

"I's glad to help, Naomi." Dawnabelle smiled and hugged her. "This was shore nice. We women ought to have us more tea parties. Our men have their stay at the Patch ever' day. 'Course, you and me both know it ain't tea they's sipping in them jugs."

Prima laughed, deciding she liked Dawnabelle

155

immensely. "We'll do this more often." She cast a worried glance outside. "Maybe next time Annie will be able to be here."

"Worried about her, are ya, gal?" Dawnabelle's eyes searched her face.

Prima nodded.

Dawnabelle patted her hand. "Well, don'tcha fret none. Annie's been taking care of herself a lot longer than most of us been on this here mountain. She knows many a burrow to hole up in if she's twixt cabins."

For more than the hundredth time this afternoon, she wished she remembered more as Naomi. If she did, she might know where to start looking for the healer. As it was, if she tried to search for Annie, she'd only get herself lost. Maybe Shaw would come by. Maybe he'd done enough traveling of the countryside and the settlement the past few days to give him a good idea of where to look for her.

"Got to git, now," Dawnabelle said. "You go on with your party. Miz Annie'll be back 'fore you drive off the lollygaggers."

Prima laughed.

"They's afraid their best bonnets'll shrivel up," Dawnabelle confided, glancing at the circle of women who filled Annie's main room to its full breadth. "Wore their Sunday best, every last one of 'em."

"Thanks again, Dawn."

"My pleasure, Naomi."

Prima watched her new friend plaster her arm on top of her own bonnet to keep it firmly on her head while she ran out and downhill toward home. A twinge of guilt crept in to sour the sweet feeling of friendship the afternoon had awarded her; Dawnabelle was nothing like any of her friends from Quest. Still, the young woman was genuine—and that meant Prima should take her as she came: real.

It had been a long time since she'd felt that way about anyone, that what she saw in the person was exactly the way the person was. Dawnabelle was real to the bone.

Taking a deep breath, Prima turned back to her guests and found them still talking about floods. She'd heard so many subjects this afternoon that her ears hurt. Some quiet time to think about all she'd learned and what it all meant would be wonderful. Trying to make polite talk, to remember which name belonged to which woman, and to keep Skillet and Jug from running amok had been a bigger bite than she should have tried to chew in one afternoon.

Though rain always made her drowsy, a nap seemed unlikely after all her company left. The few times she'd actually caught herself only halfway listening, it had been the remembered feel of Shaw's embrace distracting her. Whenever she'd allowed her mind to drift at all, the direction it took was the same. Sleep would be impossible.

Prima reseated herself beside a chubby red-haired woman who had eaten at least a dozen cookies by herself—Cora, if she remembered correctly. "Feeling better?"

Cora fanned herself, speaking around a mouthful of sweets. "Thank ya kindly for opening the door. Love the smell of new rain on clover. Always cools me down. Why, I remember the spring of fifty-seven. Rainbow season, if ever I saw one. Showers started in early March and lasted plumb past summer. River rose so high we thought we'd have ta move the Patch clean up the holler. You oughta remember that rain spell, Naomi. Washed you downriver—along with other things."

Washed ashore? This was the information she'd been waiting to hear all afternoon.

"Cora, you've lived here for several years, haven't you?"

Red curls bobbed up and down in unison with her cheeks as she chewed her cookie. "All my days."

Prima waited patiently while the woman gulped tea, cleared her throat several times, then took still another bite. The woman's appetite was inexhaustible! "Things are still kind of jumbled in my mind," Prima admitted, then pressed her fingertips to her bandage. "I don't remember much about when I came to Moonbow." Seeing that their discussion had drawn interest from the others, Prima quickly added, "Annie says that's natural, though. The hit on the head mixed things up. It'll all come back to me."

Cora licked her lips and wiped crumbs from her lap. "Cooper'd be only too glad to remind you. He's plumb crazy outta his mind worried if ya's gonna remember him."

"Cooper?" Prima had heard that name before. That was the person Annie visited every Monday, so it seemed.

"Well, Cora, ain't that just like you. Brung up the subject we skirted around all afternoon," reprimanded the oldest of the ladies.

Kathleen O'Toole. She was one of the more educated women, Prima decided, from her better use of the King's English.

Mrs. O'Toole cast a cool look upon Prima. "But now that she has, just what are your plans for Cooper? We've seen that river peddler paying you call after call. Do you still plan to marry poor, besotted Cooper, or will you be tossing him back to us so that city fellow can court you?"

"I'm engaged to Cooper?"

"You don't remember Cooper Kingsley?" Suspicion narrowed Kathleen's eyes into gray slits. "You haven't remembered a lot of things today. That must have been some knock on the head."

"I told you, it'll all come back to me." Though

she hated lying, Prima wasn't about to show the woman she had been shaken.

"Oh, leave her be, Kathleen!" Cora pulled down her blouse so it didn't gather around her bulging middle. "You just want Cooper free to marry Bertha. Naomi just wants to make sure her head's clear before she sees Cooper again. You know how that man can make a gal swoon. I think she's a wise woman to set her head straight 'fore she takes on that long, tall drink of water. Otherwise she might just do something foolish 'fore she gets that ring on her finger."

Before Prima could say anything, the heavy-eating Cora continued her admonishment. "Kathleen's just jealous 'cause he come acourting Bertha 'fore you come to live with Annie. Bertha done had her heart set on Cooper. And everybody knows that what Bertha wants, Kathleen gets for her."

"Stop your jawing, Cora."

Cora ignored the older woman's warning. "Don't have to, 'cause we all know it's the truth. You just can't stand it because the handsomest man in the hills done set his cap for Naomi, here. That really churns yer butter, doesn't it, Kathleen?"

"It's time I said good-bye." The unhappy matron stood and motioned to the woman next to her to do the same.

Bertha. The other woman was Bertha. Prima

had wondered why the pretty blonde had studied her all afternoon. She'd caught the glances a couple of times, but thought them just curiosity. Now she knew the blonde was gauging her competition.

Cora rocked forward until she gained the momentum to launch herself from the chair on which she sat. "I think we all should skedaddle and let Naomi rest. We've done jawed so much, even *my* head is hurting—and I ain't even been knocked senseless." She leaned in and whispered to Prima, "Not that I can say that about your other guests."

The rest took the opportunity to make a quick escape from the animosity between Kathleen and Cora. As polite thank-yous and invitations to visit their cabins were extended to Prima, she simply said, "I surely will, once I'm feeling myself again."

Kathleen led the exodus to the door. Prima took curious pleasure in hearing the woman and her daughter squeal as they hurried out the door and into the rain.

After they'd left, Cora rolled up a sleeve. "Where does Annie keep the washtub?"

Appreciation took root in Prima. The afternoon had given her two new friends. "That's kind of you, Cora, but I can do it myself."

Cora insisted she stay and help clean, but

Prima refused. Instead, she promised to talk at length tomorrow.

As her new friend gathered her shawl and grabbed one last handful of cookies, Prima couldn't resist asking one more question. "How close were . . . *are* Mr. Kingsley and I?"

Cora winked and crossed her fingers. "Closer'n two furless bunnies in a blizzard."

"That's what I was afraid you'd say," Prima whispered, not realizing she'd spoken her dismay aloud.

"Oh, gal." Cora waddled outside and flipped the shawl over her shoulder as a conquering Roman might have done with his cape. "If I was you, I'd have Annie pour a heap more medicine into that tea she's giving you for that brainache. You're forgetting the best part."

Not long after Prima waved good-bye and started gathering dishes, a knock interrupted her chore. She set the dishes down, then rushed to see what Cora had forgotten. "What's the matter, Cora? Did you—"

Shaw stood on the porch, dripping from hat brim to boot. "I'm not Cora, but I thought I'd give you a hand with the cleanup."

"Come in before you catch your death." She stepped back to let him through. "You haven't been out there all this time, have you?" Prima reached up and took his hat, setting free a stream of rainwater from its brim.

"Now I've gotten us both wet," he apologized, bending to grasp the lower flounce of her dress. "Shake it a bit and it won't soak. And yes, I've been out here since the ladies arrived. I wanted to be around if that man you saw earlier decided to show up."

"I got *myself* wet." She wiped the damp hair away from his face and became enamored with the blotches flushing his cheeks. Were they a product of the cold or her touch? Prima fought an urge to kiss him and see if his body heated in response. It seemed he had his own urge to resist—and was failing—for he started unbuttoning his shirt. "What are you doing?" she demanded.

"Pulling off these wet things. If the stove's still hot, they can begin drying while I help you clean up."

As he peeled off his shirt and bared a solid wall of well-carved flesh to her, Prima became speechless. *Lord have mercy!* seemed to be the extent of her thinking at the moment, inwardly and outwardly. Her heart slammed against her chest like a battering ram. She licked her lips, feeling suddenly quite thirsty.

"Tell you what: I'll heat some water for the dishes. I remember Annie said something about storing her husband's old clothes in a trunk under her bed. Would you mind looking through them and seeing if you think any would fit? I wouldn't want her returning home and finding me here half-dressed. I'll just drape my shirt on the back of a chair and set it in front of the oven to dry."

Prima nodded and nearly ran from the room, afraid she'd see more of him than she ought, yet curious enough not to want to miss a single moment.

Something wet hit the floor as she reached the landing, and Prima wondered if it was his trousers.

"I'm in serious trouble here," she muttered, trying to close off the image that invaded her senses: a vision of the rest of his body—bare, muscular . . . slick. "Deep, deep trouble!"

Now, where was Annie's bedroom anyway? She hadn't yet gotten up the gumption to inspect each room in the house; it seemed an invasion of privacy, despite the fact that she'd lived here for two years.

"In case you don't know, her room is the second one on the left. The one where all the herbs are drying. It's getting kind of cold in here. Need any help?"

"I can manage." *Unless you show up to help me.* Having a bed and a nude Shaw Lawson within kissing distance was simply tempting fate too much. Ignoring the possibilities was practically impossible—especially when those possibilities involved the body and lips that belonged to Shaw.

The next curtain yielded the room of which Shaw spoke: Annie's bedroom. In it there were more shelves like those in the main room, and walls and walls of crocks and baskets. A small bed in one corner with a tiny rug was placed over an earthen floor. There were no fancy furnishings like Naomi's room though. The room was as practical and no-nonsense as its owner.

Prima looked under the bed and found the trunk in question. Triumph filled her at finding the masculine garments, but disappeared like the wind gone from a sail. "These won't fit one of his legs, much less two."

JickJack Romans must have been a short man, plump and barrel-chested. She doubted anything he wore would fit Shaw's powerful physique. To her surprise, she also discovered a brocade dressing gown made in the colors of a peacock's tail. She giggled, thinking the gown quite the garment for a hill-town alchemist. Smiling, she turned and headed back.

She almost dropped the gown when she returned to the main room, for there, washing dishes, was her near nude Adonis.

His hair fell in waves to his shoulders, uncorraled by a hat and untethered by the strand of rawhide that usually held it in place while he worked. He might as well have stripped off his trousers, for the soaked cloth was plastered to his buttocks and thighs so tightly it left nothing to the imagination. The other clothing she'd heard him discarding had merely been his boots and socks. The sight of his bare feet seemed so personal, so intimate. His bare back glistened with such a sheen, she licked her lips to rid herself of the moisture that beaded her upper lip. Shaw turned and grinned.

Heat fused Prima's cheeks as all playfulness escaped her. A nearly nude Shaw was no laughing matter; he had always looked far too dangerous, and was even more so soaked to the skin. In defense, she thrust the dressing gown forward. "Here, cover yourself with this."

"My hands are soapy. Will you wrap it around my shoulders?"

"Mr. Romans was a colorful dresser, I take it."

"Apparently."

When he turned his back to her, she draped the gown over him, lifting his hair free of the makeshift collar, unconsciously letting her fingers glide through the thick, damp curls.

"Thank you," he whispered. "I feel much warmer now." Then he spoke again as she began to back up. "No, don't, Prima. Please don't move away."

His voice was so low it could have been only a feather's rustle. Prima felt his shoulders tighten slightly. In a slow motion he turned, a fraction of an inch at a time, and pulled her closer. Her fingers splayed over his chest, feeling the warmth of his body and his breath moving slowly across her neck.

His hands slid to her waist and drew her solidly against him. "Would you deny me a kiss?"

Prima marveled at the way he felt—like marble bound in velvet. She loved the steady pounding of his heart beneath her fingertips. She couldn't stop the sigh of longing that escaped her, yet neither could she give in to her yearning. "It wouldn't be fair to any of us." *Naomi or me*.

She would not play this game—steal kisses, rouse passions, only to leave Shaw wanting a woman whose future was uncertain. It was always dangerous to fall in love, and for Shaw to fall for her when she didn't even know who she herself was, who she wanted to be . . . But how could she possibly make him understand?

"Let me decide what's fair," he whispered, pressing his lips against the path she'd accepted before—her forehead, her eyes, her cheeks. Each kiss became firmer, more demanding.

She sucked in her breath as his mouth halted only inches from her own. Would he stop? Could she stop him if he didn't? Did she even want to?

Shaw's arms tightened around her, molding Prima to him. God, how she wanted him to demand the kiss, to lose herself in the delicious wonder of his embrace.

His breath mingled with hers, sending hot tingles to every pulse point in her body.

"Don't tell me it's because you don't want me to." His hands traced the curve of her hips, her waist, lingering just below her breasts. "That would be a lie."

Her fingers skimmed down the strong slope of his shoulders as her body leaned into his of its own volition. He shifted slightly nearer, igniting every sensation within her. The need to touch and be touched was too strong, the pure joy of being held in his arms too powerful to deny herself this moment of heaven.

Yearning swept through Prima like a fire out of control. The hunger in Shaw's eyes held more than passion. It offered a promise to see her through this confusing time.

"Naomi."

The name chilled the blood boiling in her veins. "I'm not Naomi!" she blurted. "I won't care for you," she repeated, as if saying the words would make them true.

The rhythm of his heart slowed against her breasts; the warmth of his leg moved away from her thigh. It felt as if someone had tossed a bucket of water over them to cool their ardor.

"I'm sorry. I met you as Naomi—and everyone else in town is calling you that." Shaw moved away from her, shrugging off the dressing gown.

"I'm having a hard time thinking of you as Prima."

He was right. It had to be just as confusing for him as it was for her. In fact, he was the one person who might give her away too soon if he slipped up and called her by her real name. Though the idea was distasteful, it seemed best to keep him at a distance for most of the time she spent in Moonbow. So no mistakes would be made. And so she wouldn't have to fight her own desire. . . . "The townspeople need to believe you're just here to sell your jars, and that will keep us from making any mistakes. I know it's hard for you to remember not to call me Prima. Maybe it's best we stay away from each other for a while."

"Stay away so we won't make mistakes? Every moment you aren't in my arms is a mistake, and you know it." Frustration filled Shaw's tone. He grabbed his wet shirt and put it back on, though it had not had time to dry. He stormed to the door. "But if that's what you want, so be it."

It *wasn't* what she wanted, not really, but she had no choice. She had to meet Cooper Kingsley and find out more about her relationship with him. And that would not be easily accomplished with Shaw always close by. She would have to pretend to show real interest in Cooper. Surely if she had been engaged to the man, he knew more about her as Naomi than anyone else. If that were true, then the passion aroused by the river peddler was something that might not be easily hidden from a fiancé's discerning eye. But still, she had to do it.

The enticing aroma of wild plum tarts and saffron cakes wafted through the doorway that led to the general store. Prima's stomach growled in complaint. Annie had stayed gone most of the day, and Prima's own cooking left something to be desired. Even the coons refused to hoard her cookies.

She nervously adjusted the mutton-sleeved shoulders of the one dress she'd found in Annie's closet that looked presentable enough to wear. It seemed Naomi didn't own one.

The general store provided the center of activity for the community, for Annie had said she would be able to find Cooper Kingsley among the men who paid a visit there just before sunset when he was in town. The store seemed to be the gathering place of young men and women in search of future spouses.

Not that she was looking. But she had to see this Kingsley fellow for herself. Better in a community setting the first time than alone. She wasn't sure exactly how well the two of them knew each other, and she didn't want to take any chances.

Prima had listened carefully to Annie's tales of

Cooper, but tried not to ask too many questions that would call attention to her lack of knowledge of her fiancé.

"Ahh, there you are, Prima." Cora Beth Allison stood at the store's open entryway, waving her in. "Don't you look mighty pretty tonight. You look more and more like Miz Annie ever' day," she complimented.

Bertha O'Toole frowned as Prima stepped inside the hazy room. "Cain't say that I've noticed."

Cora chuckled. "All you notice is food platters and pant legs. If it ain't wearing buckskin or got a broadax hanging on its shoulder, you wouldn't take the time to see if it's buck-nekkid."

A profusion of male voices drew Prima to a portion of the store layered in thick tobacco smoke. Men crowded around a table, their eyes intent upon two struggling men with their waist-coats discarded. The sleeves of one man's shirt were rolled up over powerful forearms that glistened with perspiration.

She watched as the man arm-wrestled another man opposite him. At last, he gave one mighty flex of his shoulder and his opponent's arm threatened to slam against the table. His foe's other hand dipped below the table. Prima watched in fascination as the first man's sleeveless hand flashed to a boot and came up with a knife. A clatter of steel against planking revealed his opponent had dropped a knife that he himself had snatched up.

"Bravo!" The compliment had escaped before Prima realized her approval had taken voice. All attention now centered on her, especially that of the victor.

"Go home, Marcum, before I forget there are ladies present," the sleeveless man said in a growl, then turned his darker than midnight gaze upon Prima. A slash of white teeth made his lips lift sensuously. "I thought Annie said you were still recuperating, Naomi. Couldn't stand to be away from me any longer, love?"

Prima backed up into the aisle. This was Cooper? "I was looking for the peddler," she said. "I need to ask him something." She wasn't prepared for such a man. This man seemed tough, but not the backwoodsman she'd expected.

At the mention of Shaw, her fiancé rolled down his sleeve and grabbed his coat. "Don't know where he is, but I've heard he's been running all over the hills talking to folks. Why don't we do some catching up? I'll walk you around town and we'll see if we can run into him. I want to hear all about how he rescued you. Gotta thank the man for bringing you home."

The way he stared at her, Prima wished she had chosen to wear her men's clothing rather than put on the dress. Her hand rose to splay across the bodice; then she realized she had drawn his attention to her chest. Quickly she settled her hand against her side.

Though not as immense as Shaw, Kingsley was no dwarf in size. His shoulders sloped to hard sinews carved by rowing daily along the river. Annie had said he worked as a scout and guide along the Cumberland.

Cooper motioned toward the door. "Ready?"

No, she wasn't, but she had to pretend she felt comfortable letting him walk her home.

Once they were outside, away from prying eyes, Cooper wrapped an arm around her waist and pulled her close. "I couldn't wait to get you outside, love. Kiss me."

Prima jerked away.

"What's the matter?"

"Nothing," she evaded. *I don't know you*, she thought. "They're looking," she said.

He chuckled. "That never stopped you before."

Just how intimate were we? she wondered, thinking it would have been hard to resist such temptation as this man—if they'd shared something special.

His features softened with concern. "Annie said you forgot who you were for a while. You didn't forget me, did you?"

"Of course not," she lied. "I just need some time for my senses to clear."

"I was hoping you wouldn't make me wait any longer, Naomi. In fact, I brought this back with me this trip." Cooper dug into his pocket, cupped his hand, pulled out a small object, then held it out in offering.

She opened her palm to receive the gift. "A wedding ring!"

"See if it fits." He insisted upon slipping it on her finger. "Perfect."

Though simple, the wedding band was carved in a never-ending circle of gold leaves. "It's beautiful."

Cooper took a matching band from his pocket and slipped it on. Inexplicably, the ring he had given her felt as if it tightened around Prima's finger. She began to tremble.

He gently grasped her hand and raised it to his lips, brushing a light kiss against the ring's gold surface. When she attempted to pull away, his grip demanded her hand remain.

She protested: "Cooper, I can't take this . . . yet. I'd feel wrong." She removed the ring and returned it to the man's hand. "But I do promise to think about this very seriously. I know what we meant to each other"—*sort of*—"and I'll never forget that. But I need to think."

Cooper Kingsley gave her a long, strange look with his, handsome dark eyes. Then he said, "Take the time you need, Naomi," he urged, "but remember this, at least: a man can only wait so long before he loses his senses with a woman. I'll pay court to you again to help you remember why you love me, but don't take too long."

Chapter Thirteen

Shaw was unsure of his place, with Prima suddenly unwilling to see him. Each time he walked past her house that week, a different horse was hitched at the post in front of the cabin. Talk at the general store revolved around who paid her a visit, where she'd been, and how she seemed to be getting along with someone named Cooper Kingsley—the man Annie had visited the past two Mondays. A man Shaw had not yet met.

For the first time in years, Shaw found himself wondering what it might be like to settle down in a place like this and become part of a community. At one time, Moonbow would have been too small a place for him. He had bigger dreams, bigger fortunes to pursue.

Having lived in Philadelphia most of his life, he hadn't had the opportunity to get to know most of his neighbors. But since coming to Moonbow and seeing how the townspeople welcomed Naomi into their fold, he wondered if they might do the same for him . . . if his ambition could be content with dwelling in the Appalachians.

He supposed this sudden bent of melancholy was because Prima had banished him from seeing her, and he now felt more isolated than ever before.

If he hadn't been so envious, he might have found it heartwarming to see Moonbow rally around Prima. He'd heard one of the local women talking about how a schedule had been drawn up to ensure that she wasn't alone while Annie was gone on her doctoring trips. It seemed the community of women felt Naomi should not be alone as long as she still had a touch of the "hickory fever."

When he wandered into the Pumpkin Patch to see if the Kingsley fellow might be about, he found only women in the store. Six sat where the men usually did next to the stove—the community circle of chairs. They were obviously discussing next week's schedule to watch Naomi. He listened politely and waited until there was a break in the conversation. "I'd like to do my part, too," he offered, realizing that by joining in with the community effort, it would give him reason to be near her without arousing needless suspicion. "I feel responsible for her needing the help."

All six regarded him with eyes that ranged from distrust to caution—an experience a man of his profession had grown accustomed to, but sobering nonetheless.

"Thank you," said Kathleen O'Toole with a curt smile, "but we take care of our own."

He absorbed the woman's rebuff, but it didn't stop him from trying again. "I might like to settle here myself. How better to go about becoming one of you than by helping to take care of another of your company?"

Her chin rose to a haughty angle. "After a couple of weeks? I think not. Besides, we don't need help with Naomi. Everything has been arranged."

"I could sit with her at night." He saw disapproval mark most of the faces and knew he would be shut out if he didn't say something to convince them quickly. "Annie, as you know, had me stay those first few days Naomi was unconscious."

They couldn't argue that point.

Kathleen shook her head. "That's different. She was an invalid during those days. Now, she's . . . well . . . it just wouldn't be right for you to stay with her."

"But Mother," a younger version of the woman said in a soft voice. . . . "Why not? If he stays with her and something does happen, then Cooper could be—"

"Hush, Bertha." Kathleen turned haughty eyes toward Shaw. "How can you even ask to help? You are the reason we're all having to sit with her."

A chubby woman with red hair piped in. "Naomi don't blame him, so you shouldn't neither. Judge not lest ye be judged, Kathleen O'Toole."

"Save your sermons for Sunday, Cora Beth Allison! Do you really want Naomi to spend her nights in the company of this potion peddler? A man of questionable honor? If you have any doubts, just look at what he's trying to market to all of us. Why he's nothing but a flimflam man!"

"A former flimflam man," Shaw admitted. "But I've turned over a new leaf."

Kathleen brushed his comment aside. "It wouldn't be proper for you to hang around Naomi."

"Why not?" Cora Beth asked again.

"Because there's no telling what might happen, given the circumstances."

"Those circumstances being that I'm male and she's female." Shaw said what the matron had not.

"From his own mouth!" Kathleen looked at the others for support.

"If I were going to do anything, would I have brought her back here to your capable hands?

No. But you see, I am a man of honor and have only the best of intentions in mind. The thing is," he reminded them all, "you ladies have families who need your attention during the evening. I don't. She'll be no bother to me, and I'd appreciate the opportunity to make amends the only way I know how—by seeing after her well-being until she is better."

"I think we ought to include him," Cora announced.

Shaw flashed a smile of gratitude at the rotund woman.

"Well, I for one am steadfastly against it." Kathleen's arms folded beneath her breasts as she rose and took a fighter's stance. "In fact, I think I'll see what Cooper Kingsley has to say about the matter. I'm sure *he* will have objections."

"I'm afraid I haven't had the pleasure of meeting this Kingsley fellow." Misgiving knotted in Shaw's gut. He knew he wasn't going to like the answer, but that didn't keep him from asking: "Just who is he anyway?"

A smile of triumph slanted across Kathleen O'Toole's lips. "The man Naomi is to marry next month."

Shaw certainly couldn't stay away now. He had to find out what was going on between Prima and Cooper. He heard someone say that the Cooper fellow had visited her a couple of times this week, but he'd thought the man merely one of the locals paying a friendly call. Now all he could think was, How friendly?

Shaw left the general store as quickly as he could without seeming too anxious to leave. He headed to his flatboat and waited as long as he could endure, then took a side trail into Moonbow so no one might spot him.

He climbed the hill that formed the town's eastern edge and made his way to Annie's place. Just before he reached it, he noticed that the side window shone with dim lamplight. Someone was still awake.

He closed the distance and squatted down to observe. The corral stall was empty. That meant Annie was gone yet again. Did the woman ever sleep?

A glance at the front of the cabin revealed a single horse. That was bad, because it meant someone was with Prima. But it was good because it surely wasn't the haughty Mrs. O'Toole. That woman never went anywhere without her daughter in tow, he'd noticed, and she wasn't the sort to ride double. She was the sort to demand her own throne.

He crossed the porch to knock softly on the old wood door, only to hear two growls behind him. Shaw swung around and spotted Skillet and Jug. He held a finger to his lips. "It's just me, you two.

Remember ol' Shaw? I fed you two when Naomi was unconscious those three days . . . remember?"

Jug moved closer and his nose lifted into the air to sniff Shaw's scent. The raccoon moved closer. "That's right, buddy. It's me. I wouldn't hurt her."

Jug bumped his head against Shaw's leg. Shaw reached down and petted him. "That's a good, boy. Yeah. You like that, don't you?"

Skillet ran up and sniffed Shaw's pant leg, but when he reached down to stroke her, she moved away—but not so far that he felt rejected. "A little choosy who you let stroke you, are you, girl?"

Waiting a minute to see if anyone had heard the first knock, Shaw gave another. Still there was no answer. He was about to go around to the back when the door opened.

Having fully expected to see someone else, he was startled to find Prima. She looked waiflike in the meager light, with pale eyes in an even paler face, framed by long, dark hair. She looked lost in the comforter she had cocooned around her, and that tripped some protective urge inside him.

"I didn't meant to disturb you," he half whispered. "I thought maybe someone else might be here who needed—"

"Let's step outside a minute." Prima's voice wasn't much louder than his. "I'm going out for a short walk," she called over her shoulder, then shut the door behind her. "Dawn's . . . I mean Dawnabelle is talking with her husband in the kitchen. One of the children is sick. He came for some of Annie's remedies, but I don't know what to give him, and Annie's gone."

He linked his arm through hers, ready to move away if she objected. She didn't. "How do you feel?"

"Tired. Friends have been coming by night and day since I saw you last. I think there must be some conspiracy to make me well. They've brought food, and they see to my every need. While I'm grateful, I think I'd get better quicker if they let me fend for myself. But it's hard to say no when they mean so well."

"I'll talk to them for you."

She shook her head and sighed, looking as if she were on the verge of tears. He didn't know what to do to make things better for her. All he wanted to do was hold her, but that didn't seem right, either. "Are you sure you'll be okay?"

She swallowed and nodded. "I'd better not go too far or they'll come looking for me."

"Then I'll take you back and convince them to go. Let you have a night alone." Disappointment made his steps feel heavy. He had hoped to stay with her, even if it would be only in the next room. At least he'd feel as if he were truly helping—and satisfy this growing need to be near her.

As they approached the cabin, Shaw could hear the man and woman's exchange.

"Dawnabelle's tried to tell him what to do, but Jubal has always relied on her to take care of the children when they're sick," Prima informed him. "Apparently the boy won't lie still long enough for Jubal to get a poultice on him. He must have spilled whatever medicine they had, because Jubal left the oldest boy with the sick one and ran over here to try to get more. I'm afraid to go through Annie's things. I might give them the wrong medicine."

"Sounds to me like he needs her to go home." Shaw couldn't help but hear the loud discussion ensuing inside. The couple must think Prima had walked farther from the cabin and didn't realize every word of their conversation could be heard.

"But Jubal, what'll ya do if I ever come down sick? You're gonna have to know what to do when I ain't around."

"Don't say that. You's always gonna be with me. The Lord done promised me that, and I take Him at His word. Now all I'm asking is for you to come home for jist a while, to help me get him settled down. Once he's sleeping, me and Bill can look after him and you can come back—if you have to. She's looking kinda scrawny, but she

183

looks stout enough to make it through the night. I'm not sure our boy will."

Prima hurried into the cabin ahead of Shaw. "Go home, both of you. I'm well enough to take care of myself. Your boy needs you."

"Go," Shaw chimed in. "I'll stay with Prima until you get back."

The worried mother looked apologetically at her friend. "You don't mind?"

Relief eased the worry lines on Jubal's forehead.

Dawnabelle grabbed a shawl lying over the back of one of the chairs and motioned to the counter near the cookstove. "If you're hungry, there's enough victuals to feed a regiment," she said, with a glance at baskets that brimmed with linen-wrapped foodstuffs. "I'll settle things and come back."

"No hurry. In fact, I can stay all night, if necessary, or until the next person shows up."

"That'll either be when Annie finally gets home or dawn."

"Either is fine."

"Kathleen O'Toole will never let me live this down," Dawnabelle grumbled to her husband. "She's my dawn replacement."

"Tell you what," Shaw said. "Come back before dawn, and she'll never know."

Shaw watched as Prima waved her friends off to see about their child. As she quietly shut the door, she rested her back against the planking, closed her eyes, and exhaled a deep breath.

"Thank you," she said, finally opening her eyes to look at him. "No matter how much she means to help—they all mean to help—they still feel like company. I feel like I have to talk with them, and that's really hard hour after hour after hour. I only know so much—and that gets said quickly. It's so awkward, I feel like my shoulders are all tied up in knots."

"Turn around."

Prima did as she was told and sighed in contentment as Shaw's hands fell upon her. He began to gently rub away the tension of her day.

"Are you hungry?" she asked breathlessly.

Yes, but not for food. "Not really. And remember, Miss Powell, I'm here to take care of you. Not vice versa. What do *you* need?"

"Do you know what would truly be wonderful?"

He kept on kneading her shoulders. Yes, he knew, but he wasn't at liberty to say. If Kathleen O'Toole could hear his thoughts now, she'd be up in arms. "No, what?"

"To lie down in my room and listen to the quiet. No talking. Just listening."

"I can do that." He smiled when she swung around to read his expression. "Listening, I mean. You can do the lying down. I'll sit up and watch you listen."

She smiled. "Thank you, but you've got to be tired yourself. Sleeping on the boat in nothing but that tent has got to be hard on your back. Why don't you use the bed Annie offered you? I'll tell her I invited you to stay, since Dawnabelle couldn't. She won't mind."

"We'll see," he said, gently nudging her toward the back rooms. Once there, he noted that the cover she had wrapped around her belonged on her mattress. "Want me to help you straighten the bed?"

She shook her head. "No, I'll just sleep like this. I'm a little cold." She pulled the cover closer around her.

Suddenly it didn't matter that they were alone in the house. It didn't matter that he might be crossing a line. He had no choice but to gather her up and kiss her . . . if for no other reason than to appease the passion that blazed inside him every time he thought of her.

The kiss was wonderful.

A few minutes before eight the next morning, Shaw walked into the main room and found Annie sleeping, one cheek pressed against the table, her mouth open and snoring softly. Her medicine bag sat next to her and instruments lay on the table. The poor workhorse had probably been taking inventory and fell asleep where she sat.

From behind him, a voice said, "Let her sleep.

She doesn't get nearly enough, Lord knows."

The snoring grew louder.

Shaw turned, glad to see Prima wide-awake, looking rested. "You're looking better this morning."

"I had really wonderful dreams."

He knew how a trout felt flipping in the stream. His heart was doing somersaults in his chest. *All you did was kiss her last night, man.* What would his heart have done if the kiss had led to something more?

Prima leaned down, took the pipe out of Annie's hand, and set it aside.

The woman stirred, looking dazed. "What time is it?"

"Time to go to bed," Prima said with affection. "Your own, and not the table."

Running a trembling hand over her face, Annie wiped at her eye. "I'll be fine. A nice cup of rosemary tea will have me up and going lickety-split."

Prima touched the healer's shoulder gently. "Whoever needs you can wait a few hours more. You've been leaving here at dawn and getting home after dark for two weeks now. I'm going to see that you get some rest."

"What about you? Who'll look after you this morning?"

"Shaw's here."

"I seen that."

Shaw nodded, pleased. "I'll stay for as long as she wants me."

Annie's eyes opened completely. "I 'spect you better pack yer bag and move in, then. It don't take knowing what's coming to see she wants you, plain and simple. Only, there's one stink in the kettle that might spoil the brew."

If Annie had any objections toward him, he wanted to hear them now. He could fight the others' prejudice toward him as an outsider, but this was Annie's home. If she didn't want him here, it would be a different story. "What's that?"

Annie glanced at Prima and waited. "Cooper Kingsley ain't the sort to share his woman."

Chapter Fourteen

The pleasant smell of sizzling poplar and birch wafted from the open fireplace in the middle of the room, staving off the growing night chill. Prima moved closer to the logs burning on a bed of sand, preventing the possibility of a fire starting on the floor. The decision to wait for Cooper's return here in his cabin had really been a foolish one.

Pleasantly scented smoke rose to the open hole that was designed to allow it escape, while the drum sides of Cooper's stove glowed red from heat. Light danced in rosy blotches as she awaited his return from the search for Annie. She should have gone with him, but he'd made sense: he could travel more quickly on horseback alone, and she didn't know the forest as well as he did. In fact, she didn't want to let him know she didn't know it at all, so it made more sense just to stay put.

Something was terribly, terribly wrong. Annie's mule would never have come back alone if something dire hadn't happened to Annie. If only Shaw had been on his flatboat, at the Pumpkin Patch . . . anywhere she could have found him. She'd had no choice but to enlist Cooper's help.

For the hundredth time, she glanced at Cooper's cabin, her eyes falling uncomfortably on the log split into a half-moon shape like a giant cradle. It was his bed—one he'd hewed himself. Her pent-up sigh of tension ended in an unexpected yawn. Exhaustion hooded her eyes, and an impulse to climb into the bunk and snuggle beneath the blankets engulfed her. But she couldn't. Wouldn't.

Though the day's temperature had proved warm enough, night cooled the dense forest, and the mortar between the logs did not sufficiently keep out the elements.

Her eyes ached desperately from straining to see Cooper's black stallion emerge from the forest with Annie on his back. She closed them to soothe the burning brought on by staring intently into the night and the deepening forest shadows. Perhaps if she just lay down for a moment and allowed herself to rest . . . Then if Cooper returned without Annie, she wouldn't be too tired to go back out, to search on her own.

Though she was convinced she would only nap, sleep quickly overtook Prima. Her worry for Annie, and now for Cooper, spiraled up and out into the Tennessee night along with the birch ash.

Hours later she awakened, disoriented, sat up, and blinked. As she crawled off the bed, her feet came to rest on the earthen floor, and Prima realized she was barefoot. Someone had taken off her shoes!

Her brows knitted in confusion. Daylight shone through the smoke hole. Had she slept through the night? A glance at her wrinkled dress confirmed the answer. *Where's Cooper? Has Annie been found?*

Prima stood and nearly hanged herself on a wire stretched across the top of her bunk. A gray blanket was partially pulled to one side. "Guess I'll have to thank him for putting up the curtain for me," she admitted, then eyed her bare feet. "And for relieving me of my boots."

"You're welcome on both accounts," the familiar baritone voice greeted Prima from the other side of the divider.

A gulp lodged in her throat as she flung aside the woolen shield. Cooper stood near the fire, pouring two cups of steaming tea, looking darkly handsome with his tousled hair and rumpled clothes.

"Good morning." He took a seat near the fire.

191

"Morning?" Not one of those ladies fortunate enough to always wake with sunshine and laughter on her lips, nor sporting curls that perfectly haloed her face, Prima worried that she resembled a rooster with ruffled feathers. She smoothed wayward wisps from her face. "Did you find her?"

Cooper shook his head, setting the dark thatch of his shoulder-length hair into motion. "Couldn't see any longer. Had to wait for sunup."

Sunlight filtered through the open door. "What are you waiting for? It's past dawn."

"I knew you'd be angry if I just took off again without letting you know I hadn't found her." Exhaustion filled Cooper's midnight blue eyes. His shoulders sagged slightly.

Prima felt a moment's sympathy, but worry for Annie took precedence. If only she didn't *know* that something was terribly wrong. The night had been cold. If Annie had taken a fall, she might die out in the elements. "Did you get any sleep?"

"Nearly three hours." He offered her a mug of steaming coffee. When she took the cup, he hooked a thumb toward the woolen curtain. "Thought you'd feel better if I put that up, just in case. Not that *I* care if folks talk. We're betrothed."

She took a sip of the hot brew and eyed him

192

over the rim of her cup. "You should have awakened me."

Cooper leaned a shoulder against the door frame. With one knee bent and his hip thrown off-center, he emanated a powerful masculinity. Intimacy and intimidation blended to form the complete man. The open vee of his work clothes revealed curls of dark hair. "I should have. But I figured if Lawson had the right to watch you sleep, so did I."

"You take too much liberty." To her dismay, her pulse beat rapidly against her fingertips. Seeing such a fine physique made her aware that she was a woman—and in danger of finding this man only a notch less appealing than Shaw.

He walked toward Prima with amazingly graceful movements. "Deny that you want me, Naomi."

"I told you. I need time. You said you would wait until I was more sure of my feelings again." Her breathlessness revealed far more than her words. Prima became aware of several differences in Shaw and her fiancé and wished that she did not find Cooper even remotely interesting. Shaw's immense hands would have made her cup of coffee look tiny and absurd in his callused palms, unlike Cooper's sculptured and well-manicured hands. From the beginning, Shaw's brawn reminded her of a bear, as powerful as his nature could be gentle. Cooper seemed sleeker, and exuded a wild sensuality.

She could not deny being intrigued by the man. And before her accident, she'd obviously seen something in him worth loving.

Cooper's breath fanned the top of her head as he loomed above her, standing so close she could see the pulse in his neck.

"You ought to drink your coffee," she said hurriedly, trying to distract him. "It'll keep you warm while we're searching."

She lifted her cup to her lips, staring at him through the steam that rose from the dark liquid. He turned and glanced at the open doorway as if aware of something that didn't seem quite right.

"Did you hear anything?"

Straining to listen, Prima could not discern anything unnatural from the hundreds of noises of the forest. "The wind's getting up. I can't really tell."

Dust motes spiraled in the light and outlined Cooper's intense profile as he stared into the distance and listened. Suddenly he swung around and focused his attention on her. "It's time we were honest with each other."

Apprehension filled her, and she sensed danger in his declaration. "I don't know what you mean."

Cooper held up his hand to prevent her from

interrupting. "I know why you really want to put off the wedding."

Her cup rattled against the saucer, punctuating her discomfort. Prima assured him, "I just want to be certain of my feelings. That's all."

"It's because of that river peddler." He rose and stepped to the door. "He's turned you against me somehow. Made you think I'm not good enough for you." Measuring her from hip to toe, his gaze darkened with disapproval. "You thought I was good enough until he came along."

For not the first time since she'd met him, Prima wondered just how intimate Naomi and Cooper's relationship had been. Surely she would remember *that?* A woman would know consciously or unconsciously if she'd made love . . . wouldn't she?

Reason warned her to proceed cautiously with the man. "I'm sure we'll resume where we left off once I feel completely myself again."

One raven-colored brow lifted, followed by a slight tilt to his lips. "I'll look forward to that, love. If that outlander thinks I intend to sit back and let him take you from me, spoil what we had, he won't find me an easy foe."

The darkness in the blue of his eyes cautioned Prima that she was playing too near the fire. There was a great possibility of getting scorched.

"Cooper usually means what he says."

A shuffle of feet diverted Prima's attention

from Cooper's penetrating gaze to the much-anticipated voice at the doorway. A scream reverberated through the cabin, echoing in Prima's ears until she realized it was her own.

Annie crumpled into a bloody heap over the threshold.

Chapter Fifteen

"Lend me a hand." Cooper lifted Annie Romans from the floor and cradled her in his embrace. The crimson stain darkening the left side of Annie's dress grew wider. "She's bleeding."

Prima rushed forward to check the wilderness woman for injury. "Are you all right? Annie, say something!"

A muffled groan emanated from where the woman's face was buried in Cooper's collarbone. "S-somebody nicked me."

"Did you see who it was?" Prima stared in amazement as Annie winced with pain yet didn't utter a single sound. Was it someone still lurking nearby? Fear settled deep into Prima's bones.

"Couldn't get a good bead on him. He hid behind a line of trees."

Annie demanded that Cooper let her stand.

Though he protested, Annie was insistent. The old woman managed to stand and teetered slightly, allowing Prima to help. Annie's hazel eye focused, looking slightly less dazed than before.

"The Lord was smiling on me, though. Let it all happen close enough to drag myself here. Least I won't have to git home all by m'self now. This hip's feeling a mite poorly." She grinned weakly.

"Maybe we should stay put." Prima offered her shoulder under Annie's right one. "Use me for a crutch. I'll help you over to Cooper's bed, and you can rest there."

Annie shook her head. "Want my own bed, thankee kindly."

"But whoever it was may still be out there," Prima insisted. "We shouldn't take any chances."

"I'll take a look around." Cooper shared a glance with Prima. "You sure you've got her?" When she nodded, he added, "My guess is whoever it was won't try anything else in broad daylight."

Cooper grabbed a rifle from the gun rack on the wall and took ammunition from a drawer below it, then he looked at Prima. "Take a look at the wound and see if it's something that needs to be seen to immediately or whether she can wait until we get her home. I don't have much in the way of poultices here. Always relied on Annie when I needed that kind of fixings."

198

He motioned to a board standing at a slant against the wall. "Bolt that behind me and don't open it until you hear this. . . ." He rapped his knuckles on the wall three times, repeated the action, then gave one last knock. "That way you'll know everything's clear and it's me."

Prima nodded, assuring him she would do just that as soon as she could release Annie long enough to barricade the door.

"Do you feel well enough to stand on your own a minute so I can bolt the door?" she asked, waiting to see if the old woman's trembling had eased any.

"Let me lean against the wall. I'll be fine. But ye might grab that sheet there. Wouldn't want to mess up the boy's place no more than necessary. Don't know how badly I'm bleeding, but it don't seem more than a flesh wound or I doubt I'd be awalking."

"We'll worry about the mess later," Prima assured her. "Right now let me get the door closed and see if I can put some water on to boil in case we need it. I'll bathe the wound and see how bad it is." She studied Annie's pale face. "Are you sure you won't faint again?"

"I'll do my best to oblige ye, granddaughter. But I'd take it kindly if ye put a little spur in ye steps."

Prima rushed to bolt the door and grabbed the pitcher of water sitting on the counter near the fire. *Please have some left*, she prayed, hoping Cooper had not used it all for making coffee. She couldn't go out to the creek behind his house and get any at the moment.

Luck was with her. About a third of the pitcher of water remained. She poured it into a pot and set the pot directly on the fire, listening to its bottom crackle and sizzle as it heated. "Maybe it won't take too long," she told Annie.

"Can't rush a kettle, but I 'spect I need to sit a spell." Annie swayed and grabbed the wall, steadying herself.

Prima grabbed a cloth, dipped it into the water, and wrung it out. A cool compress would have to do until the water heated. She rushed to Annie, wrapped her arm about the old woman's waist, and helped her to the bed.

"Easy now," she said, gently helping Annie to lie back. "Now which would be the less hurtful way to get to the wound?" she asked, not certain whether to lift the hem up or to unbutton it at the waist.

"Hitch it up. Thataway I'll still be covered if ye have to let Cooper inside quick."

That made sense. Prima was so worried about Annie, she hadn't thought that Cooper himself might be in danger. "Let's see what we have here."

Annie tried to bend and help lift her skirts, but Prima gently pushed her backward. "Lie still, sweet. It's time for someone else to do the doctoring today."

The healer did as she was told.

Prima lifted the homespun and was surprised to see that Annie wore red longhandles underneath. That presented a new problem.

"Don'tcha say a word about me long johns." Annie flashed her a look of belligerence. "Ye ride old Bert as many miles as I do in a day and ye'd wear all the protection ye could, too."

"I'm not saying a word. I haven't envied one of your rides on that bony mule's back. And by the way, that's how we knew something was wrong. Bert came home right after twilight with an empty saddle blanket. I knew he hadn't simply chewed through his reins."

"Did ye give the old coot some oats?"

Prima patted Annie's hand affectionately. "Yes, and I asked one of the McGregor boys to brush him down for me while I tried to find Shaw and then Cooper. Cooper stayed out all night looking for you."

Annie squeezed her hand, a tear welling up in her eye. "Thank ye kindly, sprite. If something had happened to old Bert . . . well . . . JickJack gave him to me, ye know."

The woman's concern for her mule outweighed her concern for herself. Annie didn't have a mean bone in her body, no matter what suspicions she and Shaw might have had about the healer. Prima refused to believe the woman capable of anything underhanded. "I'll see that Bert is taken care of properly, but only after you've let me make sure you'll survive this without any dire results."

"Ye're a dear."

"And you, Annie"—Prima was surprised at the conviction in the words she was about to say— "mean a lot to me."

"I'm glad to hear it, granddaughter." Annie's hip jerked when Prima touched the long john where it was stained.

"May I unfasten a few buttons and pull back the material so I can see the wound?"

Annie nodded, looking suddenly quite small and fragile.

Gently Prima unfastened enough buttons to allow her a view of the hip. A layer of skin had been peeled back, but upon dabbing away some of the blood, she couldn't see an entry wound of any kind. "There doesn't seem to be a bullet wound. It looks more like you were cut with a knife."

Annie nodded. "Like I said. I think someone meant to just nick me or something. Whatever it was grazed my hip. The shot startled Bert, and the darned son of a swishtail sat down right in midstride. I sailed over his head and landed clean on a clump of pine roots. One of them was a sticking up like a picket and jabbed me right in the hip. Don't think I didn't cuss old Bert a new name for sitting down instead of hightailing it out of there. Wasn't the smartest thing he ever done. Course they don't call 'em jackasses for nothing."

Compassion filled Annie's expression. "Poor ol' dear was scared plumb off his hooves he was, just sat there atrembling. If I could have gotten up at the time, I'd have carried him home my own self. As it was, I cussed him a blue streak and told him to get on home so's somebody would wonder why he came back alone. I guess it worked. I was just hoping it would work a lot sooner."

"I'm sorry, Annie." Prima imagined the horror of lying out in the dark forest alone, hurt, and prey to any creature that roamed the night. She shivered. "I tried to get help and I . . ." How she wished she remembered more about her life as Naomi and the place where she lived. "I just plain didn't remember enough about your normal traveling routes to be sure where I might find you."

"You were here when I needed you, gal." Annie smiled at Prima. "That's what really matters. You did the best you could, and that's all a body can ask of ye."

Prima moved away, blinking back tears she didn't want Annie to see. The woman didn't know what this small vote of confidence, this simple act of forgiveness, meant to her. Morgan would

203

have criticized everything she had *not done* instead of complimenting the effort she had made.

"I'll see if the water's done yet," she muttered, needing the time to put her emotions in check. A quick test revealed that the water, though not hot enough to boil, was warm enough to cleanse. Prima wrung out her cloth and returned to Annie, carefully wiping away the blood and cleaning the wound. "I'll have to stitch it when we get home."

Home. How strange, yet wonderful that sounded. Annie's cabin did feel like home. A home she'd never expected to find, much less feel welcome in. "Is there much pain?"

One hazel eye stared at her. "Could be worse."

"If you can hold that against you for a minute"—Prima pressed the cloth over the wound and waited until Annie's hand rested over it—"we can probably get the blood to ease up a bit. I'll see if Cooper has any salve."

"In the left cabinet near the table. That's where he puts whatever I bring 'im."

Prima searched the cabinet until she found a bottle of yellowish-looking goo. Why had he said he didn't have anything here, if he knew he did? she wondered, then realized that in the concern of the moment, he must have forgotten about the half-full jar.

"That boy is taking quite a spell."

Cooper had been gone for a while, but she

didn't want Annie to become more alarmed. "He's taking his time to make sure everything's fine, I'm sure."

What would they do if something happened to Cooper out there? No one knew they were here. Not even Shaw. Prima glanced at what else had been stored in the cabinets. Dried foodstuffs. Enough to last a few days at best. A small pistol still remained in a holster hanging on a rack in the gun cabinet. Would there be more ammunition in a drawer beneath?

How long could they last if they had to make a stand against whoever had injured Annie? She supposed it was unlikely that the assailant would have waited until morning to finish the job—especially since he'd missed with his first shot—but still Prima was nervous.

Who *would* want to harm the old woman, and why? She was loved by all in the community. Prima had not heard a single ugly word uttered against the healer.

Cold realization chilled Prima to the core. There was one person who might consider Annie a threat: the kidnapper. Annie was the only person in Moonbow who knew Prima couldn't possibly be Naomi Romans. Before Prima regained her memory, Annie had been safe. The healer had played into the kidnapper's scheme—whatever that was—by making the community believe Prima was her granddaughter. Whoever had kidnapped Prima now knew that she no longer believed she was Naomi.

Everyone who had followed her and Shaw into town that first day heard her say that she had never seen Annie before. But Prima had been pretending that her claim had been the result of a head that had still been hurting from the hard knock she'd taken.

Only two people had any real reason to question her role as Naomi right now—Cooper Kingsley and Shaw Lawson. And only one of them knew what result there would be if Annie quit pretending—Prima would *have* to let her father know her whereabouts.

The same someone who had conveniently been there to rescue her.

The same someone whom she couldn't find anywhere this evening when she'd first gone searching for Annie.

Shaw Lawson.

Chapter Sixteen

An hour passed, a strange pall hanging over the forest. The air grew still, disquieting. Every sound seemed painful to the ear. Worse, Prima couldn't stand around and wait for Cooper to return. She needed to get Annie home and let everyone know of the danger. She had to take matters into her own hands.

"Annie, do you feel up to riding?" She turned from gazing out the window and noted the better color to Annie's cheeks. The old woman had dozed for most of the hour, going immediately to sleep after Prima had given her hot coffee and made her something to eat. "Cooper may have had to go a lot farther than he anticipated. No one knows we're here. I think we'd have a better chance if we try to get back to Moonbow. How far is it to town, anyway?" Prima didn't find it difficult to feign the uncertainty she felt. "I'm afraid I've forgotten just exactly how far away he lives from the rest of us."

"Not so far that I can't make it." Annie sat up and began to fasten the buttons that had been left open to allow room to apply bandages to the wound. "This ought to hold the dressing long enough till I get home. Did ye walk here or bring a horse?" A frown wrinkled her brow. "Can't say as I remember seeing nothing but Cooper's black this morning."

"He's out back. I borrowed one of the Mc-Gregors'. We can ride double."

Annie stood, letting her skirt hem fall to the floor. "Guess I'm ready as I'll ever be." She nodded toward the pistol in its holster. "Grab that gun. We can't be too careful."

Prima took the pistol from the holster and looked inside the drawer. She held up a box of ammunition. Had she as Naomi, known much about guns? *She'd* never held one in her life except to examine its historical value. "Want me to take these along?"

"Unless you plan to whack this varmint over the head instead of shooting him." Annie laughed. "Bullets would be a wiser choice."

Blushing, Prima hadn't wanted Annie to know that she couldn't tell whether the bullets were meant for the rifle or the pistol.

"Don't worry, granddaughter. I've killed me a wolf or two in my time."

Relieved that Annie knew how to use a gun, Prima exhaled a heavy breath. There was a bit of irony in the situation, if the person who was stalking Annie had "wolf eyes," as he'd said his sisters called them.

Hoping against all hope that they would hear the signal Cooper had agreed upon, Prima listened. Only silence ensued.

"Best get on with it, sprite."

"We can do this." Prima offered Annie a smile of certainty stronger than she felt.

"Together we can. Unbolt that door, Naomi."

Prima slid back the board and carefully opened the door. After a quick look in every direction, she threaded an arm around Annie's waist and helped her out of the cabin. Outside, the sky above the trees looked ominous. Annie hoisted the gun carefully, keeping it positioned at midhip.

Every muscle in Prima's legs ached as she fought the restraining weight of heavy skirts to propel her beyond the protective cabin walls and toward the small trail to Cooper's corral. Bushes and low-hanging branches seemed to reach for them, yet she dodged the obstacles in her path and continued to make as much headway as Annie's gait allowed.

Her breath quickened. Each step became a

greater effort. Prima's eyes squinted to glimpse Cooper's return, but the tangled undergrowth of bush and branches refused to offer any relief from worry.

"Should I shout for Cooper?" Prima at last whispered, unable to hide her rising concern. "What if whoever shot at you is lying out there somewhere? Maybe Cooper wasn't as fortunate as you. Maybe your assailant got him."

"He told us to stay inside. If he could answer at all, he'd be cussing ye for coming out and putting yerself in the line of fire."

"I suppose you're right."

"Ye *know* I am. If he's hurt enough to not make it back, he's beyond any help. But quit worrying, gal. He's just gone far afield. He'll be back, sure as my hair is gray. And when he does and finds the cabin empty, he'll come looking to my cabin first thing. We'll be there, and I'll have him a hot meal a waiting on him for all his fine effort."

"*I'll* have a hot meal. You, dear heart"—Prima gave her a gentle squeeze—"will be in bed resting, and off that hip. Moonbow's just going to have to do without you for a few days."

"We'll argue about that at home."

"Deal."

"Where you going in such a hurry, ladies?" a masculine voice called out, nearly startling Prima into a new skin.

Relief pumped through her as Cooper's stallion suddenly emerged from bushes to the right of them.

"Did you find anything?" Her voice squeaked from the fright.

"Nothing. Whoever it was lit out of here and was good enough not to leave any sign. I'd say we're sure enough safe from any more threats."

Jays, startled, took flight, flushing the tree crowns a brilliant blue.

A crunch of leaves beneath booted heels signaled the presence of something coming toward her. Prima nearly screamed, certain that Cooper's assurance would be the last words she ever heard. Shaw Lawson broke through the bushes with a rifle in his hands.

All Prima could do was stand and stare at him as if captured in a spell. Dread and relief twisted inside her at the sight of him. Dread that he might, indeed, be the man who'd shot at Annie. Relief that his appearance meant he had not also been a victim of the shooter—a worry that had crossed her mind, as well.

Her need to believe Shaw innocent ran deep, leaving her trembling in its wake. Emotion rushed from her very core and inspired a longing to believe in what she had felt in his earlier embrace.

His yellow-green gaze held hers, concern clouding his face. "What's happened? Is Annie hurt?"

211

Thunder sounded across the sky, jarring Prima from her stupor. They had to get Annie home and out of the elements before the rain started in earnest. Prima nodded. "We'll explain later. We need to hurry and get her home." How much should she tell him?

Deciding to hold back part of the truth, she shared a glance with both Cooper and the healer. "Annie took a fall and has hurt her hip. There's better medicine at our cabin. Can you help us get her home?"

Shaw tossed his rifle to Cooper, who caught it and settled it across the saddlehorn. "I assume you're Kingsley?"

"You assume right."

"I'm Shaw Lawson. I'm sure you've heard about me by now."

"I have."

"Good, then I'm going to count on you to get Pri— Naomi home while I saddle up behind Annie." He waved away Prima's objections. "I'm the larger of us, and she'll need someone to sit behind her to keep her from falling. You saddle up behind Kingsley and go on ahead. Get everything ready for her and we'll be right behind. That okay with you, Annie?" Shaw waited to place his arm around the healer and take her from Prima.

Annie moved away from Prima willingly, lifting her arm to allow Shaw access to a firm grip. "Fine with me, peddler."

"That's my girl. Just lean into me."

Prima watched as Shaw helped Annie to the McGregor horse and placed her up on the saddle as easily as he would have a small child. She didn't know how she would have ever managed getting Annie up there, but she would have. Still, she was glad Shaw had come along when he did. Both Shaw and Cooper.

"Saddle up. You're wasting time."

The peddler's admonishment spurred Prima's steps and lifted her ire. "Don't wait on me. Just get Annie home."

Cooper held out an arm to Prima and she accepted it, mounting behind him. She locked her arms around his middle and gripped tightly as he spurred his horse into a gallop.

The heavens belched then, erupting. Rain slanted through the trees to pelt down upon them. Blue-white light flashed overhead as thunder rumbled and echoed off the stately pines. Wind whistled through the trees' crowns, sending a bowing quiver through the underbrush. Prima's skirts whipped around her calves as the rain became a deluge.

"We'll have to slow down a bit or we'll throw a shoe." Cooper's words rumbled against her cheek. "This rain's making the going rough."

Barely able to hear him through the driving rain, she simply nodded, plastering herself against his back for fear she'd slide off.

213

A yellow-gray haze hung eerily over Moonbow by the time they returned. The town looked vacant, the streets deserted. Everyone had sought shelter from the downpour.

Smoke curled from the chimney of every house. Wagons and teams stood where they had been hitched before the rain began, revealing that no one had been prepared for the sudden storm.

Cooper allowed Prima to go inside the cabin while he saw to his horse. Upon entering Annie's home, Prima grabbed several towels to offer the others when they arrived and started heating up the stove to ward off any chill. She'd barely had time to prepare everything and turn back the covers on her bed when she heard them enter from outside.

"In here, Shaw," she announced from her bedroom, throwing back the curtain.

Footsteps quickly followed. Shaw appeared with Annie cradled in his arms. The old woman looked unconscious.

Prima touched the woman's brow, feeling for fever. "Did she faint?"

Shaw shook his head. "Just dozing. She could barely sit up on the ride back. You want her in here . . . in *your* room?"

Prima nodded and pulled back the covers. "My bed's got to be more comfortable than the one she's been sleeping on. And this way she'll be

214

closer to the heat from the main room, and I can watch her more closely."

Waiting until Shaw settled Annie gently into bed, Prima tucked the covers up around the woman. "As soon as the water finishes heating, I'll give her a nice bath and redress the wound. I'm going to have to do some stitching, I'm afraid. Not something I'm adept at, but I'll learn."

"I'll do it, if you think she'll let me."

His offer eased Prima's mind. If Shaw had intended to harm the woman, he wouldn't be trying to heal her—would he? "If she wakes up before I start the stitching, I'll ask her. Otherwise, my guess is she would want a woman to do it."

"Ever done much of it before?"

She nodded. "Not skin. But I was quite a hand at embroidery. It can't be too different a talent."

Shaw nodded in approval. "She'll know you'll do the best you can."

Prima smiled, remembering how Annie had complimented any effort she made. "I'm sure of it."

"Well, it looks like the two of you have got things well in hand here."

Cooper's voice behind them made each turn. Prima spoke up to cover her feeling that she'd been caught doing something naughty. "I'll have some coffee in a few minutes. It's brewing. And I grabbed some smoked venison Annie had left over, and it's warming in the oven. Hope that and a handful of biscuits will tide you two over until I can cook something more. Right now I'd like to finish seeing to Annie's needs."

"Take your time, Naomi." Shaw's gaze met Cooper's. "Mr. Kingsley and I can serve ourselves and get better acquainted while you do whatever you must. If you need us to bring anything— fresh water, linens, coffee . . . whatever . . . just give us a holler."

Prima nodded and shooed them out into the main room. "I'll do that. And I appreciate that you'll keep each other company. I'll be out in a while."

"She loves me, you know." Cooper accepted the coffee Shaw poured into the cup he'd offered him.

Shaw knew who the man spoke of; he just hadn't expected quite such an immediate and direct approach to the subject.

Kingsley's brooding expression indicated his clear irritation. "Mighty handy how easy you move around this cabin."

Unwilling to be intimidated by the man, Shaw shrugged. "Annie allowed me to stay those first few days when Naomi came home."

"You got a flatboat. Why didn't you sleep there?"

Shaw didn't like the man's tone, nor did he appreciate the fact that Cooper obviously knew things about him. Still, he could understand the man's temper. He'd be mad as hell if any other man but him watched Prima sleep, too. "Not that it's any of your concern, but Naomi asked her grandmother to make me stay. She wasn't comfortable around Annie."

"Preposterous. She loves her grandmother."

A true enough answer once, Shaw thought. But had it been quick enough to allay any suspicions that Cooper knew a reason why Prima might feel uncomfortable in the home of Annie—a stranger who was only claiming to be her relative?

He had no reason to suspect Kingsley of being anything but what he seemed—a frustrated fiancé wanting the love of his woman returned. But the fact that Kingsley fit the description Prima had given of the man she'd thought watched her too closely from the church was enough for Shaw to proceed with caution. "She does love Annie," Shaw admitted. "Anyone can see that from the way she's looking after her now. But she needed time to get over that knock on the head. I felt responsible to her until she was well enough to feel comfortable with her surroundings again."

"Ah. When will you be leaving Moonbow?" Cooper took a seat at the table and sipped his coffee, staring over the cup rim.

"When I'm ready." He fought back annoyance;

the man was pushing too hard. "Why?"

Cooper put his cup down and slid it across the table toward Shaw, as if returning the hospitality. "Because you've done what you came to do. Annie and Naomi are fine. No point lingering."

"I came," Shaw reiterated, "to peddle my wares. However long that takes is my business, Kingsley. Now, I'm no fool. It's clear you have a claim on Naomi. And that's all fine and good, as long as she still feels the same about you. But should that happen to change while I'm here, then that's a choice she's made. No man's going to tell me who I can be friends with—and no man's gonna force one of my friends to be more than she wants to be with him. Are we clear on this subject?"

"As long as we're clear on something else." Cooper stood, apparently unwilling to sit at the table with Shaw any longer. "I'll be around long after you're gone, peddler. You may be a new distraction to her for now, but someone like you doesn't have any stay in him. That eats at a woman like Naomi. She desires the thrill of adventure, but her heart needs someone willing to plant roots. I just don't see that's something a river peddler can give her. Always having to pick up and leave . . . chase the next rainbow . . ."

"Maybe my rainbow-chasing days are over." The truth the man spoke was bitter in Shaw's ears. He'd been wandering for years. Wandering to each next big chance at fortune. Wandering from the huge wrong he'd committed against his sister. "Maybe Moonbow is the place to end the chase."

"Maybe you better think twice about whose woman you're messing with."

He'd not fight in Annie's house, but the lines had been drawn. Whether or not Prima decided to pursue this attraction the two of them had felt toward each other since Shaw rescued her was something she'd have to make up her mind about. But leaving her in Moonbow with this demanding horse's ass didn't sit well with him.

"You know, I don't think it's up to either of us to decide whose woman she is. Naomi knows her own mind."

"Let's hope so," Cooper declared, apparently unwilling to give Shaw the last word.

The curtains jiggled, announcing Prima's presence to the men. "There." She sighed. "All done. The wound looked much worse than it actually was." She stretched her arms high over her head and yawned. "She's simply exhausted from being out there in the elements so long, and from the constant work schedule she keeps. I don't see how anyone does it, much less someone her age."

Shaw offered her his chair. "Let me pour you a cup of coffee and fix you a plate."

Prima waved away his kindness. "No, thanks. I can fend for myself."

As she worked, a silence ensued between Shaw and Kingsley.

Finally Prima broke the quiet that surrounded them. "I assumed you two would be putting your heads together to determine who might have shot at Annie and why."

"Maybe it was just some hunter's bullet gone astray," Shaw stated. Everyone he'd met in the hills that surrounded Moonbow only spoke kindly of Annie and Naomi. A hunter's mistargeted shot seemed the only possible answer.

"What were you doing carrying that rifle you handed me?" Kingsley's tone implied that Shaw was suspect.

Let the man think what he would, as long as Prima didn't harbor the same suspicions. "I was hunting. A man gets tired of fish."

Prima rushed to Shaw's defense. "Shaw wouldn't hurt Annie." Puzzlement creased her brow. "Why would *anybody*?"

"Maybe she's got something somebody wants?" Cooper shrugged. "Hell, I don't know."

"Herbs? Spices?" Prima motioned to encompass everything around her. "Surely no one would kill for this."

"That's where you're wrong," Shaw said quietly. "Lots of folks would give their soul for a cabin like this full of ordinary things. The remedies would be worth a lot to someone who was sick—or had a loved one who might need them.

And who knows, maybe it's you they want."

He was deliberately baiting Cooper to see what the man would do or say.

"Naomi?" Disapproval carved Cooper's features. "I'm the one who wants her most, but what would I gain by getting rid of Annie? Naomi would just end up hating me."

"If a man thought Naomi would inherit whatever Annie leaves behind . . . that might make him think dangerous thoughts that lead to even more dangerous deeds."

"But Annie's treasures are in her head," Prima argued, "and her soul. I *wish* I could inherit those things."

Shaw smiled at her. It was good to hear her growing affection for the old woman. He'd feared her discontentment with her true father had alienated her from ever having a comfortable relationship with anyone in a familial position—especially those with authority over her. Annie clearly ruled her own roost, yet Prima didn't seem to mind.

Perhaps that new growth would allow her to one day forgive her father and help her to reconcile with him. Lord knew, Shaw himself had learned that the only way to forgive a past was to face it and make a change for the better.

"Well, I say we don't let anybody know what happened to Annie," Cooper announced. "Sure, we'll have to say her mule ran off and she was left afoot. That will explain why Naomi got worried when Bert came back alone and why she had to borrow the McGregors' horse to go looking for Annie. Old Bert doesn't let anybody but Annie ride him."

Prima's eyes lit with understanding. "I see your point. We don't tell anyone about the gunshot or the wound. We simply say that Annie's staying home to rest for a few days. If anyone else mentions anything we haven't, then we'll know who to investigate."

"That's a good plan." Shaw thought Kingsley's idea had merit, provided it wasn't a cover-up to hide his own hand in the matter. After all, Prima had said Kingsley had been gone most of the evening looking for Annie and hadn't returned until before Annie fell over his doorstep. The man could have easily shot at Annie, then returned and disavowed any knowledge of her whereabouts. "But I plan to stick close to Annie as much as I can. Maybe I'll even ride with her wherever she goes from now on. I can sell my jars to whomever she's paying a call just as easily as I can hawk them anywhere else. This way, she'll seldom be alone."

"Oh, thank you, Shaw. That would be wonderful of you!" Prima threw her arms around Shaw and hugged him excitedly. A moment later as she realized what she'd done, she blushed.

"And I'll keep an eye on the cabin at night." Cooper's gaze met Shaw's and locked. "So no stranger lurks in the shadows."

Chapter Seventeen

Up for a birl?

The message on the parchment Willy Boy handed Shaw could mean only one thing. Cooper Kingsley had thrown down a gauntlet.

Shaw lifted the lantern that lit his tent and held it up to peer into the distance. "Does your ma know you're out this late?"

Willy Boy shook his head. "But my pa does."

"Where?" Shaw asked, scanning the river to see if he saw lantern light anywhere else along the course.

"Around by our cabin where the river takes a new bend."

"Lead on," he said, making sure he held the light high enough to give Willy a clear view of the road ahead.

In minutes they approached a small cove beyond the main bend of river. The lantern was unnecessary, for the moon shone high over the Tennessee hills, bathing the cove in enough light to cook by.

Shaw noticed the shadowed figure of a man. A quick glance told him only one other person had been invited to this game. As he drew closer, Shaw was surprised that Cooper wanted the contest to remain so private. He'd half expected the man to extend an invitation to every man in Moonbow.

"Glad you came." Cooper's tone held none of the welcome his words offered.

"Son, you go on home now," Willy's father said, wading into the water up to his armpits. "You've done your job."

"Ahhh, Pa, can't I stay?"

"Willy."

The single word of reproof was enough to send the boy scurrying away.

"You should have given him a lantern," Shaw announced, angry at the man for putting the child in jeopardy.

"He can walk these hills blindfolded. And if I gave him a lantern, he wouldn't be able to hide behind a tree and watch, now, would he?" Willy's father grinned and grabbed a log that had been pushed parallel to the shoreline. He shoved it closer to the competitors. "This is cedar. It rides high in the water. You know what to do?"

"Well enough," Shaw said noncommittally. He was no expert at birling, but neither was he a newcomer to it. Riding a flatboat made a man aware of how to save his life if the logs holding it together broke apart, and he wasn't the best swimmer that had ever ridden the river's currents.

When Shaw and Cooper faced each other from opposite ends of the log, Willy's father gave a final warning: "Remember cedar rides a bit more stubborn than most. Now, boots to bark!" He held one hand high in the air. With a downward sweep, he yelled, "Spin!"

Cooper's lankier legs gained control immediately. As he pedaled slowly, the bark beneath his boots began to rotate. He laughed from the sheer thrill of his power. "What's the matter, sister? Got a cramp in your stockings?"

To his amazement, Shaw managed to fight the force that would have flung most men off. Though his own legs were built more powerfully, they seemed less agile than Kingsley's. Cooper hooked his fingers beneath his gallus straps and increased the stakes. As he jogged the log faster and faster, the slop and squish of water beneath his boots took on a rhythm of its own. In seconds the cedar became a spinning blur beneath him.

Shaw's boots jogged and broke with each unexpected twist, turn and stop. For ten minutes each man countered the other's strategy. With arms stretched wide for balance, and his boots a constant blur, Shaw felt as if he were dancing upon the water's surface.

A scowl wrinkled Cooper's brow, signaling time for a different tactic. Again he hooked his thumbs beneath his galluses and rolled the log hard to the left, then jerked it back sharply to the right, making the bark shudder as if it were alive. Back and forth, back and forth the log spun, kicking up waves that broke over the bank. Miraculously Shaw stayed standing.

Then, without warning, the log went into a high-speed spin, as fast as Cooper's legs could drive it. He threw the bark into reverse and succeeded in ruffling Shaw's composure. It was the moment the man must have been waiting for. Shaw attempted to rebalance himself.

Teetering precariously, he was unable to shift around and jog into the spin. All he could do was pedal backward. Wet bark spun in the moonlight. "Want to call it a draw?" Shaw challenged.

The idea of a tie was, apparently, something Cooper couldn't stomach. He made a final desperate attempt to upset his opponent. But, as he did so, his boot twisted at an awkward angle. His thumbs unthreaded from his galluses, and Cooper flung his arms wide to regain balance. He roared with fury but the bark no longer supported his boot, and he was dunked into the lake.

When Cooper broke the surface and slung water from his eyes, Willy's father offered the man one of the two towels draped over a nearby pine branch. "A fair challenge, Cooper."

"I thought you didn't even swim," Cooper complained. "Naomi said you didn't."

"I didn't have to," Shaw reminded him, jumping off the log as close to the shore as possible. He accepted the other towel from their referee.

"You better watch yerself. Ye've made yerself a powerful enemy," Willy's father warned.

"Just tell your son this was not something he should ever try." Shaw wiped his face and handed the towel back. "Only grown men trying to act like children should make such asses of themselves."

Chapter Eighteen

The woods enveloped Shaw as he brooded and walked farther into the late-afternoon shadows. The slanting rays of sunlight waned, and he was reminded that yet another day had escaped him. His days left in Moonbow were shortening, and still he'd not convinced Prima that she should head for New York with him.

Hell. Admit it, man. It wasn't her obstinance about returning home that bothered him; her time spent pursuing her relationship with Kingsley was the true issue tightening his gut. He hadn't told her about the birling contest the other night. Hadn't thought it necessary. Figured it would serve no purpose but to feed her ego. What woman in *any* of her right minds wouldn't feel flattered that two men were battling for her affections?

228

But her attention had not been granted equally—not since she'd discovered her engagement to Kingsley. Shaw had been left to stand at the wayside, forced to watch Kingsley ingratiate himself with the heiress.

He'd put the time to good use, discovering all he could about his rival. What he'd discovered had given Shaw more than a measure of suspicion that Kingsley had been involved in Prima's staying in Moonbow—not just as his future bride, but as his captive of sorts.

Kingsley worked as a scout, sometimes overland, other times along the river. It was his work along the waterway that caused Shaw to suspect the man. If Prima and her friends had hired the man to escort them downriver, Kingsley would easily know that Prima did not belong in Moonbow as Naomi. He would know her true identity. If that was so, why hadn't he talked to the authorities? Why had he gone along with Annie's claim? Were he and Annie cohorts in crime?

Inhaling deeply, Shaw allowed the ripe air of summer to fill him with new purpose. He would pay Prima a call and ask her if she had any memory of Kingsley *before* her awakening from the amnesia.

A movement ahead brought him up short. The cracking of leaves underfoot signaled someone approaching. His senses alert, it was then that he saw them; Skillet and Jug were scampering through the rough, chasing each other up and around the tree trunks. Did Prima follow closely behind? Pleased he started to say something, then thought better of it. They might not be her pets, after all—just normal raccoons—and he was simply inviting trouble if they weren't.

It was then that he saw her, strolling toward him through the brush. She hadn't yet seen him. Prima's lively step and pretty features revealed ease from worry or deception. She looked very much like the wood sprite Annie called her.

Shaw watched as Prima stopped to pick a cluster of violets, sniff the inner nectar, then place them in a basket she carried.

A gentle breeze carried her scent to fill his awakened senses and brought with it the sound of humming. The melodious sound graced their natural cathedral-like surroundings. Wanting to enjoy the moment and not disturb her contentment, he stepped back into the shadows of a huge chestnut tree. But Skillet and Jug would have none of it and came running up to greet him.

"Hello, you two," he said begrudgingly, and bent to scratch Jug's ear.

Prima drew herself up sharply, a question shadowing her face. Her nankeens hugged her hips suggestively, playing with Shaw's willpower. To be this close and not touch her . . .

"What are you doing out here?" she asked.

"I could ask you the same."

"Gathering herbs for Annie." She turned and waved at the clusters of violets, giving him a pleasant view of her backside. "When she gave me her list and told me to fetch these for her, I was just glad they were things I could identify. She would have been suspicious if I'd said I didn't know what to look for."

"Let me help." He bent to retrieve her basket, grateful for something to keep his mind and hands busy.

She grasped its handle firmly, refusing his assistance. "It's all right. I can do it." Prima passed him and began to stoop and gather clusters of flowers and vegetation.

He liked the way she moved, particularly the way her bottom rounded so firmly with each bend. Prima glanced up and blushed at his blatant perusal. "Don't you have more important tasks to tend to?"

"None more urgent than this." And Shaw meant his words. He'd had a good day selling. It seemed vitally more important now to spend time with Prima. He half expected Kingsley to appear any moment to destroy the stroke of luck that had led him and Prima down the same path.

"Annie did remind me that leaves of three should be let be. Don't gather anything like that."

Nodding, Shaw settled down to work beside her.

Evening stretched into twilight. Prima picked and refrained from speaking further. Shaw lost himself in thought, reliving their kisses and wondering if each had been a figment of his imagination. She didn't seem at all aware of him as anything but someone to help her gather herbs. Disappointment darkened his once peaceful mood.

Yet, despite his discontentment, watching her carefully handle each herb as if it contained a magic spell, he fell under her enchantment once again.

As promised, he concentrated on gathering herbs. If she wanted to forget the kiss, then, by Solomon, he would suffer the same memory loss. Knowing how to *store* food was one thing. Now if he could only remember which of these herbs was worth picking.

Very much aware of Shaw's nearness, Prima thought he looked like a big old bear foraging for honey that lay just beyond his view. Every time he lifted an herb into the air with a sound of triumph, she forced herself not to giggle at his little-boy sense of pride.

Little boy? The words hardly described the man she couldn't stop watching. He looked even more handsome than he had on the day she had awakened in his arms. Each time those yellow-green eyes glanced at her to seek approval, her heart beat a new rhythm. Though she glanced away swiftly and pretended to concentrate on the task, her thoughts lost themselves in the wonder of his presence and the power he held over her.

She suspected that his mind mulled over the kisses they'd shared, and she wondered why she had insisted that she not see him alone for a time. At first she had thought it best so that Cooper would feel no reluctance to resume his relationship with her—so she could learn as much as possible as quickly as possible. As days passed, she realized she had wanted to keep Shaw at bay until she was sure, herself, who *she* liked best— Naomi or Prima. She didn't want him falling in love with someone she wasn't. . . .

The more she learned about her time as Naomi, the more she realized that her years spent in Moonbow had simply allowed her to live out some of the yearnings she'd had as a child. She went barefoot, if she wanted to. She made her own bed, worked alongside someone else, and had pets. Glancing affectionately at Skillet and Jug, who played nearby, she realized how much having pets had given her pleasure in the past week.

She always woke to find their warm little bodies curled up beside her on the bed. Their eagerness to go with her wherever she went made her feel like she mattered. Even their mischievous antics and the subsequent scoldings she had to give them were endearing. She felt like the fond trappings of their lives joined to enrich everyone involved.

"You're humming again."

"Sorry," Prima whispered, realizing not for the first time how happy she was since discovering herself in Moonbow.

"Don't be." Shaw smiled at her. "It's a lovely sound."

The compliment warmed her like a blanket offered to ward off a chill. Prima found it impossible to be in Shaw's presence and not desire the feel of his arms around her. Forgetting for a moment how many of the plumwort she'd gathered, she wondered if too much would spoil the pot. *Pay attention to what you're doing,* she scolded herself, *and not the man in your company.* But ignoring Shaw was more difficult than anything she'd had to do in the past weeks she'd spent in Moonbow. He was too much man, the taste of his lips on hers too great a memory to disregard.

Gooseflesh rose along Prima's neck, warning her to put an end to her task. Shaw worked alongside her, choosing the same type of plants she placed in the basket. He'd probably forgotten which they were seeking and didn't want to ask for help.

The warmth of sunset had quickly cooled, bringing with it the evening twilight that shadowed the forest in layers of darkness. Prima reached for a last cluster of tansy, smiling as she noticed Shaw's show of pride. Both grabbed for the same plant. Neither seemed able to move away.

"Excuse me," he whispered, yet his fingertips remained pressed upon hers.

Suddenly the cooling forest no longer chilled Prima's skin. Her gaze refused to turn from Shaw's direct stare; she became aware that the source of heat that warmed her smoldered in the yellow-green fire of his eyes. His lips opened slightly, as though he would steal another kiss.

Then Shaw's hand jerked away as if scorched by her touch. He stood, shoving both fists deeply into his pockets. Though the twilight made him appear more shadow than man, she sensed his muscles tightening, fighting for control.

"You look almost dreamlike in this light," he said softly. "A wood sprite, like Annie calls you."

All her thoughts to keep him at bay fled into the shadows, something within her refusing to let another moment pass before experiencing more than a simple pressing of fingertips.

She needed to know if their kisses had been as real and thrilling as her daydreams since. She needed to know if her feelings toward him were more than gratitude.

His attempt at control only made the desire to have his arms around her greater. An ache had consumed Prima this past week—the need to believe that Shaw truly cared for her.

"Is this reality?" she whispered, wanting the world to pause and allow her a haven—a cessation of time in his arms. But she didn't want it to be merely a fantasy or the product of a mind that wasn't altogether healed.

"If it is reality, who are you?" he asked softly.

She was compelled to honesty by the huskiness of his tone. "A woman who wants to learn of love." She now knew Shaw was a man of his word. He had left her alone all week, given her time to be courted by Cooper. Yet, silently, Prima knew that it was Shaw she wanted to pay court to her. Shaw who made her heart alter its beat. "Will you teach me?"

"Have you changed your mind, then? It's all right for me to come around?" Seduction—the forbidden—deepened the huskiness of his voice. "I'll stay away as I promised."

When he closed the distance between them, the air stilled . . . as if the forest and its inhabitants listened to the thunder of her pulse.

Since Skillet and Jug had informed her of his presence along the forest lane, she'd battled the passion he aroused by his mere presence. Now, though he offered her a chance for retreat, she wanted nothing more than to plunge headlong into trouble. Prima caressed his cheek. "Don't stay away anymore."

His fists shoved deeper into his pockets. His words of caution belied the emotions he held in check. "Are you sure you know what you're saying, Prima? Is this something you want, and not simply a lesson to learn as Naomi?"

The use of her real name whispered over her skin, tickling it with anticipation. *Prima.* Despite Shaw's self-control, longing echoed in his half-hearted warning. Prima gathered her own courage, pressing a hand against his chest. "I know only one thing: I can't survive another moment without knowing if what I've come to feel for you has a chance to grow into something meaningful or whether it's just an illusion my mind told my heart was too good to be real."

The sudden erratic beat of his heart beneath her fingertips thrilled Prima, making her even more determined to satisfy her impulse. A smile grew on her lips. She leaned closer to smell the heady scent of this man, stirring her already heightened awareness of him.

Even if they had no future, she needed to believe he wanted her, cared for her . . . if only for this fragile time of truce. Shaw didn't know, but like the herbs gathered for Annie, he held within him a power to heal. But the patient was Prima. And as with medicine used to stave off illness, she needed a small dose of caring to get through the days when she would leave Moonbow and return to her life in New York. It was life that, without Shaw's arms around her, would now seem far lonelier than any she'd led as either Naomi or Prima.

His body emanated a heat that drew her like a morning glory to the dawn. "What would you imagine our future to be like, sprite?" he asked. "If we should elect to spend it together?"

Prima let her imagination soar. "There would be children."

His breath blew gently against the top of her head. "I've always wanted three sons." He paused, then smiled. "Not all at once, though. And at least one black-haired, blue-eyed daughter named Naomi—ouch . . . I mean Prima," he teased.

The pinch she gave him freed her playfulness. "Brace, the oldest, will be strong like his father, but he'll be a healer. One who will always remember which herbs can cure his patients."

Shaw's hands demanded possession of Prima, one resting against her left hip, the other threading its fingers through hers to capture her in a dancer's embrace. He began to waltz among the tansy, making her head spin as her emotion rose.

"Powell, the second, will be a world-class dancer, known for his artistic ability and"— Shaw's eyes deepened in hue—"his devotion to one single lady."

Prima raised her head slightly, losing herself in the promise of his gaze. Her dizziness eased into a delightful haze of yearning. She could almost taste the night air that caressed his lips, feel every muscle of his chest pressed against her breasts, though clothing still formed a barrier between them.

"And Shaw Morgan will be our baron. The rowdiest river peddler who ever rode the current," she whispered.

"Shaw Morgan?" Laughter swelled in Shaw's chest and rumbled forth in a husky baritone.

Her heart paused in appreciation. "Our daughter *Naomi* will name him."

The dancing stopped. "She'll be good at name-calling, I suppose." Shaw's words teased, but everything about his touch seemed intently serious.

"Naming," Prima corrected in a breathless rush. "There is a difference, you know."

"Yes, I've noticed. More than that; I see the difference in *you*." His words became a whisper upon her lips. "And in me when I'm with you."

His kiss was long and tender, urging her to savor the taste of passion slowly. She moved her fingers across his shoulders and into the thick hair at the back of his neck. The silken texture, the heady wine of his taste, and the way their bodies responded to one another filled Prima with a certain knowledge that, fantasy or reality, being in Shaw's arms felt right.

Breathless, she opened her eyes to find him

studying her closely. He seemed to hesitate, as if she might dart away.

"You taste like heaven."

"And you, like magic," she whispered, loving the way their breath mingled. Prima leaned closer and brushed another kiss against his lips. "If I'd known kissing you could be so incredible, I would have whacked my head a lot sooner."

He pressed his mouth along the cool softness of her neck, chuckling seductively. The steady pounding of her pulse rushed up to greet every place his lips advanced across her skin. Prima breathed in deeply, her soul aching for some unknown release.

"Kissing you makes a man want to lose his own senses." Shaw's hissed words were hot and full of promise.

Before she could admit feeling the same, his mouth demanded more, seeking all that her heart might share, offering something indefinable. Prima molded herself against him, accepting every unspoken vow.

Shaw's heart felt as though it might drum through his chest. Prima came willingly into his arms, setting his every nerve ending alive until he thought he might explode from the sheer pleasure of touching her. For once in his life he wanted to be lost, with no sense of direction but the one that led to her arms.

His hands caressed the swell of her hips, sliding up her body until his fingers rested under her arms. With each breath, the slight swell of her breasts strained against his thumbs, urging him to a much bolder touch.

Her lips trembled as his palms brushed over her bodice, caressing each breast's peak. When her mouth opened to protest—"I'm not very big"—he whispered, "It doesn't matter," and kissed her again.

Longing changed to pure passion as his tongue found hers, and he tasted deeply of her eagerness. Skillet and Jug ran around them, chattering like children demanding that the attention be focused on them instead.

But nothing could break the spell of holding Prima. Every muscle in Shaw's body yearned for the feel of her beneath him, but he forced himself not to hurry. Though he doubted she would frighten away easily, he sensed the pathway to true passion was new ground for her. The thought endeared her to him all the more. Though she played the role of world traveler and sophisticated socialite, in truth Prima was an innocent. An innocent who might be tasting these sensations for the first time.

Given the fact that she'd probably been sought after by fortune hunters all her life, he doubted she'd ever been able to trust a man's interest in her. She'd probably been afraid to trust her own feelings for him.

Forcing his hands to leave her sides, he threaded his fingers through the long silk of her hair. So fragile she seemed. Passionate yet yielding. Still, he would never make love to her until she was sure of what she wanted, who she was, and all that that entailed. Once that happened, if she still wanted him to be part of her reality, he vowed to lead her gently to passion. He just prayed that his desire for her would not consume him before then.

"Teach me more." Prima's fingers traced a sensuous trail from his neck, across his shoulder blades, to end clenched at his waist. "I want to know everything."

Shaw groaned with suppressed lust. He would go mad if she continued to look at him with such stark yearning.

"Sprite," he whispered, and found it difficult to think, to reason with his own needs. *Do you know what you do to me?* "What you ask for can work more wonders than any illusion. But I need to be sure you know what you really want." He exhaled a long, hard breath. "I'm not sure you've had enough time to know that yet."

Everything within him wanted to honor her request, but deep in his heart, he knew she wanted more than the act of lovemaking. Prima wanted to be courted. Not as an heiress to a massive fortune, but as a woman who needed to be loved for herself alone. Just as he needed to make love to her for no other reason than that he wanted to spend his life with her and no other. He himself still wasn't even sure of the reasons he had decided to help her, and until he was . . .

His past filled him with a raging guilt, and it was all he could do not to flee into the woods. How could he tell her he had been a cad of a man? A man who'd used any means to further his future. He could easily be one of the fortune hunters who preyed on young beauties like Prima Powell—women who rebelled against their parents' wills in order to find a foothold of their own. Women whose parents loved them enough not to disinherit them, as he had been disinherited by his.

But touching her and being touched was too great a treasure to relinquish. There was a fortune here unlike any he'd ever dreamed of finding. A fortune that could last forever and be worth more than any bank contained. A providence of passion.

She pushed his shirt open, pressing her fingers over his heart. The tentative touch became warm and loving, and much, much bolder. Her lips traced a trail across Shaw's chest and then down, leaving him shuddering in their wake.

"I want to know more." Her breath fanned the hard plane of his abdomen.

243

"We'll learn together," Shaw murmured, promising himself as much as he promised her. He had vowed to change. To be a good man. He wanted to. No . . . he *had* been since meeting Prima.

God knew the prospect of having her at his side was worth whatever it took to straighten out his life and make amends for his past. His lips branded the top of her head, searing it with a silent pledge to be the kind of man she thought he was.

He urged her chin upward to deliver the kiss that would forever seal his fate. If he kissed her now, there would be no going back to the man he was, no giving her up to Kingsley, no walking away from her when the month played out.

Her lips tasted of tomorrow.

The crackle of turf beneath booted steps shattered the moment and brought Shaw crashing back to reality. Prima's body stiffened beneath his touch.

Skillet and Jug ran up into the nearest tree, screeching like angry bobcats.

With one hand, Shaw pulled Prima behind him. The other seized the knife hidden in his boot.

Chapter Nineteen

"So there you are!" Cooper pushed aside the bushes and stepped into the tansy patch. He pulled off his hat and dusted it against his trousers. "Annie said you'd probably wandered too far, but I told her I'd know where to find you." He shot Shaw a look of disapproval. "All I had to do was find someone who saw the peddler last and find out which direction he took. The man seems to always be looking anywhere you are."

"If you're implying that the lady has anything to fear from me"—Shaw's threat echoed with deadly intent, but he lowered his knife a bit—"then you'd better back that statement up with some hard facts."

Prima stepped out from behind Shaw and blocked him from doing anything rash. Her eyes offered a silent plea for him to let her handle this.

She spun around and faced Cooper with a fierce glare. "I'm flattered that Mr. Lawson has taken his valuable time here in Moonbow to see to my welfare, as he surely must have more important matters to attend to. Also, it just so happens that it was quite the other way around. He was about his own business when *I* happened along." She motioned to her basket of herbs. "In fact, he was kind enough to help me gather the plants Annie needed. Something *you*, on the other hand, said you were too busy to do this afternoon . . . remember?"

Cooper's face clouded. "But I didn't expect you to run off and—"

"I think, Cooper, that you are presuming too many certainties where I am concerned."

His eyes blinked once, then narrowed coldly on Shaw. "This man needs to know we're more than friends, Naomi. You promised *me* your hand, and I have a right as your intended to expect you to—"

"You have no rights but the ones I allow you, Cooper."

The man started to say something, then seemed to think better of it. Though his tone offered apology, she noticed the almost imperceptible tightening of his jaw. "A man can't help being a little—"

"Jealous?" Shaw finished, replacing his knife in his boot. He reached for the basket of herbs at the same time Prima did and as their fingers met and lingered, a shared glance hinted at his disappointment at the loss of their interlude. "I'll carry this home for you," he offered.

Prima shook her head. "I'm not heading in just yet. I told Annie I'd pick some cattails down by the river. Thought I'd go for a swim, too. Told her not to wait supper on me."

Shaw gently tugged the carrier from her grasp and offered it to Cooper with a sly glance. "I'm not much for a swim, but here, Kingsley. Take these to Annie and let her know I'll walk Naomi home so she won't be out here alone."

Kingsley didn't accept the basket. "You take it. I could use a swim, myself. *I'll* see Naomi home." A sneer twisted his lips. "Besides, Mrs. O'Toole came by asking for you while I was at Annie's. She said she needed to buy some more jars. Said if I saw you to send you in her direction. Might as well kill two birds with one basket, so to speak. Who knows . . . Bertha might even begin to fancy you—since you're interested in local girls."

Prima grabbed the basket from Shaw's hand and glared at both men. This was getting them nowhere. She wasn't a piece of property the pair had to wage war over. "*I'll* carry the blamed thing and you two can stand here acting like angry bulls. If anyone's going with me, they'd better come on now. Maybe a swim would do both of you good. You could use a little cooling off."

Slapping his hat against his leg, Cooper fell in step beside her and grabbed the basket. "Ah, Naomi. Don't get riled. I'll take the damned thing to Annie; then I'll meet you at the river." He glared at Shaw. "Hell, I'll even bring you back a new basket to fill."

Shaw said nothing.

Thirty minutes later, as it neared dusk, Prima was holding on to the side of the flatboat, waiting for Shaw to join her and Cooper in the water. Instead, he sat on the edge of the boat, his legs dangling over the side.

"Won't you come on in?" she urged, irritated that he was spoiling the good time they could be having. Upon returning, as he'd said, Cooper had gotten over his anger. He'd been fun, swimming like a fish. She had marveled at his ability to do flips off the boat and hold his breath for a long time underwater. However, a man acting boyish seemed charming for only so long.

"What's the matter, Lawson? Afraid of the river at night?" Cooper taunted. "Or is it swimming that sets you on edge?"

"Shut up, Kingsley, and just keep flipping. You're bound to impress her at some point—if you don't bore her to death first."

Cooper wiped water out of his eyes and swam toward the boat. "You know, I'm tired of all the politeness between us. We've both been wanting to knock the other's teeth down his throat since we met. Want to settle up now and just be done with it?"

Shaw swung his feet out of the water and stood. "If that's what it takes to make you quit acting like a jackass, then yes, I'm game."

Prima heaved herself aboard the boat, accepting Shaw's help only because she wanted to stop this nonsense before it got too far along. "Why must fists be the only way to resolve anything between men?"

"I won't fight if you ask me not to." Shaw's hand lingered at her waist. "But don't ask. A man gets tired of taking taunts, and he has a right to stay dry if he chooses."

Cooper's wet frame stood only a few feet away. "Gonna hide behind a woman's wishes, peddler?" he asked.

Shaw's gaze met Prima's. Finally, after a moment of silence, he conceded and took a step backward. "She's right, Kingsley. This can be settled in other ways."

Pleased that Shaw cared enough to control his temper for her sake, she offered him a smile of gratitude.

"Afraid you'll lose?" Cooper's stance broadened as he readied himself for the fight.

"Stop it, Cooper," she demanded, moving between the men to form a blockade. "You're acting childish."

"He's worried you're going to break off the engagement for good." Shaw's words were more effective against his opponent than a well-aimed fist—and only made Cooper angrier.

"Damn you, Lawson. She's mine!" The man swung with his right, throwing his whole body into the motion. Shaw's hand shot out and grabbed Cooper's clenched fist an inch away from impact. Momentum carried the other man forward, though, making it impossible for Shaw to prevent their fall. He let go of his foe's wrist and bear-hugged him instead, disabling him from using his fists any further.

"Let me go, damn it!" Cooper pushed his back into Shaw's stomach, plowing him into the boat bed, but Shaw had locked Cooper's arms against his sides, making it impossible for him to free himself.

"Not till you listen to reason," Shaw said in a growl, withstanding backward head butts to his face. "I said I don't want to fight you and I mean it! What satisfaction will you gain by beating a man who won't hit back? That'll *really* impress her, won't it?"

Cooper went still. "Then let me go," he demanded again, and this time his voice held more than simple anger.

Shaw released the bear hug and twisted as if he anticipated a blow. But Cooper surprised

Prima by not taking advantage of his foe's awkward position on the ground.

The look on the man's face could have sawed bark, but surprisingly Cooper offered Shaw a hand up. Wondering herself if it were a trick, Prima could see Shaw's hesitation. After a few moments, though, he tentatively accepted the offer.

The handclasp lingered, as if the two men were testing each other's strength.

Cooper was the first to let go. "This changes nothing."

"It's a beginning." Shaw dusted off his trousers.

"You still have no clue why I despise you, do you?" Cooper's laugh was bitter. "You offer her a life outside of here. How am I supposed to compete with that?"

Understanding dawned within Prima; suddenly she could sympathize with Cooper's frustration and resulting actions. He had come to know Naomi well enough to realize that she wanted more than what a place as backwoodsy as Moonbow could offer. He understood her enough to feel threatened by what Shaw represented, not just the peddler's attraction to her. Though she was angry at his method, she was flattered and impressed that Cooper had the sensitivity and insight to discern her needs—especially from the actions of a girl who'd thought she was someone she wasn't. Prima couldn't entirely rebuke such devotion. "Coop, if you're the man I'm meant to marry, it won't matter where we live. Here or in New York."

Shaw's head spun to glare at her so fast, Prima didn't realize until too late that she'd just given away another clue that her memory had returned. "I mean wherever . . . whatever big city might lure me. Just because a city man comes along doesn't mean he'd turn my head."

"I'd like to think not, Naomi. But you've been acting awfully strange lately. *Too* strange for me, maybe. You said you needed some time to think about us. Well, take it. You won't have any more argument out of me." He grabbed his hat and plopped it onto his wet head. Giving it a curt bob of the brim, he muttered, "I hope you enjoy the rest of this evening. I'll stop by Annie's and see if she needs anything before I head home."

Prima refused to let him leave on bad terms. "That's kind of you, Cooper. Annie always enjoys your company." Cooper seemed a good man, even if he had a hot temper. Heck, Shaw had been just as willing to fight. . . .

When Cooper's shadow blended into a thousand others, Prima felt a touch on her shoulder.

"I'm sorry, Prima. I didn't mean to overstep myself . . . to ruin what the two of you have enjoyed the past few days."

She shouldn't have let Shaw's hand linger for

a moment before she moved away, but she did.
Still, he was implying she'd given Cooper liberties she'd given no man—and that annoyed her.
But she did have such mixed emotions about her
two suitors. Didn't she? "He's really a much nicer
fellow when you're not around."

"Do you like him?"

She had to be truthful. "He's attentive, and he's
kind to Annie. He seems to be well liked in the
community and is respected as a businessman.
Still . . ."

"What?" Shaw disappeared inside the flatboat
tent and lit a lantern, holding it up to ward off
the growing darkness. "Sounds like you could
easily keep Naomi's promise and marry the man.
It's clear he wants you for himself."

"He does. But I'm not sure how I feel about
him."

"Because you don't know what the two of you
shared?"

Prima wasn't sure how she felt about discussing this uncertainty concerning Cooper . . . with
Shaw, of all people. But it felt good to talk with
someone about it. "Partly. I mean, it is rather
awkward being unsure about whether or not I've
made love to the man."

Shaw chuckled.

"I find no humor in the matter." Prima's temper flared at his lack of sensitivity. "It's awful trying to pretend to remember everything Naomi is

supposed to know about him, and yet I have no clue how close they've been."

"You haven't, you know," Shaw said softly. "The two of you haven't made love yet."

"How would *you* know?" She should have been pleased by his certainty, but her irritation only grew.

"I can tell by his frustration, and by the way you react to me when you're in my arms. If you had been with a man, I would sense it, Prima. Oh, now, don't bunch up your freckles. If you truly loved him, you wouldn't be able to hide it from me. You couldn't hide that from any man who had any experience with women. That's why he's so frustrated. He senses you pulling away from him. I'd almost bet you two haven't kissed since you hit your head. It certainly makes me wonder why Naomi ever agreed to his proposal."

"I'm sorry you think me so fickle and inexperienced." She refused to answer him concerning her kisses with Cooper.

"That's not what I said, and even if I had, you should take it as a compliment. When a man kisses a woman and she kisses him back the way you did me, he wants to believe that no other man has made her feel the same way." Shaw set the lantern down and pulled out the trunk she had so admired the first day on his craft. "I believe that. Now come sit here and I'll grab a towel so you can dry off. Let's not end the evening in a quarrel. I was just trying to reassure you that nothing happened between you and Kingsley, no matter what he may try to lead you to believe."

He unlatched his trunk of belongings and opened the lid. Sifting through, Shaw held up several items—an ivory dragon, a silver wizard's hat, a bolt of lightning carved from turquoise. They were all items that had been duplicated on the outer sides of the trunk.

Prima's gasp of delight made him swing around to peer at her.

"Are you all right?" Shaw surveyed her from head to foot.

"Did you draw that?" she asked, staring at the artwork that lay in partial shadow at one side of the trunk. The drawing was nothing short of masterful. The artist had sketched a single tree, whose roots lay partially hidden in a foglike mist. Pink calypso and passionflowers grew at the part of the base that was visible, but the tree itself drew her most rapt attention.

"Sketching is something I do when I'm alone," he admitted. "Selling from town to town has given me plenty of that kind of time."

A woman's image was molded into the tree's trunk, her arms lifted as if they were branches, long, sculptured fingers spreading and tapering into foliage that had been formed by endless ten-drils of hair upswept by the wind. The facial contours clearly resembled Prima's.

Prima felt her irritation dissolve. Emotion twisted her throat, making it difficult for her to speak. Finally her awe could no longer be silenced. "That is wonderful. You've drawn me as if I were something more than myself—part mystical being, part seed of something generations old."

Shaw's yellow-green eyes searched hers, asking a question she couldn't quite discern. She gauged each stroke his charcoal had created and found it all a mystery.

"Look twice, Prima. Look at it as you would have when you were Naomi. Then as *you*, heiress to an empire, Prima Powell, would."

His request would have surprised her had she not immediately seen a difference. Prima would never have bought such a painting. Her parents would think it too whimsical for manor walls. Naomi, on the other hand, would have hung it in a special place where she could study it repeatedly, finding new subtleties to marvel over every time.

Tears sprang to her eyes when, with sudden clarity, she realized that this was exactly what Shaw was trying to elicit with the painting: she was both Prima and Naomi—a complicated creature of both fantasy and reality—a blend of forest sprite and deeply rooted Powell seed. Her time as Naomi had not been an aberration; it was not something she should fear. This whole episode had taught her so much!

The mist in the sketch? It could represent so many things: the confusion of the amnesia, the fog of deceit that seemed inherent in her relationship with Morgan, the sense of needing to clear something from her life.

Maybe it was all those things or none of them. But one thing shone through with great clarity: Shaw Lawson knew her as no one else ever had. He had looked past what she pretended to be, seen through what he had heard and read, and saw her as she must become if she ever intended to be happy.

"You believe I must find a balance between my fantasy life and my true self," Prima finally answered. "A cross between me and Naomi."

"Exactly." Shaw searched her eyes, but she could not read their depths. "You will never be one without the other. You were meant to experience both of these lives you've been given—so that you can find the right one." His gaze averted to somewhere just beyond her, as if he were looking into some distant horizon. "I know whereof I speak, Prima. I'm on a path not unlike yours."

"But Naomi can't survive in my world," Prima insisted. "A wide-eyed believer in miracles, a lover of frivolity, doesn't fit in my family."

"Then just be Prima," Shaw said softly, sadness filling his eyes as his gaze returned to hers.

"Let me take you home to your father. You can't just let him continue to think you're dead. Go back to New York."

"I can't." Prima felt trapped by all the things she was learning about herself. Her true wants. Her true needs. And she didn't know where she'd be headed after she discovered her true self. It was easy to *say* she wanted changes, to be treated differently. But actually making those changes and doing something about them was much harder. Old habits died hard. Being responsible for her own actions, not blaming everything on Morgan, was wonderful, but it required a greater effort than she'd ever truly understood when she'd been a young socialite with her friends in Quest. But could she ever go back to her father's controlling guardianship?

She had virtually run headlong into reality and now faced exactly what she'd prayed for all those years under her father's roof—the right to be herself. How ironic that the one true obstacle to that possibility might end up being herself. "I don't fit there anymore either."

"Where *do* you belong, sprite?"

"Nowhere," she said with finality, handing him back his disturbing drawing and wishing she'd never seen it. "I belong nowhere. Not even to myself."

Chapter Twenty

"How much farther?" Prima asked, stopping to take a deep breath. Though they hadn't climbed hand-over-foot yet, the path leading to the meadow where Annie demanded they go this morning was becoming steep and physically taxing. How the older woman managed to walk with her sore hip was beyond admirable—it was impossible! "Aren't you even tired?" she asked in amazement.

"Gotta keep going even when the road's rocky, lass." Annie shifted the blanket she carried to her other arm and halted a few yards above Prima. She turned and pointed to the hill's crest. "Just a wee bit more. It always feels the most troublesome just before ye get where ye're headed."

As they rested, dawn played across the sky, brightening into mauve, orange, then saffron.

The surrounding peaks blossomed in panoramic color as sunlight warmed the mountain's face and evaporated the morning mists that rose from the foothills.

Though it was summer, Prima was glad she wore the longhandles Annie had suggested she add beneath the calico blouse and trousers she'd selected from the few pieces of apparel folded in Naomi's trunk. She really needed to buy a dress for herself, even if she was still pretending to be unchanged, but she'd grown accustomed to attiring herself more comfortably. Besides, she doubted she had any money stashed away; she couldn't see how Naomi would have made it. It seemed everyone paid the Romans in barter instead of coin: chickens, flour, wood—whatever material a patient could afford to trade for services rendered.

Her men's clothing made climbing easier and helped to stave off some of the chill in the air. Annie seemed unaffected, even invigorated by the cool morning.

"You never said why you're in such a hurry," Prima reminded her, picking her way along behind the healer. Skillet and Jug ran past, rushing over the mountaintop to see what was on the other side. Annie was not long behind them and disappeared over the crest. "Why did we have to do this at dawn?" Prima asked loudly, not liking the fact that Annie was out of her line of vision.

She was afraid the dear woman might stumble and fall, exacerbating her hip injury further.

Annie would be the aspect of Moonbow she would miss the most when she returned to New York, Prima decided. The thought of not seeing the healer again filled her with a sadness she didn't want to think about. Didn't want to examine any closer. To do so would be to admit that she had grown very fond of her life as Naomi.

" 'Twas a promise I made. A promise to be kept." Annie's voice seemed to echo as if she were in a deep valley, and it reverberated off the granite walls that rose up around them.

Prima hastened to catch up. At the top of the rise, she halted to gape at the magnificence stretching before her.

Mountain peaks reached for the sky as if carven stair steps to heaven. The horizon shimmered with a haze of blue mist as far as the eye could see. Faraway crests wore caps of white, a sign that winter never left parts of the Appalachians. The peak rising above Moonbow swept up over a blue-green lake surrounded by a mountain meadow blanketed by summer wildflowers. In the center of the meadow stood a dozen or more wooden crosses. Annie had brought her to a graveyard.

A cathedral-like hush lay over the land.

"Who's buried here?" Prima asked, watching

Annie hobble down the path that led to the burial ground.

Annie removed the blanket she carried and spread it out over the ground near two graves that were slightly separated from the others. "We'll rest here."

Prima joined her and sank down, glad for the respite. Tiny needles of pain jabbed at her knees and calves. "Goodness, how do you do it, Annie? I couldn't have walked much farther."

Annie patted Prima's cheek. "Ye have it in ye to do what ye must, child. Ye're a strong lass, full of spit and vinegar, ye are. Ye made it here fine, didn't ye? And ye were thinkin' ye couldn't. Ye just had to keep going no matter how long it took to get here. The *trying* is the thing, lass. That's the glory of everything about ye. It only takes the trying to see things done eventually."

Annie spoke of more than their journey to the meadow; Prima was sure of it. The woman was looking into her troubled soul and offering words that made Prima believe she could find her way past this fork in the road her life now offered. Maybe trying was all she could do at this point— try to find which road was the right one to take.

Looking around at the graves, Prima asked, "Where are we exactly, and more important, why are we here?"

Annie's hazel eye slanted toward the taller of the two graves. " 'Tis where my JickJack is laid to rest, bless his dear, departed soul."

"I'm sorry, Annie." Prima noticed the name carved on a cross and the date of his passing: *Beloved husband. March 24, 1838.* She felt as if she had intruded upon a private sanctuary.

Annie looked at her strangely. "Ye must still be thinkin' ye're that Powell person, aren'tcha? Ye know this place as well as I do. Ye planted those flowers there."

A glance at Annie's face made it difficult to lie to the woman; she'd come to mean so much to Prima. "Sometimes I think I'm her—but it seems she's becoming more memory to me now than anything else."

" 'Tis a good thing, lass. Change comes to everyone." Annie motioned for the basket Prima had toted uphill. Prima handed it to her. "The sooner a body welcomes change instead of fighting it, the sooner she can learn why the change be necessary."

"Annie?" Prima watched as the healer lifted out some biscuits and fryback she'd wrapped in cloth to keep warm while they climbed the mountain. A crock of cold milk and two tin cups followed. "May I ask you something without your getting angry with me?"

"That important, that I don't howl at ye?"

Prima nodded. She could take all the shouting her father tendered, but a harsh word from Annie might break her heart.

"Then I'll do me best, lass, to keep an even temper." Annie's one eye winked. "But don't rile me too greatly, or old JickJack will roll over in his grave, he will, if I don't act like the banshee he bedded for thirty years."

The great affection in Hazel's voice urged Prima to delay the question she wanted to ask and say something else instead. "He's been gone for some time," she said, looking back toward the cross.

"Twenty-one years, four months, eighteen days," Annie agreed quietly, her eye shining with unshed tears.

Almost as long as Prima had been alive. She reached out to clasp the old woman's hand and found it trembling. Prima squeezed gently and let her hand remain curled over it. "You must have loved him very much."

"Aye, that I did, lass."

"And that one." Prima noticed the date carved into the smaller of the two wooden crosses. *Sprite.* The date of passing was only a day sooner than JickJack's. "Who is that?"

"A child," Annie whispered, and moved her hand from beneath Prima's. She poured the milk into the tin cups and offered one. "Nary more than two years old when she left this fine earth, she was. One of God's angelhearts now, I be certain." She handed Prima a biscuit. "Eat this so ye have the strength to help me gather the wild-flowers."

Though Prima wanted to ask if the girl was Annie and JickJack's daughter, the woman clearly didn't want to talk any more about the child. Prima wondered if now was the appropriate time to bring up Annie's knowledge of her arrival at Moonbow. Perhaps it could wait.

"Spit it out, lass." Annie wiped the tears from her eye and looked squarely at Prima. "Ye've wanted to say something the whole climb. Am I so fierce that ye're afraid of me?"

"I want to know what you thought of me when I came home that day saying I'd never seen you before and that I wasn't your granddaughter."

"All of us wish we was someone else now and again. . . ."

The words weren't what Prima had wanted to hear. She needed to know if Annie had any involvement in a kidnapping . . . and if so, why. "When I came to visit you . . . how long has that been now?"

"Two years, four months, nineteen days," Annie said without thinking, offering Prima a piece of biscuit. But as she realized what she said, her hand froze in midoffer.

Exactly twenty years from the date of the child's death. Prima wondered if there truly was any connection. She counted back the months. March. The month she and Quest had taken the trip down the Cumberland. "Then I arrived in March of fifty-seven?"

"About that time."

Not liking the way the facts were stacking, Prima didn't know if she wanted to hear more. She wanted to trust Annie, to believe she could be no part of any scheme to steal her away from her family. "I've had such a good time spending it with you, I've quite forgotten why I stayed."

"Yer mother passed away. Ye didna want to return home. Kept saying so, even in yer sleep. I couldna let ye go back. And, truth be, angelheart, I needed ye here."

Angelheart. Sprite. Both names somehow bonded Prima to the child's cross next to Jick-Jack's. Both were names Annie called her at times with great affection. She had to discover what the connection was.

"Then you had only one child? There was no one else but you for me to stay with?"

"Just me."

"What was her name?"

"You know yer mother's name, lass."

"Naomi," Prima said with sudden realization.

"Aye, Naomi. We'd best be getting to our chores," Annie announced, setting her tin cup aside. "Time has a way of taking things from us if we don't pay her heed."

Prima swiftly ate a bite of the biscuit, then placed the remainder in the kerchief that had held them. Annie had closed off any further discussion for now, and perhaps she wasn't the one Prima needed to ask the question of anyway. She needed to see if anyone else might be willing to discuss her arrival in Moonbow those two years before. There had to be someone who didn't particularly care how much she knew about the events of that time. There had to be someone who was not happy that she'd stayed.

Only one person came to mind—Kathleen O'Toole.

But she had to say one more thing to Annie before she let the subject alone. To let her know that no matter what her true motivations were, Prima understood one of them well beyond question. "I'm glad you loved me enough to make me stay, Annie."

Chapter Twenty-one

Now what is she up to? Shaw wondered as he noticed Skillet run past at a bounding clip. The raccoon held something in her mouth—a scrap of paper? Jug followed close behind. He anticipated the sight of Prima but was surprised to discover Cooper Kingsley running after them instead.

"Come back here, you mongrels!" Kingsley ran like a man who had the devil chasing him. "Give me back that paper."

Shaw childishly entertained a thought about tripping the man as he ran by, to give the coons a better chance to escape, but something instead made him step back into the brush so Kingsley didn't see him.

He slunk out of the pathway and crouched behind a cluster of laurel bushes. If Kingsley spotted him, Shaw would have some hard explaining to do. And as Shaw was no little man, Cooper might easily notice him. Still, Shaw's gut said to hide and watch.

Not far from where he hid, the coons decided to climb a tree and get out of reach. Shaw watched Kingsley come to a halt to catch his breath.

"You damn coons'll be supper before I get through with you!" he cursed, shaking a fist at Skillet. Neither raccoon meant to budge. Skillet merely rattled the paper for effect.

"Give me that paper and I'll let you be, you little thieves." Cooper began to climb the tree, forcing the two miscreants to scurry to a higher branch.

"I'll climb until there's nowhere else for you to go, fat-butt. You'll wish Naomi didn't feed you so well," Cooper shouted, and kept climbing, pushing the animals to greater heights.

At last, when they could go no farther, the coons stopped. Turning, Jug ran down the tree, placing a barricade between his mate and Kingsley. With bared teeth, he emitted a loud screech of warning for the man not to move any higher.

"Trying to protect her, are you, lover?" Cooper snapped. "Won't do you any good. I've got to get that letter. You and nothing on this earth ain't gonna stop me."

But Cooper was wrong. The male raccoon

dropped toward him in a cloud of fur and nails.

"Ouch, you sorry son of a . . . quit it, damn you!" For a second too long, Cooper let go of the tree to elude his attacker's fierce bites. He lost his hold on the tree and toppled backward, falling to land with a resounding thud upon his back.

For a moment he lay there, motionless . . . speechless.

Shaw started to show himself, to see if Kingsley needed any help. The man might have seriously injured himself, and Shaw couldn't let him lie there and die no matter how much he might have deserved to fall. Jug was only doing what any male would do in that circumstance—protecting his mate in any way possible.

"When I get up from here, you are dead meat!" Kingsley called from his back.

It was time to step in. Shaw moved out of the brush and walked up behind Cooper. He looked down at the man, who stared up at him, startled. Offering a hand, Shaw helped him up.

"Still holding a grudge against me, are you?" Shaw asked. He looked around, then added, "Do you always sleep in the middle of the road like this, or were you studying something up in the trees?"

Shaw could tell that it took everything Kingsley had in him not to dart a glance at the raccoons, so he, too, pretended not to be aware of Skillet and Jug's presence.

"There's an old superstition about sleeping toward the bark instead of away from it," Kingsley lied. "It helps make sure nothing will ever take you away from your roots."

"Peculiar superstition, if you ask me," Shaw said with a laugh. He watched as Kingsley dusted off his backside, and thought the man muttered something under his breath. Still, he looked no worse for the fall. There was no reason to coddle him.

Cooper twitched impatiently, and Shaw smiled. The man surely wanted him to leave.

"You heading over to Naomi's?" Cooper asked, frowning.

"Not unless her cabin has moved since the last time I saw it."

Annoyance darted across the man's features a moment before being cloaked behind a look of disappointment. "Well, for once, peddler, I wish you were. You could tell her that Mrs. O'Toole will be back tomorrow. She asked me to find out when the woman would return, and I haven't had a chance to let her know."

"Your nap was too important, I see." Shaw nearly choked with mirth when the glint hardened in Kingsley's blue eyes.

"Been up all night," the man said in a growl. "But that's no concern of yours. You'll take her the message for me, won't you?"

"No." Shaw stretched his shoulders and

271

yawned loudly. "I was thinking I'd take a nap my-self. Since you've already got the spot warmed up for me, I'll just grab the shade from this here tree." He had to dig the spur one notch deeper. "Doesn't matter if I'm not the superstitious sort, does it?" He moved past Kingsley and rested his back against the trunk. "I kind of like the idea of sleeping this way."

Frustrated, Kingsley glared at him. "Do what you damn well prefer, Lawson!" A glance into the heights of trees surrounding them made him curse. "Sleep standing up, for all I care!"

Shaw folded his arms across his middle and pretended to close his eyes. He could almost feel Kingsley's exasperation as the man stood there waiting to see if Shaw really meant to remain under the tree that sheltered his prey.

What could be so important about a letter that the man would risk his fool neck for it? "You gonna stand there and watch me sleep, Kings-ley?" Shaw drawled, opening one eye to stare at the man. "Got any reason you don't want me sleeping here?"

"Hell, no!" Kingsley snapped. "Sleep anywhere you damn well choose." And with that, he turned and stalked off down the path back to town.

Shaw was sure enough time had passed and that Kingsley had not remained behind any bushes to watch him, when he finally heard Skillet and Jug making their way down the tree trunk.

He opened his eyes as Jug used his shoulder to launch himself to the ground. Skillet followed close behind, using Shaw's head as a perch. "Hey, girl, get off there, will you? The man's right about one thing: Prima feeds you too much."

As he lifted the female coon down, he noticed that her weight wasn't all her own. She was an expectant mother! "Well, congratulations are in order, I see. Jug, you old devil."

Shaw ran his hand down Skillet's spine, finishing the stroke at the end of her tail. She dropped the paper from her mouth and she began to chirr softly. Shaw didn't grab for it immediately, as he didn't want the beast to think he was petting her just for the sake of getting the paper. At last, when she sat on her haunches, her belly more rounded than he'd ever seen it before, he moved a hand toward the scrap. "Can I take a look at this?"

Skillet stared at the paper, unblinking.

"I won't, if you don't want me to. I'm asking."

She bumped his hand, a silent plea to continue the stroking.

"Like that, do you?" Shaw resumed the petting and lifted the paper to read. "Let's see what he's so concerned about."

I have news that will interest you. Your daughter is not dead, as you believe. She's

273

very much alive, and I can show you where to find her.

Shaw sat up straight, reading the words again. This was a letter written to Morgan Powell, he was sure of it. As sure of it as he had been that Cooper might be involved in Naomi's stay in Moonbow.

But that was all there was of the letter. Just words that implied that Cooper believed Naomi's original claim and, possibly, had decided to use it to his advantage. Of course, the man could have simply recognized the differences in her since the blow to her head and decided they were too much simply to be the product of a shaken memory. . . .

The few scribbled words didn't tell Shaw what he needed to know most. Was this just a besotted beau's attempt to ingratiate himself to his ex-fiancée's father, or an abductor's last attempt to gain a ransom he had decided to exchange for other rewards?

"I'll have to keep my eye on him," Shaw told the coons. "He's craftier than he looks." He stood, folding the paper and putting it away for safe-keeping. "This will come in handy later on."

He snapped his fingers at the raccoons. "You minxes up to a little investigation? Let's see if you can grab anything else the man might not want us to see."

Chapter Twenty-two

"Am I that hard on your eyes, Naomi?"

Startled, Prima let her hand slide across the notes she'd been taking, leaving the last comment illegible. She rose from the chair situated behind the table in the main room of Annie's cabin and attempted to will the roiling in her stomach to halt its turbulence. She hadn't expected to look up in the open doorway and find Cooper standing there.

"You should get out more." His hand swept elaborately out to encompass the surrounding three walls. "You don't have to hide out in this cave to steer clear of me."

Prima had deliberately avoided Cooper since the quarrel between him and Shaw at the river. She hadn't seen Shaw all that much either, but Cooper even less. She simply needed time to gather her thoughts and analyze her feelings about both men—and her situation in Moonbow. Her thoughts about Annie.

Dressed in a black frock coat and cossacks, Cooper looked as if he might be coming from a party.

"May I?" He sauntered across the room to take a seat in the chair opposite hers.

"For a while. I'm sure you have more things to do than watch me puzzle over descriptions of herbs and spices."

"Not really." Cooper offered a disarming smile. "Watching you has always had its charms." His gaze swept over her as if she were a map and he a cartographer.

Willing herself not to blush under his scrutiny, she pretended to study her notes. "I really must finish this before Annie gets home," she insisted, hoping to persuade him to leave. "Was there something particular I could help you with?"

His hand reached out to stop hers. "Naomi, can't you take a mere five minutes and talk to me? I've missed the sound of your voice."

"Don't, Cooper." She attempted to look away, but his gaze drew hers. The pressure of his hand forced her to lay the papers in her lap so he wouldn't see her notes.

"I wore out a good horse finding O'Toole for you. The least you could do is spare me a few minutes."

She wrestled her hand from under his and pushed back her chair. "Which I appreciate, but I can give you nothing more than a few minutes."

"Then I suppose I'll have to be satisfied with that." His eyes darkened to a midnight blue. He rose and walked around the desk. She started to rise and back away from him, but his commanding voice restrained her as surely as if he'd reached out and grabbed her. "You look tired."

She didn't trust the way his eyes suddenly softened. This man ran hot one minute, cold the next.

Cooper offered a smile that would have blistered any other woman's heart with its warmth; then he sighed deeply. "Ah, Naomi, you don't know how I wish you'd marry me now and be done with this farce. You don't have to live like this." His hand caressed the soft curve of her jaw. "I can be every bit as resourceful as that peddler. Let me show you how much I love you."

And then he kissed her.

"No!" Prima opened her mouth to protest, but the action only gave him full access. Bands of iron encircled her, pulling her closer despite her struggle to push free from his grasp. Her foot connected with his shin, only to discover that his boots shielded him from the force of her anger. Finally one hand broke free of its prison. She slapped Cooper soundly across his cheek.

He let go and backed away, looking dazed. The

imprint of her hand stained his cheek a fiery red. "That was uncalled for," he said with a gasp. His voice was husky with anger and something more.

"I'll thank you to remember that *I* choose who touches me."

Kingsley ran a hand through his disheveled hair, his mouth forming a circle as he exhaled a deep breath. "So . . . you love him."

It no longer mattered that Shaw had not professed love to her, nor she to him; Prima had committed her heart and soul to the peddler nonetheless. And suddenly she saw that she had to end any false pretenses between her and Cooper right away. "Completely."

"All right." Cooper's palms lifted in front of him as if she'd aimed a gun at him. "I may be stubborn, but I'm no fool. Anyone can see you mean what you say. Truce?"

Wary, she wondered if she was making a mistake, but she didn't want to leave enemies in Moonbow. "Truce."

Noise sounded outside the cabin, drawing Cooper's attention away from her momentarily. "Damn!" he said.

"Who is it?" She noted his dark brows angling abruptly before settling back into place.

"O'Toole and her gaggle of followers. They've come to pay you the call you asked for." He quickly dismissed the view and moved toward her with a gleam in his eyes. "How about one

278

little tiny kiss good-bye? I don't think that's asking too much, not if I must resign myself to the role of former intended instead of lover."

"You have a scoundrel's heart, Cooper."

"That's one of the nicer things I've been accused of. Now, if I promise to keep my hands and my tongue to myself, would you grant me one last request? Otherwise I might waste away to sheer—"

She splayed her hands over his chest to prevent him from coming any closer. "If a good-bye kiss will relieve me of these dramatics, then I'll grant one." She held up a warning finger. "On the cheek."

"Done."

Cooper kept his word, kissing her on the cheek, and gently.

"I see you've delivered your message, Kingsley."

Abruptly, Prima pushed away from Cooper and allowed her eyes to feast upon Shaw Lawson's countenance, hungering for more than the mere sight of him. But the forbidding expression etching his face into a mask of stone prevented any rush into his arms. Dread sank into her stomach as she realized that Cooper had lied about who had been outside. He'd wanted Shaw to see her let him kiss her—"Cooper and I, we were—"

"I've talked to Mrs. O'Toole, Kingsley. She'll be

in as soon as her daughter quits throwing up. They had a rather rough journey."

His tone halted any further explanation Prima might have given regarding the kiss. Shaw walked over and handed her a folded-up piece of paper. "When you're less occupied, look me up and we'll discuss that." He turned from Prima and walked away, calling back over his shoulder, "I'll be at the flatboat. Enjoy the rest of your afternoon." And with that, he stormed from the cabin.

Recovering from what looked like shock, Cooper took ground-eating strides to catch him. "Don't talk to her like—" he began, but Prima cut him off.

"Let him go."

Turning on his heel, Cooper stared at her, pleased surprise sharpening his features. "You know what he's thinking. You're just going to let him believe it?"

Prima stuck the letter Shaw had given her into a pocket to look at later. "Yes. He believes I've made my choice between you. It's that simple." Her statement lingered in the air like a pungent odor.

"And?"

She glanced up, willing the hurt Shaw had inflicted upon her to a place so deep within her heart no one would ever again reach its pit. How dared he mistrust her, not allow herself to explain? "I'm not at his beck and call any more than I'm at yours. No matter what I feel. I'll never simply obey a man ever again. I refuse to live my life explaining what I do or asking permission to do it. And whether you deliberately intended for him to catch you kissing me or not, he either trusts me or he doesn't. I, after all, was not the one doing the kissing."

A knock sounded at the entrance to the cabin. Kathleen O'Toole and several other women stood outside, awaiting permission to enter. "Won't you come in?" Prima asked with a great deal of welcome she didn't feel at the moment. She had wanted to speak to Kathleen, not the woman's attendants.

Kathleen looked around the room, one brow arching in surprise. "There aren't enough chairs, dear. Weren't you expecting us? I thought you were having another tea?"

Smiling patiently, she shook her head. "I had asked to see you privately, Mrs. O'Toole, but since you're all here you're certainly welcome to stay. Perhaps it's best. What I need to ask of you, someone here may know as well. Cooper, would you grab the extra chairs out of Annie's room and mine?"

"Sure." He quickly came back with enough.

"Thank you," Prima said sincerely. When he waited, folding his arms and leaning against the door frame, Prima finally realized she'd have to ask him to leave. "I'm sure you have better things to do than listen to women gossip at a tea party. Now off with you."

After he'd left, Bertha giggled. "You're a lucky gal, Miss Naomi. Cooper's one handsome devil, he is."

"I'm glad you think so, Bertha. You might tell him that."

"You don't mind, what with you being engaged and all?"

"We've broken off our engagement. I'm not marrying him."

Kathleen sat up straighter. Bertha squealed and a buzz of conversation started with the others.

"If you ladies will make yourself comfortable while I put on some tea?" Prima started to get up, but Kathleen shook her head.

"That's unnecessary, Miss Romans. Since you hadn't planned on all of us coming, it was my mistake to have assumed. I'll offer them tea when we leave here. Now what was it, dear, that you wanted to ask me?"

Dear, was it now? Now that she no longer posed a threat to her daughter's marriage target?

Every eye seemed focused on Prima, every ear tuned to her intended question. "Well, I thought perhaps . . . since you are one of the"—*don't say oldest*, Prima reminded herself at the last second—"founding mothers of this settlement, that you might remember something about my grandfather's death."

A collective gasp echoed over the group of women.

Prima lowered her lashes and spoke softly, playing coy to achieve the end she desired. "You see, my grandmother won't talk much about it. It pains her greatly to discuss that tragic time in her life."

Kathleen reached out and patted Prima's hand. "As I imagine it would anyone who loved her husband as much as Miz Annie loved JickJack Romans."

"So you knew him?" Prima looked up hopefully, grateful for the woman's compassion. It might spur her into revealing the truth.

"Quite well, actually."

"How did he die?"

"She didn't even tell you that?" Bertha sounded amazed.

"Hush, Bertha."

"Yes'm."

"He drowned, my dear, trying to save that dear little child." Kathleen's voice filled sympathy. "Oh, Annie told us his lungs got too full of the river water he drank trying to pull little Naomi from the current, but all of us who knew him knew he died the next day because his poor old heart broke in two. Their daughter was the light of JickJack's life."

"Naomi?" Prima could barely whisper the name. "The child's name was Naomi, right?"

Kathleen nodded. "Just like yours, my dear. That's why you could imagine our surprise when you washed up on shore that day after the big flood and Miz Annie claimed you were her granddaughter she'd been expecting from back east. It seems there had been a steamboat explosion upriver around that time. I see now that you must have been on it. Of all the bodies that washed ashore, I think you were the only one to come out alive. It was a miracle, they said."

"A miracle," Prima whispered, her heart sinking to the pit of her toes. Annie knew. Annie had known her true identity and had kept it hidden from her for two years. *Why?* Prima's mind screamed. "How much more fortunate could I have been?"

Puzzlement wrinkled Kathleen's brow. "The thing I found odd about the whole affair was your name. Annie said her daughter back east decided to name you Naomi. But that meant both Annie and her daughter had babies around the same time and each gave them the same name. Even stranger was that near twenty years to the date she lost her little Naomi, you washed up from the wreck. Sort of peculiar, don't you think?"

"Not where Miz Annie's concerned," Bertha

piped in. They were all aware of Annie's unusual abilities in other areas.

Prima didn't want to hear any more, didn't want to think any more. She'd just lost trust in the one person she had believed actually cared for her unconditionally. She'd just discovered that that love belonged not to her, but to a namesake she was meant only to replace. And she had just angered the only man whose love could ever lead her out of this quagmire of a town.

Prima felt utterly lost. The image of Shaw's painting crept through her mind. It invaded her senses and enveloped her in a mist of misgivings.

Chapter Twenty-three

Smiling and waving good-bye to the last woman to leave took every last ounce of will Prima had left. She couldn't wait to be rid of her guests, yet now the cabin felt utterly empty, and she felt more alone than she had since first arriving in Moonbow.

Prima glanced at the home she'd shared with Annie, remembering with too great fondness the meals they'd recently shared and the joy she'd taken in relearning how to cook, how to clean, and how to ease Annie's work with the herbs.

Annie had grown to mean a lot to her. More than Prima thought possible. But the old woman had deceived her. She had lied in order to keep her here. And there was no reason Prima could imagine that could be great enough to warrant the deception.

A noise from the corral made her step outside to see who had come back. When she moved around the corner of the cabin, she wasn't prepared for the sight. *Annie . . . home.*

"You're back early," she said, trying to keep the anger from her voice.

"Blessed be the angels' mercy. Everyone seems fit enough to let me sleep in me own bed tonight. Good thing, child, 'cause I'm needing to talk to ye and that peddler man. There's things ye must be knowing." Annie hitched a strap with a muzzle of oats around the mule's head. "Old Bert'll wait for his brushing later. For now, will ye walk with me to the flatboat and see if the peddler's at home?"

"He's there," Prima informed her, suddenly remembering the note in her pocket. "He asked me to pay him a visit."

"Good. I don't want nary a day to go by afore I do this telling."

"Do you want a fresh shawl?" Prima asked, worried at how weary the woman looked.

" 'Twill be a clear night—warm, and just right for what I be needing." Annie glanced about. "Where are Skillet and Jug? I haven't seen them with you the past few nights."

Prima shrugged, falling into step beside the healer. "They stay with Shaw sometimes. Other times I don't know where they go."

" 'Tis that time, lass."

"What time?"

"Their time to find their own way. Every one of God's creatures is granted such a time, and no amount of love can keep them home, if they must leave."

"Skillet's looking for a mate?" Prima had not given the coons much thought other than the joy they brought her, but when she left Moonbow, it would be best if the pair moved on.

"Found one. She's set to deliver soon."

"Jug?"

" 'Tis possible."

The questions concerning the coons were simply to stall the one burning a hole inside Prima's stomach. Should she demand the truth from Annie now or wait until they were back at the cabin, alone, with time to discuss everything? At last she decided that if she had anything to fear in being alone with Annie, it would have taken place years ago. Waiting won out.

She supposed reading Shaw's note couldn't wait, however, if he wanted to discuss it once they arrived. Taking it from her pocket, she unfolded the paper and read. The words shocked her.

Was Shaw planning to contact her father without her permission? Was that what he wanted to discuss? But he'd promised to wait! To give her the month! Had his anger urged him to go back on his word?

No. The note had already been written before he saw Cooper kiss her. He'd already decided to tell Morgan.

"Slow down, lass. I can't keep up with yer highstepping."

"Sorry." Prima realized that her own irritation at Shaw had increased her gait. She took a good hard look at Annie and realized how stiffly the woman walked, as if the soles of her feet hurt with each step.

Prima wrapped an arm through Annie's. "You've got to quit traveling so much, Annie. Riding that big-boned mule and sitting in that ladder-back is going to make an old woman of you yet."

A smile of gratitude stretched across Annie's sun-bronzed face, creasing the furrowed wrinkles deeper. "Soon as I get me a little money set by, I'll tell that peddler to float me one of them fancy rockers downriver."

"I'll get you one," Prima said, without thinking how it sounded.

"Oh, jist gonna take out that tin of coins you've got buried somewhere out back, huh?" Annie's laughter was playful.

It was then that Prima realized Annie had no clue how much money she was worth. Which meant Annie's reason for keeping her here had nothing to do with any ransom note being sent to Morgan.

A weight lifted from Prima's heart. Whatever sins Annie was guilty of, they weren't to gain a fortune. Somehow, for Annie, this all had everything to do with a little girl named Naomi, lying in that grave in the high mountain meadow.

"You'd be surprised what I can come up with when I want to." Prima tightened her hold on Annie, lending her balance to keep the woman from waddling back and forth with each painful step. "I'm gonna get you that rocker before winter comes. It'll have a padded back and cushion, and you can rock to your heart's content when I park it in front of the cookstove."

"Sounds good, lass."

They neared the river, and from a distance they saw Shaw. He must have caught sight of them, too, for he waved.

"Wave back, lass. The boy will break his fool arm if ye don't."

"He's waving at you. He's angry with me."

"Care to tell me why?" Annie waved back.

She supposed she should hold back the facts behind the argument, but she wanted to regain that old feeling of trust with Annie. Knowing she was not an abductor said there was hope that their relationship might be mended. "He saw Cooper kissing me."

"Jealousy, plain and simple." Annie shook her head. "It can drive the best of men loco."

"But he has no reason to be." Prima's voice

lowered as they drew closer to the flatboat. "I don't care anything for Cooper. In fact, I broke off our engagement."

Annie stopped where she stood and demanded that Prima face her. "Are you sure, lass? 'Tis ended? Cooper knows there willna be any going back?"

"He knows. I told him I love Shaw."

Annie's hazel eye closed, then flashed open. "Then be very careful, lass, when ye're in Cooper's company. He's a good man, but even a good man can turn mean when he loses something of great value to him."

Prima wanted to ask Annie exactly what she knew about Cooper, and whether or not *he* knew her true identity as well. Could the pair be conspirators of sorts? She didn't like the idea.

"Hello, Annie." Shaw helped the older woman step aboard as they reached his boat. "I hadn't expected to see you this afternoon."

"I have something to tell ye, peddler. Something that will please ye, no doubt."

"Can I get you some coffee? I just made some." Shaw finally acknowledged Prima. "Miss Romans. Good to see you again."

"Mr. Lawson." So they were back to formal address? "My grandmother asked me to come along. She said she needed to tell us both something."

"Did you read that note I gave you earlier?" His eyes searched hers.

"I did." She wouldn't argue with him about it here, though. Not in front of Annie. The less the healer knew, the better.

"What do you think?" he asked, helping Annie inside his tent to settle into a chair.

He turned to get Prima a seat, but she didn't wait for him. She sat on his ornate trunk. "I think someone's out to reap a lot of money from such a transaction."

"My assessment exactly."

"A new venture on the horizon, peddler?" Annie looked inquisitive about the conversation between them. "Gonna be leaving us soon?"

"My question exactly," Prima practically spat.

"My work here is almost done. The month almost up. I've taken plenty of orders. A few more, and I'll have enough to satisfy my backers."

"What would ye say if I told ye I would be willing to tell every man jack in the hills of yer jars?"

"I'd be delighted," Shaw admitted, smiling affectionately at the old woman. "But what did I do to deserve such kindness?"

Annie set down her cup. "I had me a vision. The fields will soon be overrun. My people will be fighting instead of tilling the land. War's coming, and we got to count on them jars of yourn to salvage the food and keep it safe for hard days to come."

"War?" Prima couldn't hide her skepticism, though she didn't take Annie's predictions lightly. "With whom?"

"There is a huge conflict stirring in Washington," Shaw admitted. "Talk is, some of the Southern states may secede from the Union."

"You must be joking."

"Not a joke, lass." Annie sighed heavily. "Real as anything I ever seen." She faced the peddler. "How many of them jars ye got left, Mr. Lawson?"

Shaw mentally counted. "Several cases, but if you can give me time, I'll get more. All I have to do is let Mason know how many."

"Then get ordering, son. Ye'll need more than ye've got stocked here." Annie stood. "And I have a small favor to ask of ye."

"Name it."

"There's a special herb that grows near a big falls upriver just across the border into Kentucky. Got about a sixty-foot drop, about a hundred and twenty-five feet across. Ye know the place?"

"I've passed it."

"I'd like ye to escort Naomi to the falls and help her gather the herb for me. It only grows one other place I know of, and that isn't even on this side of the ocean." Annie looked at Prima. "Gotta preserve it for times to come. Can't let soldiers trample it to death."

"I can go by myself," Prima spoke up. She didn't know if she could be in Shaw's company long enough to make such a journey.

"Ye'll get lost. Besides, ye need to go now, while the weather holds. If ye leave within the hour, ye might make it by midnight. Perfect timing to pick the centaurea. The strength of the soil stays in their stems if ye pick 'em at midnight and wrap 'em carefully. Don't just tear; pull up their roots so we can replant one or two—whatever I don't preserve. They'll grow better if ye bring some of their homesoil with 'em. Go, lad and lassie, and make an old woman happy. These old bones can't make the ride themselves this time."

Chapter Twenty-four

Tree branches reached out like sharp-edged tentacles as she tried to keep pace behind Shaw's mount as they crashed through the woods. They had been riding full-tilt for some time. The mane of the McGregors' horse she'd borrowed whipped into her face, stinging her cheeks and bringing tears to her eyes. Yet Prima dared not rise an inch higher or she might lose her precarious balance on the saddle.

Suddenly a tremor rippled the horseflesh beneath her, giving a quick warning before the beast's massive shoulders jerked upward, slamming against her cheek. Then the horse hurdled an unseen barrier, catapulting her into midair. Her breath sucked in, caught at the back of her throat, and held—until it exploded from her mouth as she slammed into pine needles and hard earth.

Shaken and stunned, she lay there trying to assure herself no bones were broken, feeling a deep pressure within her lungs, and wondering if her breathing would ever return to normal.

Calm down, she silently commanded, willing herself to move, to test the pain stabbing at her palms and knees and discover whether or not it would eventually go away. Her lashes fluttered. A cough forced itself from the pit of her stomach. She gasped.

Prima turned to see how her mount fared. It was continuing to follow Shaw's horse. "Oh, Lord . . . no! Stay, damn you!"

Her shout only spurred the horse faster. Prima attempted to jump to her feet, but couldn't. Her left knee hurt too much to put pressure on. "Come back!" she yelled.

But her pleading was useless. The horse knew only one home, and the McGregors lived back in Moonbow.

"Don't panic," she told herself aloud, finding some comfort in the sound of her own voice. "Shaw will notice you're not following. He'll come back for you. In the meantime, get up and start walking."

She took up Shaw's horse's trail and began to walk out the soreness in her arms and legs. Her knee was bruised but not broken. That knowledge reassured her. Resolve filled Prima with each step. If she had to walk all the way to meet Shaw at those damned falls, she would.

He'd said their destination was due north. After a while, watching for the collection of mildewed moss that bordered the trunks became tedious, but she reminded herself that she had to get as far as possible while she could still see at all.

The forest shadows were growing and would soon obliterate any sense of direction. It was a good thing the weather was particularly warm and the stars bright overhead. If she'd been out here any other time, she might have frozen to death before she reached safety.

"Catch up, Prima," Shaw shouted into the wind as he rode but not looking back, though he was aware of the lessening of sounds behind him. She wasn't following as closely as before. He'd deliberately allowed his anger at her to set their pace.

When he didn't hear any change in the speed of the hooves, he turned to see what was keeping her. The sight of the riderless horse behind him pierced him with terror. Where had he lost her? How far had he ridden before he'd noticed? Why had he allowed his anger to rule his actions?

He spurred his horse into a gallop, and he returned down the path he'd just taken.

A prayer formed on his lips as he silently beseeched the power that had brought her into his life not to take her out of it so soon. He hadn't told her that he realized he'd made a mistake not explaining that the letter hadn't been from him. He hadn't told her that he'd realized it was Kingsley who'd kissed *her*, not she, him. He hadn't told her loved her.

She had to be all right.

Prima rubbed her hands back and forth against her arms, trying to stir her blood into new warmth. A chill of fear swept through her. The night shadows had grown deeper, and she tried to ignore the fact that she was terribly alone in a strange place with even stranger things around her. What she wouldn't give to have Skillet and Jug beside her right now.

Her knee ached fiercely. Hunger gripped Prima, reminding her that she had eaten little more than a biscuit all day. She'd been too upset about her suspicions of Annie and her argument with Shaw.

Forcing herself to concentrate, Prima searched the forest ahead of her. Tall, strong pines intermixed with a greater outcropping of chestnut.

Prima cupped her hands over her mouth and shouted. "Help! I'm lost! Can you hear me, Shaw?" How long had it been . . . minutes? An hour? When would he realize she wasn't following?

She strained to listen. Only the sigh of a gentle wind whistled through the treetops. Desperation filled Prima, urging her to shout, "Is anybody out there? I'm over here. I need some help."

The sound of a tree bough shifting under the weight of something scampering over it seemed inordinately loud in the silence.

Her hope wavered, making her shudder. Gooseflesh tingled at the base of her skull, sending a chill across her shoulders and along her forearms, to end as cramps in her fingers. She formed fists and released them, attempting to work warmth back into them. Something out there watched her. She could feel it, sense it waiting. Shaw might not find her if she didn't let him know where she was. She had to take the chance of shouting.

Prima resumed her rapid walk, determined not to give in to the uncertainty and fear creeping into her thoughts. So intent was she on watching every shadow that moved, one foot hit something hard. She stumbled and fell forward. Her hands splayed out to break the fall. Knees and palms impacted roots, jarring her already bruised joints. Though she was shaken, only her pride seemed hurt. If she kept this up, she'd have no knees left to bruise.

Determined not to let the stumble shake her resolve, she trudged forward. With every step she became more aware of the soreness in her left knee. She gritted her teeth against the pain and allowed her steps to take on a rhythm and cadence. Her body moved methodically, as if she were a soldier marching in a parade. She concentrated on keeping one foot in front of the other and watching for hidden obstacles.

Her jaw hurt from biting back the pain.

"Wait there!"

Prima's head jerked up at the words echoing through the forest and blinked several times at the pathway ahead. The shape taking form in the distance was real and not a figment of her imagination. "Shaw!" she yelled, never more glad to see him.

He spurred his mount toward her.

She waved broadly. "Thank God you found me."

"You're alive." Relief filled his beloved baritone as he reached her and dismounted.

A thousand emotions welled within Prima, spilling over her lashes into tears of relief. "You came back."

Like rapids racing to join a calmer flow, the two rushed into each other's arms. She felt herself captured and lifted high above Shaw's head, then lowered into an embrace that promised never to let her go.

"My love, my love, my love." His hot breath fanned her ear. "I thought I'd lost you. Are you hurt?"

She hugged him just as tightly, afraid that if she let go she might discover he was merely a figment of her imagination and longing. "I'm all right now. All that matters is that we're together." She laughed joyously, grateful to be alive and in Shaw's arms.

His kiss seared her lips. The passion had been building between them for so long now, since their first embrace. The terror of wondering if Shaw would find her thawed within Prima, as if melting away from her bones. All concerns with danger or safety fled against the onslaught of sensations sweeping through her. Though their clothing formed a frustrating barrier, she could feel the hard wall of his chest pressed against her breasts, granite thigh against silken counterpart, the flush of his skin as it heated then flexed beneath her searching fingertips.

Her fingers' journey ended at the nape of his neck, where she threaded them into the thick mass, glorying in its texture. Deep pleasure voiced itself, and she wasn't sure if she had moaned or if the sound had been Shaw's.

"I've wanted to make love to you"—a rush of breath whispered against her cheek as he allowed her a moment to steady herself—"ever since you woke in my arms."

"And I, you." Her breath mingled with his until she could no longer resist the impulse to satisfy the craving that had been throbbing in her for

301

the past weeks. With a moan she pulled him closer, and tasted of the intoxication his lips offered. Desire rippled through her like banners welcoming a hero home.

His fingers trailed down her back, caressing, leaving shivers of anticipation in their wake. Clasping the flare of her hips and more, Shaw pressed her closer, driving Prima wild with a yearning she sensed only he could fulfill.

She became aware of the strength of his ardor and experienced a certain triumph in knowing that it was she this wonderful man desired. It no longer mattered who he desired, Naomi or Prima, for she was a happy mixture of both women.

Any misgivings she felt about being inexperienced fell away from the need to show him what he meant to her. "Are we far from the falls?" she asked, praying their journey would not require much more time.

"I was almost there when I turned back to find you. It's not far, love. We'll have to ride double. I didn't take time to grab your horse when I turned back for you."

She mounted first, then reveled in the feel of him nestling into the saddle behind her.

He spurred the horse into a trot. "Don't want to throw a shoe now. Better to make our way carefully and get there. Once we reach the falls we'll break through the lanes, and the moon will guide us the rest of the way."

Minutes later, it seemed, the sound of thunder woke Prima from the comfort she'd found against Shaw's chest. "Has the weather turned?" she asked, worried that they would be caught out in a storm. "How long have I slept?"

"An hour." His breath was warm against the top of her head. "And there's no storm. We're close to the falls. That's what you hear."

Almost immediately, the horse broke through the copse of trees that bordered the river. In the distance a mighty curtain of water stretched across the land, plunging sixty feet or more to billow into puffs of moonlit mist.

"It's beautiful," Prima whispered with reverence.

"Nowhere else like it on earth." Shaw urged the horse forward. "And if our luck holds, you'll see why it's so special. This is the place. If the conditions are right, you'll get to see the bow I had carved on the trunk."

"The moonbow?" Prima suddenly found it fitting that she would experience the sight with Shaw instead of the Quest team. "Are conditions right?"

"It's a clear night. The stars can be seen for miles." Shaw pointed at the heavens. "The moon's in the right place. About forty-five degrees. Just as everything gets its darkest, the moon will shine on the mist. That's when the white moonbow occurs."

She waited until Shaw dismounted, then accepted his help in doing the same. Sliding down the length of him, she was aware of how well their bodies molded to each other. When her feet touched the ground, she was so enraptured with his presence she forgot about her sore knee—for a moment. A painful gasp escaped her.

"Want to stretch out somewhere and rest? We can pick the centaurea anytime during the night."

"I'd like to bathe, actually." She looked at the falls with longing. "That ride and those two tumbles were hard on me."

Though her suggestion had been made out of practicality, Prima realized the moment the bath was suggested, it implied much more. Their eyes met.

"I'll spread out a blanket near the bank. Why don't you go ahead and get undressed?"

She hesitated.

A knuckle tucked itself tenderly beneath her chin, lifting it gently so that her eyes were forced to focus on his. "You're beautiful to me as you are, sprite." The knuckle unfurled and his finger traced a sensuous trail down her neck. "I love those freckles. That stubborn chin. The slim silkiness of your neck."

She shivered with longing as his finger mapped

its claim. When he reached her breasts, she breathed in and forgot to breathe out for a moment. Would her somewhat smallish breasts be too small for Shaw? She knew she shouldn't let such things bother her, but they did.

"You are more woman than I've a right to worship," he murmured.

Prima exhaled a deep sigh of contentment, pressing closer to show him that she would go willingly into his arms. There was no more fear.

"I've longed to kiss you again."

"I've longed to be kissed again."

For a moment neither of them moved; then Shaw's palms cupped her face, slid into her hair, and gently clutched her as if he were afraid she'd leave him.

"God help me, but I love you," he whispered. "*You*, Prima. I should have told you before. I wanted to. But I let jealousy blind me and my pride get in the way. And about that paper I handed you—I didn't write it!" He explained how he'd taken it from Skillet and why. "You've got to believe that no fortune means more to me than you do."

"I believe you, Shaw," she whispered in return. And she did.

With an overpowering gentleness and hunger, his mouth possessed hers. She wrapped her arms around his neck and pressed her body hungrily against his. Adrift on a rush of desire, Prima parted her lips in a sigh of invitation.

His mouth was soft and seeking at first, compelling her hands to slide his shirt's buttons free and delve beneath his shirt. Curls of hair lightly covered his chest like thistledown, a sharp contrast to the supple firmness of his flesh, the iron hardness of his shoulder muscles that flexed beneath her exploring touch.

When he finally ended the kiss, Prima buried her face against him and breathed in the musky scent of all that was Shaw.

"Put your arms around me, love," he entreated.

Her hands played over his muscled back as Shaw's palms rose from her waist and over the gentle swell of her ribs to cup each breast, contouring them, igniting fire in their tips. All of her stood expectant, waiting, breathless, as he lavished first one nipple, then the other. Through the barrier of her clothing, his tongue aroused each straining peak.

A moan escaped her, deep and full of a raging hunger she'd never known existed.

"Please." She said the word aloud, not meaning to, not even realizing she had. Prima moved away as if she were drugged and sleepwalking. She slowly unfastened each button of her blouse and moved closer to the bank. She shrugged out of her blouse and let it slide to the ground. Her trousers puddled in a heap around her ankles. As she stepped out of them, she turned, her heart

pounding so wildly she could scarcely breathe. "Bathe with me."

Her heart sang as those wondrous yellow-green eyes stared at her so intensely they sent gooseflesh racing across the surface of her skin. Her gaze drifted over the broad expanse of his shoulders to the thick tawny hair that framed his face.

The husky groan that exited his lips blazed through her like a bolt of lightning, burning at every pulse point. Desire—bold, overwhelming, unrestrained—compelled her to walk backward into the river.

Slowly Shaw followed, shedding the clothing that would keep her from a closer touch. Prima's throat dried at the sight of the washboard planes of his abdomen. Her lips felt hot and in need of moistening. Her tongue darted out, just as his pants fell away to reveal his magnificence.

She stared at him, afraid that if she shut her eyes for one moment, he would disappear into the mist rising from the falls.

"You're beautiful," she whispered in awe.

"Come here, Prima."

The invitation in his voice went through her senses like a warm wind, igniting the passion that smoldered within her. She swayed beneath the impact of the desire that threatened to consume her.

Mesmerized by his gentle command, she

moved toward him, and he, to her. At the exact moment they touched, a shimmering light arced overhead, illuminating them in a soft aura of white.

His fingers threaded through her hair, coiling the ebony mass. He kissed her then with sweet abandon, his breath moist, demanding, hot. She wanted to imprint his taste, the way he felt, the rhythm of his heart upon her memory, but he pulled away.

Then hands, mouths, thighs touched. The intensity of his ardor pressed him hotly against her, forced Shaw to sweep Prima up into his arms and carry her to the bank.

Laying her down on the blanket, he stretched out beside her. "We'll bathe later . . . together."

His voice sounded husky, resonant against her cheek as the words rumbled from deep within him. Shaw began to caress her shoulder, building a fire within her that radiated in ever-widening circles from his trailing touch. Shivers danced along her shoulders and neck. He hesitated at the base of her spine, then drew tiny figure eights along the rise of her hip, soothing, caressing until she relaxed.

The brilliant light of the moonbow arching over the bank played over Shaw's features, revealing the raw passion in his face, the extreme effort he made to guide her gently into lovemaking.

"Any second thoughts, Prima?"

Her heart answered with a shake of her head.

One of his long legs threaded itself over and through hers, pressing her more intimately against him.

Breath rushed from her lungs. Within Prima grew the knowledge that he waited for her to offer him what he would never take from her against her will. He was every good thing she'd ever been deprived of. He lived by a code of honor, had never been anything but honest with her. She trusted him as no man before.

The solid wall of Shaw's resistance crumbled beneath Prima's touch. He stared into the face of an angel, a woman who'd never known passion, yet who came willingly into his arms. He threaded his hands in her hair until the raven-colored curls poured over and through his fingers, cascading past her shoulders like a silken waterfall. With a groan of pleasure, he rolled so his entire length was stretched upon her. A whole new flurry of sensations erupted inside him, funneling into the nether regions of his control.

Take it slowly, he reminded himself. *It's her first time. Talk. Get your mind on anything but the feel of her beneath you.*

"I wish this were a grand hotel, and this"—he fingered the blanket—"the finest feather bedding."

"*You* are my comfort, Shaw," she whispered

sincerely. "You bring me peace. Fill me with a joy I've never known."

Joy? Did she know what her words did to him? The tiny beat of the pulse thrumming in the hollow of her throat was about to drive him wild with desire, testing his will. Yet she needed time to experience every sensation, every shiver of anticipation.

Shaw nuzzled the underside of Prima's chin, unable to resist kissing the rhythm of her desire where it revealed itself to him. Her pulse quickened and kept pace with the beat of his heart.

"I want to be closer." Her voice was low and sultry. "Show me how to get closer."

His skin grew flushed, and he grew harder with wanting. Shaw claimed her mouth with his tongue and rocked his hips against hers. At last he had found a home in this woman's arms, and nothing and no one would ever again raise a barrier between them.

Trembling with longing, he felt sensations gush through him as the kiss deepened and her warm, hungry tongue challenged his in its thrust and parry. A marvelous anguish built within him, reflected in Prima's face as her head leaned backward of its own accord. Her ribs rose, arching her spine as her fingers threaded through his hair, pressing him closer still. Shaw moaned softly, knowing he had to tell her now, before he was unable to think coherently.

A throaty whisper escaped him as he braced himself above her, poised. "I don't ever want to hurt you, sprite, but the first time may—"

She kissed away his words, unwilling to wait any longer for the final blending of their bodies.

Ever so gently he entwined his fingers with hers, rocked slightly forward on his knees, and in one slow, exquisite motion filled her.

Prima gasped with the initial pain, but that gave way easily to awe as she realized how perfectly their bodies adjusted and molded to one another's.

When her breath steadied once more, she discovered he'd begun shallow, lingering movements that forced her to respond. Prima wanted to flow into his being like a brook meanders to a greater river. Their breath became labored as they found a rhythm all their own. Shaw's shallow movements deepened. In that moment she knew she belonged to him, and he to her—heart, mind, and soul.

Currents of desire surged through her as she rushed toward fulfillment. She clutched his sweat-glazed shoulders as they moved back and forth with each thrust of his hips. She could feel something inside her growing, knew it compelled him, too, for Shaw's moans of joy echoed her own. The countryside began to spin as he made love to her, hot, wet, deep. And in that final moment of headiness, a light more radiant than any the moonbow offered shattered her into a million pieces of blinding ecstasy. The light of love shone in Shaw's eyes.

His fingers threaded in her hair went still, and he whispered her name over and over; then the hot seed of his satisfaction warmed Prima as he collapsed in exhaustion upon her. He cradled his head in the curve of her neck.

Several moments passed before either could speak, yet they clung to each other possessively. She felt his heart slow to a steadier rhythm, trembled at the sweet stirring of his breath against her skin. As the slick, warm tip of his tongue brushed her ear, a single shattering sob escaped her.

"What is it, sprite?" he asked. Rolling to his side, he pulled her with him.

She forced her face sharply away and covered her eyes with a forearm, shaking her head and unable to speak.

He withdrew from her, stroked the arm she held over her eyes. "Please, love, tell me what I've done wrong."

"N-nothing," she choked.

"Why are you crying then?"

"I don't know. I just feel like crying. Please understand."

"Did I hurt you?"

"No!"

His big hand stroked her hair helplessly.

Shaw's voice was full of apology. "Was it not what you . . . expected?"

She moved her arm, staring into eyes filled with love and concern. "Oh, no, Shaw. I never really knew what to expect. It was just so beautiful . . . so soul-shattering. Something magnificent happened between us just now. Something that made me feel as if, together, we have no limits. Nothing can conquer us as long as we face it together. Even the moonbow seems to agree."

"And that makes you cry?"

"I'm being foolish. Or maybe just a little superstitious. You said a moonbow points the way to the right path. It shone on us, Shaw. That means, if you believe in such things, that we are right for each other."

He hugged her—an action that asked nothing of her and offered only love and tenderness. Moments passed as she reveled in his thoughtfulness. Finally he kissed her gently, cupping her bottom to press their bodies even closer.

"Nothing's foolish if it's what you truly feel. I'm a man of potions, a snake-oil peddler. I deal every day with what's real and what isn't. This, my love, is the first real thing I've ever been sure of—my love for you. So the legend must be true."

She pressed an eager kiss upon his lips, needing the taste of him again. She couldn't imagine her hunger ever being truly satisfied. "Maybe we should run away together—not tell my father that I'm alive and just go somewhere else to live." With a laugh she looked up into his eyes, but something strange lurked there. Not wanting to know if he was considering rejecting her, she quickly changed the subject. "Have I thanked you properly for finding me when I fell that first time? And for now, today?"

Challenge flared in Shaw's eyes, even as he chuckled. It made her realize she must have been imagining whatever she'd seen earlier. "I'd rather you thanked me a little more *improperly*, Miss Powell," he said.

Seduction newly learned filled her with anticipation. She slid one foot up and down the length of his leg as she leaned closer for another kiss.

"Rest for a little while, sprite." His lips brushed the tip of her nose instead. "You'll be sore from more than the fall, and we still have work to do for Annie." Seeing her disappointment, he tapped the pout of her lower lip and promised, "I'll wake you up in a very special way in an hour or so."

And he did.

Chapter Twenty-five

For a long while Shaw pretended to sleep, telling himself the best thing for him to do was to wake Prima and insist that they gather the centaurea and leave as soon as possible.

He had reason enough. Dawn would be upon them soon. The plants must be taken from their soil before first light, Annie had said. But that wasn't the problem; something she'd said had truly bothered him. And he couldn't make love to her one more time without her sensing the change in him. He wouldn't be able to hide his decision from her.

All night they'd gloried in each other's touch; each had claimed and given in equal measure. He knew every silken inch of her skin, and she, every nuance of his face and form. They'd spent

315

the night basking in the radiance of the moon-bow and its blessing of their love.

He'd lain awake long after she drifted to sleep, unable to quiet the fierce knowledge of what he must now say. Of what she would do as a result of the decision he'd made.

"Prima," he whispered against her ear, gently shaking her. She only snuggled closer, murmuring something soft he couldn't quite discern. *"Sprite."* He shook her gently, moving away with great dread of the words that might now part them. Duty beyond any he'd ever felt before insisted he speak. He stood and gathered his clothing. "It's time to wake up, love. I've let you sleep as long as I could."

She sat up and yawned sleepily, then started to comb her fingers through her hair to tidy the ebony mass. "Good mor—" She looked about. "Oh. It's not morning yet, is it? Still, you shouldn't have let me sleep so long."

She looked so beautiful, he wanted to prevent the coming storm that would cloud her face. "I would have let you sleep longer and picked the plants myself, but Annie said she'd told you which ones would be the most likely to survive the journey and which ones wouldn't. I didn't want to take any chances."

She accepted his assistance to rise, then stood on tiptoe to offer him a kiss. He drank fully of her lips, savoring the taste of Prima as if he were a man to be left without life-giving water.

"What's wrong?" Breaking the kiss, she pulled away to stare into his eyes.

He handed Prima her clothes and turned away, unable to meet her intense concern. "I've made a decision. You have to contact your father."

Hurt and something that nearly killed him—a quiet note of distrust—echoed in her tone. "I don't understand. You said Cooper wrote that letter, that you didn't."

"All of that's true," he said, facing her. "But that has nothing to do with our need to contact your father." He couldn't bear the hurt in her eyes, the anger in her voice. His heart would mourn her long after he left her in New York.

"Remember the children we want? Brace, Shaw Morgan . . . *Naomi?* Think of what it would be to have a child and not know if she were alive. I couldn't breathe if my daughter's safety wasn't certain. If I didn't have a body to prove she was dead. I'd be haunted the rest of my life if I didn't find her. Think of your father in that situation."

He willed her to understand. Needed her to. "I can't live with myself if we don't do for your father what I would want any human being with half a heart to do for me. I'm not the kind of man who can walk away anymore; don't you see that? You've made me whole again. I'm a man whose heart is no longer stone. A man who loves enough to love more than himself."

Prima whirled and started pinning her hair up. "Oh, please. Save the fable for someone else, Shaw. You're slicker than most, I grant you that. I'm no backwoods believer ready to buy a whimsy or potion, but you've played me for a fool, as surely as you must have with many a customer. Go ahead, contact my father. I'm sure the reward will be quite handsome."

He hadn't wanted to tell her about Hannah. But now he had to—otherwise she'd never understand why he couldn't just leave her whereabouts a secret. So he did; he told her about the day he'd taken the dare and gone over the falls in a barrel. His voice broke as he confessed, "I saw what she meant to do, Prima. I could have stopped her, too. I knew she was only trying to impress a brother. A brother who should have had more sense."

Shaw's eyes began to sting with tears he hadn't shed since watching Hannah's broken body being pulled from the river. "I was thirteen at the time, Prima. Shame is a terrible weed that grows within you and strangles you. I didn't let anyone take care of her after that. She was my responsibility. I put her in that wheelchair as surely as if I'd been the one to push the barrel over the falls."

"You're lucky you weren't the one hurt yourself," Prima added.

"You don't know how many times I wish I had been." Shaw wiped his eyes with his forearm. "Especially as I grew older and resentful of always feeling so responsible. I got tired of everyone counting on me. Of always doing the right thing. Of being so dependable that everyone knew what I would do or say before even I did. Do you know what that does to a man—no, make that a boy who thought he had become a man?"

"It doesn't sound like such a bad thing to be." An edge of scorn filled her voice as Prima began to pick the clusters of herbs they'd been sent to gather. "To be dependable."

He grabbed one of the cloths Annie said had been specially treated with one of her concoctions to protect the centaurea until they were returned to her. Studying the ones Prima chose, he began to choose similar plants to harvest. "It was hard at the time. Like you said about your father and wanting to be out on your own, proving to yourself what you could do. You searched for adventures with that team of thrill seekers. I wanted just the opposite, in ways. I didn't want to lead. I didn't want to be counted on. I didn't want to feel responsible for my sister's every happiness. I wanted out, and I was foolish enough to tell Hannah so one day when I couldn't take it all anymore."

319

"You told her that?" Prima looked up from her picking. "Then your family made you leave." It was not a question.

He pulled the next centaurea too harshly, nearly ripping it in two pieces. "Disinherited me. Not that there was much to lose. I had never intended to take my portion, either. Hannah's medical needs required a goodly sum each year." He reached out to touch Prima. "Do you really think I played you false, Prima, because you believe I wanted to fool you into having to marry me? Do you think I took your virginity and now insist upon seeing your father in order to gain a fortune? It isn't so." His eyes met hers, locked. "I've had a handful of fortunes since I left my parents' home. All of them I give to Hannah. I've never kept any money for myself."

Prima reached out and pressed a palm against his cheek. "This is why you dislike swimming so much, isn't it? It reminds you of Hannah's mishap?"

"And of being so caught up in myself that I could allow someone else to suffer needlessly." He pressed his hand over hers, wishing it would always be offered to him in compassion. "Now do you understand why we have to go to your father? Any reward he offers means nothing to me. And if he did feel he needed to give me something, I would just ask him to send a draft to my sister's account. It's the idea that he's being needlessly hurt that forces me to make this decision. It's only right that he knows you're alive."

Prima's hand slid from beneath his. "You go if you must, Shaw"—her spine straightened—"but I'll not be going with you." The graying edges of dawn streaked across the mountains rising up around them. "We'd best be on our way," she added quietly, glancing at the sky and at their horse, who cropped grass nearby.

As they'd saddled up, she cradled the cloth-covered plants they'd gathered against her as if they were the children she and Shaw had discussed. Though she was nestled against his chest, he knew she was far away, distanced by the words he'd said. He nudged the horse into a trot, dreading the miles and the silence that awaited them on the way back.

"You should take the reward, if he offers it," Prima announced as they moved away from the falls and into the forest. "I'd like to think some of Morgan's money will be put to use for something other than building more for himself."

Chapter Twenty-six

"Why are we stopping here first?" Prima demanded, wanting nothing more than to get back to Annie's cabin.

"Something's wrong. I can feel it."

Prima searched the flatboat in the distance. It looked the same to her. How could he tell anything was amiss?

He spurred their horse into a ground-eating gallop.

"Be careful or I'll lose these plants." She pressed them tightly against her for fear the horse's fierce pace would jar them from her hands. A few moments later, Shaw reined to an abrupt halt and dismounted so quickly she had to hang on to the saddlehorn in order not to slide off.

Something *was* wrong, but she couldn't quite

pinpoint what. The boat looked emptier. One of the ropes that tied a corner of the tent sagged. Shaw disappeared inside. A loud curse rent the air.

"What happened?" She dismounted, careful not to break any of the centaurea. She laid them carefully on the ornate trunk that she now realized no longer remained inside the tent where it had once sat.

Shaw flung back the tent flap that provided a door and announced, "My jars. The ones that people ordered but haven't picked up. Most of them have been stolen. The ones inside are broken. Now I've got to leave, I have to get more. There may not even be enough to save *those*." He motioned to the plants in her arms. "There sure won't be enough to do what Annie plans."

He slammed a fist into his other palm. "I guess this decides it. I'll head back to Philadelphia to see Mason, put you on a stage to your father, and be back here as quickly as possible. That's all I can do."

"I told you, *you* can contact my father if you have to, but I'm not going to him. I'll stay here with Annie."

Frustration creased his brow. Shaw reached out to hold her, but she moved away. She would not be seduced into anything she didn't want—and while she was angry, she was aware that one touch from him could make her lose all sense.

She had to keep her mind about her concerning this one thing.

"You have to face him, Prima, as an adult. You have to go back and let him know you're alive. Let him know that you will live your life the way you want, but don't make him suffer just because he hurt you. . . ."

Not wanting to hear any more, she demanded, "Please just *go*. Do what you must. I will see that these plants get back to Annie. I'll tell her what happened and why you had to leave in such a hurry. She'll understand."

"Do you really want this?" His eyes searched hers as if he were incredulous that she would ask him to leave.

She nodded, unable to speak. She could hardly stand—her legs felt weak, her heart so heavy it felt as if it had plunged into the pit of her stomach. Her entire body was already beginning a deep mourning at the loss of him. She wanted to do nothing more than return to Annie's and fling herself on her bed and weep. What would she do when Shaw was gone? When she couldn't walk out to the river and see the one man who'd set her free? But he had his principles, and she could not go back to her father. . . .

"Will you be here when I return?" he asked softly.

She had to think about it for a moment. There were many reasons she should run away, but there were two reasons she shouldn't. With a deep sigh she admitted, "I can't do that to you. Morgan will demand proof of my whereabouts. He'll send someone back with you. I wouldn't want anything to prevent you from gaining the reward he'll surely offer. Your sister needs that money. You deserve the reward, if anyone does. After all, you were the one who rescued me from my amnesia."

"Keep this, will you?" Shaw grabbed his trunk and placed it on shore. "I want you to have it."

Prima shook her head, her heart breaking. "I can't. It's your special place, where you keep all things precious to you."

"Look inside."

She lifted the lid. "It's empty!" Glancing about, she feared the worst. "Did someone steal your art? The carvings? All your treasures?"

"No. I pitched them into the river just before you and Annie arrived yesterday—when you thought I was the one who'd written the letter to your father." His laugh was bitter. "It's funny. I was so angry that you thought I'd go to your father . . . everything else seemed meaningless."

"You can replace those things. Put new things inside it."

"No." He looked upriver. "It is fitting you should have it now."

"Why?"

Shaw faced her, something terribly sad written

in his expression, and something even worse in the depths of his eyes, "Because you, my love, have yet to learn that a prize is not worth gaining if the victory is hollow."

Chapter Twenty-seven

"What happened between ye and Shaw?" Annie turned her head first one way, then the other.

"Hold still, Skillet . . . Jug. You'll make me spill the medicine." She watched the old woman's face grow pale merely from the effort it took to wait for the pair of raccoons to stop reaching for the spoon as if it held something sweet.

Prima had returned to find Annie ill and in bed, the raccoons pestering her for attention. "You're tiring Annie. Now stop it, you two!" *And you're tiring me.* She allowed herself a moment of self-pity before willing it away. The healer was being obstinate enough about being a patient, and Prima didn't have time to deal with two coons who had been cooped up for too long.

She needed Annie to be well. To live. So that there was a place Prima could always call home.

Because, mistakenly or not, the woman had provided just that—along with the love and concern that her own father had never been able to display.

Chastised, Skillet and Jug ran under the covers and hid.

"I'll take the medicine, if ye tell me the truth." Annie's head stopped its swiveling, her mouth poised in front of the spoon.

Exhaustion swept through Prima. The spoon shook. The elixir banked along its edge. She sighed heavily, exhaling the pent-up tension that had filled her since having to say good-bye to Shaw. "Take this, and I'll tell you," Prima finally conceded. As accurate as Annie was in foretelling things, she probably had already guessed that a quarrel had separated them.

While Annie swallowed the medicine, Prima quickly told her what had transpired between herself and the peddler.

Annie's gaze locked on something behind her. "It took a lot of courage for him to tell ye about his sister and his mistake, lass."

Prima sensed that Annie was trying to find courage of her own.

"Talking it out is the only right way to set straight crooked things." The healer pulled the covers up around herself, the wrinkles in her face furrowing more. In a voice deepened by an emotion only she could define, Annie informed her,

"I hope ye'll be kind after my straightening-out."

"What is it, Annie?" Prima suspected—no, hoped for—the direction the conversation might lead. Her anticipation got the better of her. "Is now the time you feel comfortable enough to tell me why you claimed me as your granddaughter when I'm really not?"

Annie sighed deeply, pressing a palm against Prima's cheek. " 'Tis a smart lass ye are, but then I knew that. It's been hard to keep ye a secret, and I knew one day ye'd have to know the wherefores. I hoped ye'd be old enough to understand when that time came."

"I'm old enough, Annie. Trust me. Help me understand."

"How much do ye know?" The old woman bowed her head.

Prima repeated what she'd learned from Kathleen O'Toole and the others. "Why did you tell me I was Naomi?"

Annie's head rose and her hazel eye blinked, shimmering with tears. "I thought the river had granted me my wish—to give my child back to me. There ye lay one day on the bank, the very image of my Naomi. What she would have looked like at yer age, so my heart said. Ye seemed the right age, had she lived. When ye didn't remember anything about who ye were or where ye came from, I decided ye needed me as much as I did ye. I gave ye a name—my Naomi's.

I meant ye no harm, lass. I just needed someone to love again . . . and ye needed a place to belong." Her tears fell unchecked. "An old woman's folly," she whispered. "An old healer's much-needed remedy. Can ye ever forgive me, child?"

Prima patted Annie's hand and sighed. "Forgive you for loving me, Annie? If that's the only crime you've ever committed, we should all be so evil."

"Then ye don't hate me?"

"I never could."

A change came over Annie's features, as if she were delving into some hidden source of strength and willing it to the surface. "Then do one thing for me?"

"Anything, Annie. Just get better. We all need you."

"The thing that will cure me quick is to see ye and yer young man together again. Ye belong with each other."

Prima shook her head. "I'm not so sure—and you must not be or you would know what our future holds."

"No, sprite." Annie smiled affectionately, if somewhat sadly. " 'Tis the one thing this old eye can't see. Ye have to look into yer own heart and decide. I just think ye're a good match."

Unable to meet the certainty in Annie's gaze, Prima moved away. Her attention was averted to the trunk Shaw had given her. The beautiful, empty trunk.

A look into her own heart revealed how much she would miss what he had brought into her life: Joy. Love. A knowledge of her true self. Shaw Lawson might have once been a scoundrel—though she had never seen him act that way—and he might still prove to be one, but the one thing he had never done was left her feeling empty inside. Maybe she could face anything with him by her side—even her father.

"Annie, I've got to go after him," she announced, spinning around, never feeling more certain of anything in her life. "I've got to let him know I love him. I can't live without him. I don't care if he wants to go to my father anymore. I'll go with him. You're right; nothing's as important as our staying together."

Annie whipped off the covers and stood, nodding in approval. "Then go, lass, and tell him. Show him that ye finally know who ye should be—the other half of him." But then the old woman wobbled on her feet.

Prima's heart sank. "I can't leave you like this."

"I'll go fetch 'im myself, if you don't."

No doubt Annie would. Prima urged the healer to sit on the bed, at least, if she wouldn't lie in it. "What if I don't catch him in time? Before he leaves?"

"Have faith, child. Ye know where he's headed.

He'll have to take the flatboat instead of a horse if he's bringing back more jars. 'Tain't easy rowing upriver. If he's left, he can't be too far ahead of ye. Worse come to worse, ride there a'fore him." The raccoons scrambled from beneath the covers, nearly bumping Annie off the bed.

"And take these two rascals with ye."

Chapter Twenty-eight

Prima rushed down the path to where Shaw docked his flatboat. The way seemed infinitely longer now that she needed to get there in a hurry.

Skillet and Jug scampered alongside, hindering her steps. "Come on, you two; don't slow me down. I can't play now, but we'll have plenty of time once we're aboard. We'll miss Shaw . . . if we haven't already."

They ignored her, bounding along the path as if they had nothing better to do than weave in and out between her legs. Prima managed to sidestep disaster a few yards farther until, all of a sudden, Skillet stopped still, rose on her haunches, and sniffed the air. Her teeth bared and she issued a low growl.

Prima stumbled. Unable to stop her momentum, she gritted her teeth and crashed to the ground. "Oof." The air escaped her as one knee hit and her hands splayed to break the rest of her fall. She got up instantly, glad it hadn't been too hard of a jolt. As Naomi, she'd certainly had her share of falls and head knocks; she was ready for a little more of Prima's steadiness. With a laugh, she hoped her tendency to fall was only the result of her brain's having been knocked around for two years.

"What do you see?" She peered ahead, trying to view what had provoked Skillet. The sight of a curling plume of black smoke made Prima blink. A stench began to fill the air, making her throat convulse in reaction to its acrid taste. Fire!

She shouted and broke into a run. In seconds her eyes focused on the flatboat, adrift in the current. A bright orange light was growing in one corner, flames licking heavenward to blacken into the greasy trail of smoke that now marred the sky.

Her gaze swept over the boat, seeing nothing but the tent in one corner and the oar lying across the deck. The craft was adrift with no one aboard.

Relief washed over her. For a horrible moment, her imagination had run away with itself and she'd imagined Shaw to be trapped abroad. But something wasn't right about the scene— even if the fire was merely an accident. Apprehension prickled her scalp. The peddler would never have left his boat unsecured. He always tilted his oar skyward and let the handle rest in a downward position—always at the ready to leave, if necessary. He wouldn't ever have left it lying on deck.

The tent. The canvas was moving as if a great wind blew it, yet there was little wind at the moment. Was someone inside, unable to get out?

The sound of wood splintering erupted, and the boat sent a spiral of flames into the air. "Shaw!" Prima screamed, praying she was wrong, willing him to be ashore, but sensing he wasn't.

Frantic, she flung herself into the river, hoping she was a strong enough swimmer to reach the boat in time.

The fire burned white-hot, sending long tongues of flame licking out over the water. Prima swam closer, fighting the burning ash that was released from the wreck, making her eyes water and her lungs fight for fresh air. The smoke billowed from the boat, surrounding it and moving down the river, making it difficult to see clearly.

Calm down. You'll reach him. Don't panic. Call to him. Let him know someone's coming. That he's not alone. "Shaw, I know you're there. Just hang on a little while longer. I'm coming!"

She thought she heard something. The shout

of her name? She strained to listen for something that would direct her, assure her that Shaw had not been overcome by flames or smoke, but the black ash was too thick, the sound too indistinct. "Hang on, Shaw. You can make it."

Intense heat threatened to hold her at bay. If she could just find a handhold—a part of the boat that wasn't too hot to touch . . .

Her fingers lifted up and out, searching, testing, but everywhere she grasped she found nothing but overwhelming heat. Touch and jerk back, grasp and recoil—it seemed to go on forever. Finally, when she thought there was no place left to try, she touched damp wood—logs the fire had not consumed. She planted both hands upon the deck and started to heave herself up.

Something yanked at her, pulling her backward, shoving her under. She gulped for air that wasn't there, gasping as her mouth filled with water. She slammed it shut and sank.

Flailing her arms, she thrashed her legs, at last clawing her way to the surface.

Arms locked around her, jerking her upward until she broke the surface like a leaping trout.

"You!" she cried, gasping for precious air and flinging the water from her eyes, fighting the man's bruising grip upon her hair.

"You wouldn't let him go, would you?" Cooper accused, jerking her around so he could grab one of her flailing arms. He pulled her into his canoe, forcing her against the wall of his chest. "Wouldn't leave well enough alone."

"You aren't a killer, Cooper. Let me go!" Prima fought like a wildcat, jabbing her captor with her free elbow and trying to maneuver to stand. Though she was wet and couldn't have been easy to hold, his powerful arms, accustomed to rowing, easily subdued her.

"You should have married *me*, Prima," Kingsley reminded her, tying a rope around her arms to keep her still.

She struggled to break free of her bonds, but he only added another loop. How would she free Shaw with her arms tied? "You knew who I was all along, didn't you? You *were* the one who sent my father the ransom note two years ago."

"I'll admit I knew more about you than I let on to Annie, but no, I didn't send it."

"Annie didn't."

"No, she didn't, either. And I've never quite figured out why she claimed you as her granddaughter. Still, she is powerful enough in these parts for me to hold back what I knew for a while. A while stretched into two years." He grabbed a paddle lying in the canoe bed and shoved it against the side of the flatboat, pushing away from the burning craft. "By the way, if Lawson dies, blame your own greed. Not me. You should have been content to be a backwoods bride."

Prima swung around as far as her bonds would

allow, trying to peer through the roiling smoke for sight of the tent on the flatboat—anything white to assure her the entire surface had not already been consumed by flame. She cursed Cooper, cursed herself for not listening to the voice that had made her mistrust him. "If he dies," she warned in a voice full of loathing, "I'll use every resource within my power to hunt you down and see you hanged—even if I have to spend my entire inheritance!"

"That's quite a threat from someone whose hands are tied. Don't make foolish threats, Prima. It will only up the amount of ransom I'll ask for your return."

Shaw had told the truth. Cooper *had* written the more recent ransom note to her father. Had he already contacted the man? "You'll never get away with this," she vowed. "Once I'm free, I'll see there's nowhere you can show your face. You'll be a wanted man."

"Versus a man unwanted by the woman I love?" Cooper leaned against her ear and whispered seductively, "The Powell fortune is a wonderful consolation prize."

"You don't know what love is."

"Now, that's where you're wrong, Prima. I loved you once. Loved you enough *not* to accept the ransom the first time."

* * *

Shaw rocked back and forth, vying for a better position where he was tied. If only he could reach the jar that had rolled against his right thigh when the boat shifted a minute before. For a moment he'd thought he'd felt someone board, but then nothing. Probably just one of the burned logs breaking away from the tethers that bound them to form the deck.

Fear pulsed in Shaw's veins, drumming in his ears. He could barely see for the smoke, and between it and the gag Kingsley had tightly secured around his mouth, his lungs felt as though anvils had taken up residence in them. His head hurt like sin from whatever Cooper had used to hit him from behind. When he'd revived enough to retaliate, Kingsley already had him bound by hand and foot. If his luck didn't change soon, the ash was going to kill him before the fire ever did.

Moments ticked by as Shaw worked the jar to knee level, praying the boat didn't shift and send it rolling away. After a few minutes more, he managed to capture the container in the bend of his knee. *There!* At least he had it securely between his legs. If the jar rolled now, it would still be within his control. He could bend and try to grab it with his teeth, but that would take a contortionist. He couldn't exactly flip it over his head and into his hands. But maybe, if he rolled the jar down to his ankles and maneuvered around so that his body was in direct line with the stones that formed the bed for the cookfire, he might be able to push the jar hard enough to break it against the stones.

He could then bounce over to the glass and use a piece to cut his bindings. The stones themselves were useless—too many fires had softened their surfaces—but the glass would work perfectly. Plus, it was the only real possibility. He probably wouldn't be able to do it, but it gave him a chance, and if Shaw believed in anything, it was in not wasting an opportunity.

Water seeped under the flap. The boat was sinking! Just what he needed. If he somehow survived the fire and smoke, he'd drown with his hands and feet tied. If the deck became too wet, the wood and the stones would soften. The jar would be harder to break. Shaw cursed against the gag, straining against the ropes that cut into his flesh.

One chance, his mind warned.

One good kick, his body promised.

Cooper's duplicity sickened Prima. "You just contradicted yourself," she shot back over her shoulder. "You said you didn't send the ransom note."

"That was no contradiction. Your good friends from Quest sent the note. I just attempted to follow through on it."

"Q-Quest?" She didn't want him to know that

he'd rattled her with such a claim, but it made sense. Otherwise why hadn't they contacted Morgan and told him she'd hit her head and fallen overboard?

It was then that the truth hit her full force. She knew him. She swung halfway around, trying to see her captor better.

Cooper stopped paddling and shoved her around to face him finally. "Ah, so you finally recognize me, do you? I wondered how long it would take. I didn't really expect it to be this long, but then"—his eyes glinted with hardness—"you really didn't pay much attention to me that day, did you? I was just the river guide playing escort to a bunch of spoiled darlings out to anger their papas."

That was why she had never quite been able to pinpoint what it was about him she didn't like. Well, she wouldn't sit here now and take his scorn. "You took the money easily enough, and I remember quite well that we paid you extravagantly for your services."

Cooper nodded. "Well enough, but you didn't pay me any attention yourself, Prima."

"I'm Miss Powell to you, sir."

"Very well, Miss Powell. You didn't pay me any mind until later. Then you were only too happy to be . . . courted."

"I was confused, Mr. Kingsley. Hardly something I think you'd want to boast to other men—

341

that you were engaged to a woman who didn't know her own mind."

His sneer faded into a grim line. "Don't be nasty, Miss Powell."

"Then don't imply anything happened between us when I was Naomi. I already know that didn't transpire."

Fury carved his face, made it even harder. "There's only one way you could be certain of that."

"And now I'm certain." She wasn't going to discuss her and Shaw's lovemaking, the fact that she had felt that it was her first time.

"What an unfortunate circumstance to have to tell your father. If that peddler should happen to get out of this alive, then he certainly will find a cold welcome in your father's house."

She understood his plan now. He would contact Morgan, gain the ransom, and blame Shaw. But what would he do to keep her from talking? "He won't believe you. You don't know my father. You'll have to have believable facts. He'll think you're just some madman who's taken up an old opportunity to make quick cash."

"Believable facts, huh? How's this for believable?" He began to count off the facts on his fingers. "One, I'm hired by a team called Quest to take them downriver. Two, when I return from scouting out an area ahead, I discover that one of the team—you—has taken a dare and fallen out of the boat, hit your head, and been swept downriver. Three, they're so afraid of your powerful father, they'd rather lie and pretend they're going to hold you for ransom instead of admit that a senseless joke might have killed you. Four—"

"Stop it. I don't want to hear any more." She knew the truth when it was spoken. Quest had sent the note. The betrayal humiliated her and sent tears rushing to her eyes. Her friends. . . .

"No . . . I've waited a long time to tell you how it happened. To let you know that by *my* grace you've been treated well."

"I can guess the rest." She stared at the curtain of smoke growing more distant behind them. She only wished Shaw had not suffered from her stupidity.

"Can you?" Cooper grabbed the oar and aimed the canoe toward shore. "I think you'll be surprised. You see, I only heard bits and pieces of their plan and started to head to Nashville to tell the authorities of the accident. A steamboat explosion sent some bodies ashore, and I heard that one washed up in Moonbow. Hazel Annie claimed you were her grown granddaughter who had suddenly turned up from back East. You fit the description of the woman I was going to contact the authorities about. But there was no need to send the message, if you were alive."

"How thoughtful of you."

"My motives were pure kindness to your father at that point, yes." Cooper frowned at her expression of disbelief. "Fine, think what you will. But when I found you alive, I decided that I needed to investigate why Annie was calling you Naomi—and her granddaughter. As I said, I had to be very careful in countering her claims. Then your friends—in what I can only believe was a misguided attempt to cover up what had really happened—sent that ransom note. I imagine they wouldn't have collected the money, but who knows? I could never understand the minds of rich brats. . . . I decided to use the situation to my advantage."

"You decided to get the money that would come of Quest's attempt at a cover-up," Prima presumed. "You threatened them with telling my father what had really happened—except that I was alive and down here!" Her friends might have been fearful of her father, but they wouldn't truly have wanted to get money out of her death. Would they? They would have had no choice but to give Cooper the cash to repay him for his silence.

"Well, they sent the note! And when word leaked out in the papers that your father had made it clear that he would pay the ransom without any question . . . When he even refused to allow law enforcement officials to try and trick the abductors . . . Your friends were clever enough to indicate a 'he' had stolen you, not a 'they,' so the police were looking for a lone man, not a group. Then, for some reason, they must have gotten scared. They must have decided the stakes were too high, the game too risky. And they had achieved the end they wanted, your father believed you had been abducted."

"But weren't they afraid that you would tell on them?" Though a long way from forgiving them, Prima felt relieved that her so-called friends had not been able to profit from such a cruel act. "Or didn't you go to them? Why didn't you force them to collect? Why didn't *you* try to go take that money? You obviously have little conscience!"

"Unfortunately, I made one unalterable mistake, Miss Powell."

Surprised that he would admit it, she asked, "And what was that?"

"I spent time around you and Annie. I fell in love with you."

His words sank in slowly. She saw the truth of it in eyes, in his jealous actions toward the peddler. "Annie didn't know about any of this, did she?"

Cooper shook his head. "She still doesn't, as far as I know. But then, the woman can see things others of us can't, so I can't be sure how much she guessed."

They neared the shore. Skillet and Jug ran up and down the bank, screeching their outrage at

Cooper. Prima couldn't endanger their lives, nor Annie's. She might have already cost Shaw his. "If you ever once loved me, Cooper, then promise me one thing."

"No guarantees, of course." Cooper let the front of the canoe slide up the bank. "But I'll consider it."

"Leave Annie out of the rest of this. Let her go on believing you are the good man she thinks you are."

Flames danced around the canvas walls like demons. Shaw's fingers stung, raw with cuts from his dropping the glass and having to search for it behind him again in the rapidly rising water. Only a miracle had kept the flames from consuming the tent already. He might be a few feet from its open flap, but it wasn't far enough away that he wouldn't suffer seriously once the fire spread to the canvas.

Had he been sawing for minutes, an hour? Time seemed lost to him as his senses reeled with the effects of the smoke. The rope chafed his wrists and the glass nicked his hands as he continued to saw through the remainder of the rawhide that bound him.

Images of Prima invaded his thoughts—of their first kiss, their night together beneath the moonbow. It couldn't have all been a lie. He might not have believed the legend before, but he willed it to be true now. For if it were so, their paths were destined to continue. To join again. His life couldn't end here in a sinking ship, away from Prima. He sawed harder.

The pressure at his hand broke free, and his wrists swung forward. *At last!*

His wrists hurt like the devil, but he didn't have time to see how badly they were wounded. Untying the gag from around his mouth, Shaw gulped in badly needed air. But the air was foul, full of fire and smoke.

His feet. He had to unbind his feet. Shaw swung around and grabbed the jagged piece of glass and sawed powerfully against the rope at his ankles.

Flames caught one of the ropes that moored the tent in place. Shaw watched in horror as fire ran up the rope like a snake flicking out its tongue.

The canvas burst into flame. Shaw bit back the pain that stung his wrists and sawed for all he was worth.

"There you go. That's a good boy, now." Cooper jabbed at the coon that refused to let him come ashore. "Let Uncle Cooper out of the boat."

Every time Cooper stuck a leg out of the canoe, Jug ran up and tried to bite him.

"Don't you hurt him!" Prima shouted. "He's just being protective of Skillet."

"I'll hurt them both if he doesn't back off." Cooper jabbed at one of the coons, then the other. The pair easily dodged his awkward thrusts. "Stand up, Miss Powell. You get out first and move up to higher ground. That ought to distract them long enough."

"The canoe will tip . . . remember? I'm not the best there is at standing up, especially with my arms tied."

"All right, I'll untie you." He cradled the oar beneath his armpit while he worked the knot he'd made in the rope that held her. "But don't try anything stupid, and don't try to run. You might get away, but I know where Annie lives. I hurt her once, remember? I'll do it again if you try anything."

His threat halted the plans for escape she'd already been making. So Cooper was the one who'd hurt Annie! What had he been thinking? Had he believed that Prima would be frightened enough by the danger that she would find safety in his arms? She went completely still, terrified by his crazy logic.

"Smart woman." He quickly unlooped the rope from around her. "Now distract those coons."

Prima stepped out into the water, rubbing her arms to revive them from the numbness of captivity. "Skillet, Jug. Back off, darlings, so he won't hurt you."

The tactic seemed to work. The coons bounded

up the bank and toward the path that led to Moonbow. Prima's heart sank as she dared a glance backward and saw the flatboat. It had been caught up on some rocks in the middle of the river and was now encompassed in flames. "Shaw!" she cried out, unable to believe the sight.

She'd failed him utterly. Sinking to her knees, she let her hands cover her eyes and began to sob bitterly.

"Prima!" a beloved voice shouted above the din.

Prima's head shot up, her eyes straining to see through the roiling black smoke and orange flames. A precious outline, standing . . . diving off the flame-lit edge of the flatboat. She jumped to her feet, racing toward the river again. "Swim, Shaw, swim! Don't be afraid, darling. You can do it!"

"Damn you, peddler!" Cooper nearly stumbled out of the canoe as he moved to block Prima from joining the man in the river. Skillet and Jug raced past and directly into the path of danger. They bit at Cooper's heels, weaving in and out between his feet as he tried to hit them with his paddle and wade to shore. Stumbling, he fell face-first into the water. He batted at them with his fists, but the coons would not back off. At last, the villain managed to rise.

Powerful strokes carried Shaw to shore, but Kingsley was waiting. Prima watched in horror as Cooper discerned the moment Shaw would be upon him, then kicked at the peddler's face. A hand shot from the water and grabbed Cooper's boot, sending him backward. Prima raced to help, but Shaw shouted "Stay back!" as he rose.

Prima retreated, calling Skillet and Jug to her. She knew she should run for help from the townspeople, but she didn't dare leave Shaw. He'd been on that boat for a long time. He must have inhaled a lot of smoke. She didn't know how weak he was or how much strength he had left after that swim. And swim he had. She didn't think he knew how, either, but he'd managed to reach Cooper well enough.

The coons! They could sound the alarm. But how? Prima grabbed the end of her shirt and tore it, offering the piece to Skillet. "Go get Annie, girl. Take her this piece of cloth. She'll recognize it. She'll know something's wrong. And you." Prima patted Jug's head. "You go with her, little protector. See that she returns, all right? I'm counting on you two."

The coons seemed to understand, for they headed up the path, back toward town.

Prima couldn't watch them any longer; she had to see if Shaw was holding his own against Cooper. The men still wrestled, thrashing and sending the water spraying, looking like gators spinning in a fight to the death.

Shaw might not want her in the thick of things,

but she could set the canoe adrift so Cooper couldn't have access to it or escape on the river. As practiced as he was at traveling the water, if he escaped he might disappear before anyone could obtain a vessel of any other sort. She pushed hard on the birch bark, sending the canoe sliding into the Cumberland.

The battle moved closer.

Cooper managed to stand on the shore. Shaw slipped and fell to one knee, one fist bunching Cooper's shirt at the neck. Cooper's hand was slipping toward his boot.

Anger filled Prima as she realized he meant to go for the knife he carried there. She couldn't just stand aside and do nothing. Taking a running leap, she threw herself onto Cooper's back.

Shaw used the distraction to throw a mighty fist into his foe's midsection. Cooper's howl of disbelief ended in a rush of air leaving his lungs. He toppled, sending Prima into the water.

Shaw grabbed her just before she went under, and he clutched her to him, half dragging her to safety. She suppressed a shudder, thinking how nearly the Cumberland had claimed her again. She'd had enough of this river for a long time!

"Are you all right, love?" Shaw asked. She found herself enveloped in the beloved embrace that had come to mean so much to her. Prima threw her arms around him, hugging him and trying not to laugh from the sheer joy of being in his arms. "I thought I'd lost you forever. I came after you, but I found the burning boat and—"

"I'm fine," he whispered an inch away from her lips. "Just a few cuts and burns. Nothing your love can't heal. Will you marry me?"

Shouts echoed from the forest. Skillet and Jug came bounding toward them. The coons' mission had been successful.

"Pull Kingsley from the water before he drowns," Shaw informed the first man on the scene.

Prima refused to move away. Let the people of Moonbow decide what punishment Cooper would receive. Right now, all that mattered to her was giving Shaw the answer to his question and thanking him for rescuing her yet again— for rescuing her from a life without love.

She cupped the strong line of his jaw in her hands, looking up into the beloved eyes that hungrily searched hers for a promise and a commitment. "I found my true self here with you, my love. The moonbow didn't lie. I could easily blame Cooper for everything that happened, but the truth is, I, too, am a guilty party. I set this all into motion. I was too eager to rage against my father, but it was me who frustrated me the most. You see, darling, it was easier to blame Morgan instead of finding out what I could or could not become on my own. That's the gift I gave myself as Naomi. I will never be sorry I lost those two

Moonbow in the Mist

years. I gained more from them than I could ever repay."

Her heart sang with truth, her soul humming in sweet harmony. "You came into my life because of it. You loved me enough to help me find the strength in who I am." Tears of happiness welled from her heart to brim in her eyes as she spoke of the gift the peddler had given her: "You helped me remember what counts most . . . *love*. Yes, Shaw, I'll marry you. I'll go back and confront my father, but only under one condition."

"What's that?"

"Tell me how you managed to get away. I thought you couldn't swim."

Shaw laughed. "I never said I couldn't swim. I said I didn't like getting wet."

She laughed joyously as he encircled her in his arms and claimed her lips with a kiss that would linger in her dreams for all her years to come.

353

Chapter Twenty-nine

"Well, this is it." Prima sucked in a deep breath and exhaled it into the crisp New York dawn as the driver reined their rented buggy to a halt in front of the marble estate. She'd forgotten how imposing and untouchable the peach-colored marble walls of Powell Place appeared from the road.

"I'll go with you, love." Shaw's arm remained around her, hugging her closer. "You don't have to do this alone."

"Yes, I do." Her gaze savored the compassion and concern etched in those wonderful wolf eyes. "But it's incredible to know that you'll be out here waiting for me. I do want you to meet him, make no mistake. But I've got to walk in there alone, of my own volition, and face him with everything

I've done and all that was done to me because of it."

"My love goes with you, Prima."

"That's why I'm not afraid." She squeezed his hand gently and accepted the driver's help out of the buggy. Turning, she offered Shaw a brave smile. "Why don't you have the driver show you some of the new park? They say it's almost completed now. Imagine a park amid all this brick and stone."

"We'll see it together later. I'll wait for you here."

Though she felt guilty about leaving him outside the gate, she was relieved that he would be there should she be thrown out of it.

She rang the bell hanging on the gate that barred entrance to the long drive, letting the servants know that company had come. Then Prima opened the gate and started the long stroll. In the distance, the main doors opened and one of the servants stepped out.

Prima took her heart in hand and waved, announcing her arrival home.

The servant shaded her eyes, peering at the visitor hard. All of a sudden the hand removed itself and lifted into an excited wave. "Miss Prima?" the servant yelled. "Is that you? Oh, my Lord. Miss Prima's home. Somebody wake up the master."

The servant disappeared through the door,

then instantly returned, running down the path toward Prima, her skirts flying.

It was dear little Carrie, the housekeeper's daughter, followed by the parlor maid and the door attendant. Apparently she was not so little any more, Prima thought as she noticed Carrie's newly developed figure. Two years had wrought many changes.

Carrie halted a foot away from her mistress, suddenly aware of her station.

Prima hugged the girl fiercely and stood back to regard her at arm's length. "Carrie, it's so good to see you. You've grown so."

"Oh, Miss Prima." Carrie's eyes filled with tears. "We thought you were . . . Well, your father . . . he's gonna be so surprised. I sent Jenkins up to wake him. I knew he wouldn't believe me, but he will Jenkins. Jenk had to see for himself first, though. He stuck his old bald head out the door and nearly dropped his false teeth when he saw you. Started blubbering all the way up the grand staircase, he did."

"Prima!" a deep baritone shouted from afar. "Is that you, daughter?"

Emotion fisted Prima in the belly, raw and full of need. "Father!" she shouted back, and had to keep her legs from racing toward him.

Her father, who had appeared at the front door, catapulted himself from the top of the marble steps and rushed down the drive. "Prima!"

Tears flooded her eyes as his arms opened wide in welcome. She met him halfway, flinging herself into his arms. He hugged her fiercely, his body shaking as if a great tremor rent the earth beneath him. "Prima, Prima, Prima, my beloved child! Where on earth have you been?"

"Lost, Father," she whispered through her tears. "I've been so very lost all these years."

"And now you've come home to me," he said, great joy shining in his eyes as he pulled back to study her. "Safe. I can't believe you're safe."

"Yes, Father, safe and much different from when I left."

He wiped the tears from her eyes, a thumb caressing her cheek. "You must tell me everything. Where you've been. Why I couldn't find you. You may not know it, but—"

"I know, Father. Everything." She wrapped an arm around his waist. "We'll talk about everything after I've seen Mother."

Morgan wrapped his arm about her shoulders and walked side by side with her to the great house. His fear had truly changed the man. Prima couldn't remember a time he'd ever made her feel more welcome. For once in her life, she felt that she was truly loved by her father.

Epilogue

Two months later

Shaw stood in the grand foyer of Powell Place, waiting for Prima to finish packing. She exited the room on the second landing, and Morgan followed behind holding a wooden rocker. Mrs. Powell trailed behind, offering instructions on how to carry it properly without banging it against the banister.

Shaw had expected to see a gaggle of servants carrying Prima's belongings out to the rented buggy. Yet nothing but the rocker seemed to be going. "Is that all you're taking?"

"I have everything I need. The bare essentials." Prima smiled, her eyes shining with love. "You and me and the trunk you gave me to store a lifetime of memories in. The rocker's for Annie so she'll have somewhere to rock a passel of great-grandchildren."

"Are you sure you've got to leave so soon, Prima?" her mother asked, growing teary and grabbing a handkerchief from her reticule. "Oh, now, I wasn't going to cry."

"Well, I am, so you might as well." Morgan looked solemn despite the tears reddening his eyes. His gaze locked with Shaw's. "You'll remember she's a headstrong woman who knows her own mind, son."

"I will."

"Don't try to mold and shape her into something she's not."

"I won't." He rather liked the shape she had.

"You remember to bring her to visit now and again." He cleared the emotion from his throat. "Christmas. The Fourth. Of course for any christening."

"You can count on it, sir."

Montgomery handed the rocker to Shaw as if he were passing the responsibility of Prima to him. They were both responsibilities—and a pleasure Shaw gladly accepted.

"Let her become all she can . . . not just what you expect of her. Take the advice of a stubborn old man who learns lessons the hard way."

"Advice taken, Mr. Powell."

"We really must be on our way, if we're going to catch that train to Philadelphia, Shaw. Hannah said that if you didn't catch the eight-fifty, you'd get in too late to watch the play."

"I can't believe she's working. Who would have thought sitting in that wheelchair all day had made her a writer?"

"A playwright," Prima corrected. "A soon-to-be-produced playwright now, thanks to you." Her parents had insisted on awarding the ransom money to Shaw, but not the interest it had accrued. Morgan wasn't that generous. "And she wouldn't want you to miss opening night. She wants the whole family there."

The whole family. How wonderful that sounded to Prima as they waved good-bye to her parents. Knowing she had been a part of reconciling Shaw with his family was one of the happiest moments of their wedding ceremony. The Lawsons had come to the elaborate wedding Morgan had thrown two weeks after Prima had returned to New York. He'd made certain it proved difficult for them to refuse the invitation. He might have had a change of heart toward Prima, but he was still the influential and cunning dealmaker who had made himself such a success.

She'd forgiven his methods, knowing that he'd forced the Lawsons to be there for one reason only—so Shaw could reconcile with them. And once there, Shaw had taken matters into his own hands and confessed his shame to Hannah and his parents. He admitted being horrified by how he'd treated them and apologized for his selfishness. Hannah proved to be a true angel, for she broke the jam of resentment. When she agreed to be Shaw's "best man" at the wedding, the Lawsons could only follow suit and forgive their son.

Yes, everything was good. Cooper was in prison, Annie was healthy, and both Shaw's and Prima's families were whole at last. And her darling husband didn't know it yet, but their own little family was also about to increase in size. And not just from the raccoon kits soon to be born to Skillet and Jug.

But that was a surprise she would wait to share with him back in the Appalachians, under the light of moonlit mist. Under the light of their very own moonbow.

THE GENTLE SEASON
DIA HUNTER

Nicodemus Turner is in a bind. Not only has the handsome gambler just found out that he has a daughter he's never met, but in order to get custody he has six months to become a proper father and marry. And while Nick is head-over-heels in love with his best friend Alewine Jones, the stubborn lady freighter doesn't take kindly to the notion of a wedding. The solution: a poker game where the prize will be a full house. Nick is Aly's closest companion, her best fishing partner, and he can make her insides go mushy with one lingering glance. That still doesn't mean she will up and marry him. But that mushy feeling comes back every time she looks into Nick's eyes. Suddenly Aly realizes that Nick has won more than her hand, he's won her heart.

___4705-5 $4.99 US/$5.99 CAN

Dorchester Publishing Co., Inc.
P.O. Box 6640
Wayne, PA 19087-8640

Please add $1.75 for shipping and handling for the first book and $.50 for each book thereafter. NY, NYC, and PA residents, please add appropriate sales tax. No cash, stamps, or C.O.D.s. All orders shipped within 6 weeks via postal service book rate. Canadian orders require $2.00 extra postage and must be paid in U.S. dollars through a U.S. banking facility.

Name_____
Address_____
City_____ State_____ Zip_____
I have enclosed $_____ in payment for the checked book(s).
Payment <u>must</u> accompany all orders. ❑ Please send a free catalog.

Savage Honor
Cassie Edwards

Shawndee Sibley longs for satin ribbons, fancy dresses, and a man who will take her away from her miserable life in Silver Creek. But the only men she ever encounters are the drunks who frequent her mother's tavern. And even then, Shawndee's mother makes her disguise herself as a boy for her own protection.

Shadow Hawk bitterly resents the Sibleys for corrupting his warriors with their whiskey. Capturing their "son" is a surefire way to force them to listen to him. But he quickly becomes the captive—of Shawndee's shy smile, iron will, and her shimmering golden hair.

___4889-2 $5.99 US/$6.99 CAN

WHITE DOVE

SUSAN EDWARDS

White Dove was raised to know that she must marry a powerful warrior. The daughter of the great Golden Eagle is required to wed one of her own kind, a man who will bring honor to her people and strength to her tribe. But the young Irishman who returns to seek her hand makes her question herself, and makes her question what makes a man.

Jeremy Jones returns to be trained as a warrior, to take the tests of manhood and prove himself in battle. Watching him, White Dove sees a bravery she's never known, and suddenly she realizes her young suitor is not just a man, he is the only one she'll ever love.

___4890-6 $5.99 US/$6.99 CAN

Dorchester Publishing Co., Inc.
P.O. Box 6640
Wayne, PA 19087-8640

Please add $2.50 for shipping and handling for the first book and $.75 for each book thereafter. NY, NYC, and PA residents, please add appropriate sales tax. No cash, stamps, or C.O.D.s. All orders shipped within 6 weeks via postal service book rate. Canadian orders require $2.50 extra postage and must be paid in U.S. dollars through a U.S. banking facility.

Name_____
Address_____
City_____ State_____ Zip_____
I have enclosed $ _____ in payment for the checked book(s).
Payment <u>must</u> accompany all orders. ❏ Please send a free catalog.
CHECK OUT OUR WEBSITE! www.dorchesterpub.com

Lori Morgan

Autumn Star

Morgan Caine rescues Lacey Ashton from a couple of pawing ruffians, feeds her dinner, and gives her a place to sleep. He is arrogant, bossy, and the most captivating man she has ever met. He claimed she will never survive the wilds of the Washington territory. But Lacey sets out to prove she not only belongs in the untamed land, she belongs in Morgan's arms.

Morgan is completely disarmed by Laceys's innocence and optimism. Like an autumn breeze, she caresses his body, refreshes his soul, invigorates his heart. At last, the hardened lawman longs to trader vengeance for a future filled with happiness—to reach for the stars and claim the woman of his dreams.

___4892-2 $4.99 US/$5.99 CAN

The Cowboys

LEIGH GREENWOOD

MATT

Matt's rough-and-tumble childhood taught him to size up a situation at a hundred paces. And to end his standoff with respectable society he knows he has to take a wife. Ellen agrees to act as a mother for the two boys he's sworn to protect, if he will be a father for the two children she brings to the union. It is a business arrangement. But nothing has prepared him for the desires the former saloon girl incites. She gentles him like a newborn colt, until he longs to be saddled with all the trappings of a real marriage. Until he understands he's found a woman to heal his orphaned heart.

___4877-9 $5.99 US/$6.99 CAN

The Agreement

SECRET FIRES

Constance O'Banyon

In the midst of the vast, windswept Texas plains stands a ranch wrested from the wilderness with blood, sweat and tears. It is the shining legacy of Thomas McBride to his five living heirs. But along with the fertile acres and herds of cattle, each will inherit a history of scandal, lies and hidden lust that threatens to burn out of control.

Lauren McBride left the Circle M as a confused, lonely girl of fifteen. She returns a woman—beautiful, confident, certain of her own mind. And the last thing she will tolerate is a marriage of convenience, arranged by her pa to right past wrongs. Garret Lassiter broke her heart once before. Now only a declaration of everlasting love will convince her to become his bride.

___4878-7 $5.99 US/$6.99 CAN